KU-436-689

PENGUIN BOOKS

The BOYBAND MURDER MYSTERY

BAINTE DEN STOC

WITHDRAWN FROM DÚN LAOGHAIRE-RATHDOWN
COUNTY LIBRARY STOCK

Ava Eldred was born in London, and has spent much of the last decade writing and developing stage musicals, as well as producing large-scale theatrical concerts. Her work has been performed both in London and internationally. She is a recent alumna of Faber Academy's Writing a Novel course, and a life-long fan of boybands. This is her debut novel.

Follow Ava on Twitter
@ava_eldred
#BoybandMurderMystery

AVA ELDRED

THE BOYBAND MURDER MYSTERY

BAINTE DEN STOC

WITHDRAWN FROM DÚN LAOGHAIRE-RATHDOWN
COUNTY LIBRARY STOCK

PENGUIN BOOKS

PENGUIN BOOKS

UK | USA | Canada | Ireland | Australia
India | New Zealand | South Africa

Penguin Books is part of the Penguin Random House group of companies
whose addresses can be found at global.penguinrandomhouse.com.

www.penguin.co.uk   www.puffin.co.uk   www.ladybird.co.uk

First published 2021

001

Text copyright © Ava Eldred, 2021

The Florence and the Machine lyric in the epigraph is from
'South London Forever' written by Brett Shaw and Florence Welch
'Flying without Wings', sung by Westlife,
was written by Wayne Hector and Steve Mac

This book is a work of fiction. Names, characters, places and incidents are
either the product of the author's imagination or are used fictitiously,
and any resemblance to actual persons, living or dead, business establishments,
events or locales is entirely coincidental.

The moral right of the author has been asserted

Set in 10.5/15.5pt Sabon LT Std
Typeset by Jouve (UK), Milton Keynes
Printed and bound in Great Britain by Clays Ltd, Elcograf S.p.A.

The authorized representative in the EEA is Penguin Random House Ireland,
Morrison Chambers, 32 Nassau Street, Dublin D02 YH68

A CIP catalogue record for this book is available from the British Library

ISBN: 978-0-241-44943-1

All correspondence to:
Penguin Books
Penguin Random House Children's
One Embassy Gardens, 8 Viaduct Gardens, London SW11 7BW

Penguin Random House is committed to a
sustainable future for our business, our readers
and our planet. This book is made from Forest
Stewardship Council® certified paper.

To Bette, Emma, Helen, Philippa,
Roz, Sarah, Siobhan and Tree –
I wrote this for you.

'*Music is a moral law. It gives soul to the universe, wings to the mind, flight to the imagination, a charm to sadness, gaiety and life to everything.*'

Plato (probably)

'*Everything I ever did was just another way to scream your name.*'

'South London Forever',
Florence and the Machine

INTRO

I have long believed that loving a boyband brings with it a wealth of transferable skills, but I'd never imagined solving a murder would be one of them.

That's what I keep coming back to as Jas and I sit in a police-station waiting room, desperate to hear if we've done it – if the evidence we've given will go down in fandom legend and put a guilty person behind bars. No pressure.

It has to be said right off the bat that we didn't plan it. All the things we did – gate-crashing press conferences, learning how to hack CCTV and, um . . . breaking into someone's house – were completely outside the realm of my imagination three months ago. A week ago. Some of them even yesterday.

Eventually, though, when thinking about all that becomes overwhelming, my mind turns to cells. Not the prison kind – the ones in your body. I'm thinking specifically of that poetic line people like to spout – that every seven years all your cells renew. One day, they tell you, you'll be a totally different person. It's supposed to be comforting, but it's not true. There are some cells, you see, that don't work like that. Some of them stay with you forever and, when it comes to boybands, you can never forget your first.

Dad would be proud, I think, as the clock strikes the hour again. *What's that saying? If you want to know what you love, look to where your mind goes when it wanders? Ironic. After all that time I spent trying to convince him that I wasn't cut out to be a scientist, mine wanders straight to biology.*

So yeah. That's what I'm thinking about in these quiet hours when we don't know if our investigation has worked or not, and nobody's telling us anything.

Well, that – and that, when I said I'd do anything for Half Light, this isn't quite what I had in mind.

TRACK ONE

Before

The Friday night was in that blurry limbo stage, somewhere between midnight and morning, where the mood could still go in either direction. The vibration of my phone on the kitchen worktop made me jump as it cut through the quiet.

'Don't be boring, Harri,' Stefan had groaned good-naturedly when I'd floated the idea of pizza and a duvet fort instead of the party, so I assumed the text was him, from the common room at the other end of the hall, letting me know what I was missing.

I probably should have made more of an effort. Stef was the closest thing to a friend I had in the uni halls I couldn't quite call home yet – when he wasn't making unsubtle comments about how he was sure we were meant to be more than that, and the logical part of my brain knew that I should be tempted. Stefan had so-dark-it-was-almost-blue black hair and the kind of bushy-but-groomed eyebrows that I'd have killed for. So far, though, the overthinking part of my brain, which always held me back in these

3

situations, had not let me get any further than admitting he was sort of cute.

The kitchen floor was cold against the back of my legs, and I sighed as I watched my pizza bubble and brown in the golden light of the oven. *Is it supposed to be like this?* Three weeks into my first term, wasn't I meant to be feeling dizzy with freedom, and throwing myself into new experiences to see which ones would stick?

'What were you expecting, Harri? A complete personality transplant?' I asked aloud, and the silence of the room felt totally fitting. Nobody around to hear me talking to myself.

My phone buzzed again and this time the vibration felt more aggressive.

Not Stef then. He's far too cool to double text. It must be one of the girls.

Messages arrived at all times of the day and night since I'd discovered Half Light, fresh off the back of the viral YouTube video that propelled them from three regular boys singing harmonies in a garage to the highest heights of superstardom. That song had become 'Closer Than You Think', their first top-ten single, and it had stirred something in me. I'd never felt anything like it before. I'd reached out a virtual hand with no real expectation at all, and somehow found myself part of a global girl gang, bonded by equal parts love and affectionate exasperation for these three enigmatic strangers.

Sometimes we joked that we needed a schedule for all the WhatsApp messages and late-night FaceTime calls. I knew how the sunset looked from Ruby's third-floor apartment on the outskirts of Berlin, and the sound of a

London street in the evening rush hour. I had shared lazy Sunday mornings here in Brighton with Gemma as she made her way home on Saturday night in LA. It made me feel safe somehow. Like at any time I could call out and there would be someone, somewhere, to answer me.

I squinted at the oven clock, promising myself that I'd look for my glasses tomorrow. It was 12.35 a.m. With friends all over the world, close to midnight was one of the times it could have been any of them. I liked the idea that my final hour before sleep would be spent with whoever was on the end of the phone.

It buzzed again as I reached for it and then three more messages appeared all at once.

'What's happening?' I asked aloud as it began to ring, and Jas's face, not a single smudge in her perfectly applied make-up despite the late hour, appeared on my screen as I accepted the call.

Jas was my closest friend, both geographically (in that we actually lived in the same country) and in the sense that we'd immediately just *known each other*. Sure, we hadn't met in person yet, but that oh-there-you-are moment that had made me jealous every time I'd heard it described by newly-in-love couples on American TV shows? That's what I'd felt when I stumbled across Jas for the first time.

Actually, what I'd stumbled across was a comment she'd written underneath a particularly delicious Instagram photo of Frankie Williams, one arm slung carelessly round Jack's waist as if it was no big deal at all that they were now boyfriends, the other cradling, for entirely unexplained

5

reasons, a baby piglet. (We'd learned by that point not to question most things Frankie did.)

I have always had one fundamental issue with organized religion, Jas had started. Let me tell you why.

I wasn't entirely sure why she was talking about religion when our famously atheist crush was not only holding baby farm animals but was *finally* ignoring the ridiculous heteronormative management team, who clearly hadn't heard that teenage girls were pretty liberal and accepting these days, and parading his oh-my-God-we-knew-it soulmate publicly on the internet for the whole world to see. As far as I could tell, God couldn't hold a candle to Frankie in that moment.

I read on.

You might imagine it's a teenage rebellion thing, but I'm all about an easy life, and mine would definitely be easier if I saw eye to eye with my parents on this. Go to church on Sunday? Whatever, I love the singing and nothing interesting happens before midday anyway. No sex before marriage? Trust me, nobody is offering and you can't miss what you've never had. Don't worship idols?

Not a chance.

I don't really know what I think about God, but I know what I think about Frankie Williams. I have never seen God, but I could talk for hours about that wrinkle under

Frankie's left eye, or the mole on his lip, or the way there's a universe in his laugh. Those things, and how completely perfect and ridiculous it is that he's standing here, holding a baby pig and ruining my life in the best way. And you all could, too. I know you'll join me in analysing every single *move* in the behind-the-scenes footage from this shoot. I know you *get it* even if we all show it in completely different ways. It's amazing, when you stop and think about what has actually happened since I first saw that grainy video of Half Light singing in a garage and felt something inside me turn on. I was looking for a song to listen to while I did my make-up, and I found so much more.

Don't worship idols, they told me.

I'm starting to think it's because they were scared of the whole world I might discover if I did.

There were some parts of what Jas was saying that I couldn't relate to. The closest my family had ever come to anything like religion was when my dad would make us stay in the car until *Crosby, Stills and Nash* had played the whole way through. The older we'd got, the less that had felt like a brilliant adventure, but, when I thought about it, maybe those endless minutes spent sitting outside our house, listening to three boys sing in harmony, is where it all started. *I should thank him for that*, I thought as I remembered.

Even so, there was something in the way Jas made words

come alive that I wanted to be a part of. I ran off a quick Hi. I felt this on a deep level and I don't even know why. We'd started with the video she had mentioned – fourteen gorgeous minutes of Frankie and Jack acting like children, as if they didn't even know the cameras were there, while Kyle looked on affectionately and their management tried to keep them still long enough for the photographers to get their shot – but quickly moved on to talking about our own lives. Hours later, it was her who said we had to stop talking, so we didn't run out of things to say tomorrow, and tomorrow, and tomorrow. We never had. Imagine searching a hashtag for something to read in bed and finding a best friend? It had quickly become my favourite example of fate.

I turned back to my phone, where Jas's eyes were wild but bright with news.

'Have you seen?' she asked before I could even say hello, her south London accent even more distinct than usual. That tended to happen when she got worked up about something.

'Seen what?'

Jas sighed, sinking further back into the pile of pillows she was propped up against in a bedroom I had only ever seen onscreen. She found it exasperating when people didn't have the exact same knowledge base as her.

'Harri, sit down,' she said, and I screwed my face up in confusion.

'Jas, it's FaceTime. I am sitting down – you can see me.'

Another thing that annoyed Jas was when reality got in the way of what she'd already decided she was going to say.

She loved a good line. Who cared if I was already sitting down? That wasn't going to stop her from delivering it.

'What's up?' I asked. 'You look like the world is ending, but you're weirdly excited to tell me.'

'Evan is dead, and Frankie is being questioned in connection.'

OK. That was not what I'd been expecting. I laughed out loud, because this was a *joke*, right? Frankie? Really? Yes, he was the *bad boy* of Half Light, if by bad boy we meant he wore ripped jeans and slightly more eyeliner than the rest, but that was just a perfectly curated act. Nobody who knew the slightest thing about him could ever legitimately suspect him of hurting a *fly*.

I replayed her sentence in my mind, the first part of what she'd said catching only on the second pass.

'Wait, Jas. Say that again?'

She closed her eyes before she spoke this time. 'Evan has been found dead, and they're questioning Frankie in connection.'

Evan.

If I hadn't already been sitting, I was sure my knees would have given way. I wouldn't have believed it no matter who she'd named as the victim, but Frankie as someone who could harm *Evan specifically*? There was just no way.

Evan Byrd was Frankie's best friend. In every childhood photo splashed across the internet as proof that Frankie had always been adorable, Evan was right by his side. In every incriminating image of teenage Frankie that his publicists tried so hard to hide, but the fans always found anyway, Evan could be seen just out of focus, always close enough to make sure that Frankie never *really* got himself into trouble. When *Let There Be Light*, Half Light's first album, had got to number one, it was Evan next to Frankie at every club they'd hit in celebration, underage but glowing so brightly with new fame that everyone forgot to mind. I hadn't seen a single picture from the last night of the Lights Up tour where Evan wasn't looking at Frankie with so much pride in his eyes that it made me want to cry. Just last week they'd been spotted leaving a tattoo shop together, even though there was no sign of the new ink anywhere on Frankie's body yet, according to the girls who had made it their mission to find it. There was constantly more to be discovered about that man.

It was true they'd spent less time together in public since Frankie had *finally* realized he was in love with Jack and admitted his feelings, but that happened at the beginning of any new relationship, right? The long-standing friendship between Frankie and Evan was completely rock solid.

'Can't be true,' I said. 'Where did you read that? A gossip blog? Or –'

'Check BBC news,' she interrupted. 'Check NBC, CNN, whatever else will make you believe me.'

I didn't need to check anywhere. I could tell by the way her voice shook, the opposite of her usual assured tone. I was silent.

'I'm sorry,' she said.

All I could think of to reply was, 'It isn't your fault,' which was ridiculous. Of course it wasn't. I lay down flat on the cold floor, closing my eyes to try to calm every instinct that was telling me to run. *Run where?* I asked myself.

'He didn't do it,' I said after a moment, my voice quiet but certain.

I opened my eyes to see Jas pull herself upright and look straight at me. I couldn't quite read her expression. Something between heartbreak and helplessness, tinged with a little bit of manic energy. I knew how she felt.

'Well, we know that, H, but it isn't looking good. They're holding him. No bail yet, and we know that isn't because his lawyers aren't good enough.'

'They can't have arrested him without evidence, right?'

'They haven't arrested him,' Jas clarified. 'Held and arrested are not the same thing. This is not the worst that could happen. Not yet.'

'God, he must be so scared. Can you even imagine? His best friend is dead, and he's all on his own, and they think he had something to do with it. I feel sick, Jas. I can't believe . . . poor Evan.' I was surprised I made it to the end of the sentence before my voice broke completely.

'I know. But us crying isn't going to help him, Harri. Come on.'

She was right. I pulled myself to my feet a little too fast, and ignored the head rush as I began to pace round the kitchen.

'So what do we do?' I asked. 'What's our plan?'

'What do you mean *do*? We can't do anything, H.'

'We've got to, Jas! How many times have we said we'd do anything for him? For all of them?'

We couldn't just sit by and watch the press destroy Frankie. We couldn't leave him locked away until the police found the real criminal, and this whole thing was written off as a seriously embarrassing mistake that caused even more trauma for Frankie in the midst of an honest-to-God tragedy. We could not *just wait*. We said over and over that we'd be there *no matter what*. I realized, though, that I'd never for a second thought the day would come where we would have to prove it. Where they'd *actually need us*. Where we'd have to step up and be counted, or admit that *I'd do anything* had been empty words all along.

Jas swung her legs round until she was sitting, poised, on the edge of her bed. Behind her I could see her makeshift shrine to Half Light covering one wall. My own had been downsized considerably in the move from the safety of home to the absolute minefield that was uni halls. '*Don't erase yourself*,' I could hear my dad say every time I looked at it, and I had to admit Half Light were a big part of the reason I was here studying music management in the first place, but a few fancily printed Polaroids placed among those of my parents and friends did seem cooler than the collection that had been creeping from the walls to the ceiling in my old room.

'What are you suggesting?' Jas asked, pulling my focus back. 'What do you actually think we can do to help here? We don't know their situation, Harri. We can't even start to guess what's going on.'

'Do you really think he'd do this? Frankie? Kind and loving Frankie, who goes around cuddling baby piglets and encouraging fans to be themselves? And to *Evan*? Besides Jack, there's *nobody* he loves more.'

'We don't know that,' Jas said abruptly.

'Who *are* you?'

'I'm just saying. We don't know.'

'So you think he did it?'

I pretended not to see the mask she threw up as she said, 'No, Harri. Of course I don't think he did it.'

I was almost convinced.

'Go on, then,' she said. 'What are you suggesting?'

'Think about it, Jas,' I said, the plan only really forming as the words came out of my mouth. 'We know these boys better than anyone. They can't make a move without one of us noticing. They say it themselves all the time. "*The fans know more about our lives than we do.*" And now we get to use those powers for good!'

The idea was generating energy as it formed, no details forthcoming, but the outline completely *there*.

'We notice when they wear each other's clothes, or tie a new stupid bit of string round their wrist, or trim their hair. We knew that Frankie and Jack were made for each other *years* before they were finally allowed to admit it. We *know* these boys. We can work out their behaviour – most of the time *predict* their behaviour – because we've spent so long analysing every move they make. We've spent years saying we'd do anything for them and now they need us. So let's do it.'

'Harri, what are you saying?'

Her eyes were sparkling. Jas put on a convincing good-girl act in front of her parents, but I'd never known anyone get quite so excited at the idea of breaking rules.

I couldn't help mirroring her grin.

'I'm saying I don't know much, but here's something I am sure of. I know enough about Frankie Williams to prove he didn't do it.'

The smoke alarm blared a soundtrack to my declaration, my forgotten pizza barely recognizable as grey fumes began to fill the kitchen. I skidded across the floor, trying to reach the alarm and pull out the battery before anyone did something stupid like call security, but had only made it as far as the window, throwing it open wider as I passed, when Stefan appeared in the doorway, the concern on his face turning quickly to laughter once he realized I was OK.

'Harri, you didn't have to start a fire to get my attention, girl. Put it out!'

I definitely wasn't going to engage with his terrible flirting when Frankie needed us. Instead, I smiled at him as I pressed the reset button and silence fell over the kitchen.

'That's exactly what I'm going to do.'

TRACK TWO

There was going to be a press conference. That's what I gathered from the fifty-two unread messages waiting when I picked up my phone again, having finally convinced Stefan that I was going straight to bed and he should get back to the party.

Pulling back the duvet and nestling into the freshly washed sheets, I sighed as my toes wriggled against the cotton. I had almost allowed myself to relax for a second when the light of my phone screen pulled me back to reality. I only skimmed Jas's more and more irate texts, sent as stream-of-consciousness thoughts from the moment we'd hung up twenty minutes ago.

I called her back, and she answered on the first ring, as if she'd been waiting, phone in hand, the whole time. The only thing that betrayed her was the fact that her face had been scrubbed completely clean. I found her only slightly less intense without the eyeliner.

'That was quick.' Her voice dripped with affectionate sarcasm.

'Sorry, Stefan was –'

'He was cute actually, but you didn't call me back to talk about him.'

'No. Sorry. You're right. What's the latest? Who knows?' I asked.

'H, the whole *world* knows. It's all over the news.'

'I meant who have you spoken to, Jas. About the plan.'

I knew that just because she hadn't been talking to me, it didn't mean Jas hadn't been talking.

'I kept it close,' she replied. 'Gemma and Ruby, and I've texted Alex, but she's not replied.'

Her answer made sense. In a far larger group, Gemma, Ruby and Alex were our closest allies, despite the fact that only Alex even lived in the same country. I hoped one day that I would get to feel the sand between my toes as I walked along Venice Beach with Gem, or queue all night for a Berlin super-club with Ruby (ignoring the fact that clubbing made me nervous), but for now I knew what their bedrooms looked like, reduced to the size of an iPhone screen, and I knew how their hearts worked, because they worked like mine. Surely, I thought, that was more of a basis for friendship than deciding to love someone because they lived on your street, or you took the same classes? In a whole world of people, what were the chances that the ones meant for you would be dropped right into your path? No, I thought, our way was much more logical. Magical too. We were proof that if you were meant to find someone, you would. Screw oceans and borders. You just had to know where to look.

I slipped further under my duvet, the night settling heavily over me now.

'So. What do we actually know?'

'Are you sure you're ready to hear this?'

No. 'Of course I am.'

'OK. The police were called earlier tonight – or I guess yesterday now – to that rehearsal studio in the industrial park near Wembley. Albany Road. You know, where –'

'They rehearsed the Lights Up tour, yeah,' I interrupted. I'd recognize that studio anywhere from the hundreds of fan photos taken through the railings by girls just hoping for a glimpse.

'A woman working in one of the other units called to report a man falling from the studio roof. She was too scared to go and check alone, which I think is fair enough. Anyway, the police turned up and found him. Evan. In case that wasn't clear.'

'It was.'

'Sorry.'

'So he fell, then? Or . . . he jumped? Why would they connect that to Frankie?' I asked. I couldn't make the link between what sounded like a horrifying accident and Frankie being questioned by the police. Maybe they'd just called him in for background details; to find out what they could about Evan's life from the people who loved him. That would be routine, right? That was completely different from them thinking Frankie was involved.

Jas paused before she spoke again, and I gripped my duvet nervously. Something told me the worst was still to come.

'That's the thing, H. Albany Road was almost empty that day.'

I knew before she said it – but I still needed to hear it.

'But Frankie was there. Holed up in a studio, music blaring I assume, all on his own. He probably had no idea what was going on right outside the door, H, let alone up on the roof. But . . . yeah. Frankie was there.'

Stay calm, I urged myself. *Remember what Jas said. Us crying right now is not going to help him.*

'Have they said anything about evidence yet?' I wondered aloud as I reached for my laptop and flipped it open.

'No. I guess they can't if it's an active investigation, though. That's a thing. They can't comment.'

'How do you even know that?' I asked.

'Podcasts.'

Her answer was instant. Of course it was podcasts.

'They're going to question Jack, too,' I said. 'I bet they have already.' They'd suspect Jack, because they'd say he was jealous of Evan and Frankie's friendship, and the whole world would turn against him, and –

'He has a solid alibi,' Jas said before I could finish my train of thought. 'Check the Half Light Instagram. He was in a writing session with Kyle the whole afternoon.'

It was a fandom conspiracy theory that whoever ran the official Half Light channels loved to remind the world that it was Jack and Kyle who wrote the songs. Frankie was undoubtedly the frontman, but what he had in charisma he apparently lacked in creativity. I didn't think their social-media manager was that calculating. Frankie was the golden boy. Any attention on the others was welcome in my book.

'Well, that's something, I guess. Have they said anything?'

I was already typing Half Light into Google as I asked, and I had to close my eyes as the results filled the screen. Pictures of Kyle Barber, and their strategy-manager-slash-best-friend Molly, and gorgeous, heartbroken Jack, all with red-ringed eyes, trying to hide beneath completely out-of-character baseball caps that couldn't cover their puffy faces or the fact that they'd all been crying, appeared next to articles declaring with little doubt and even less subtlety that Frankie had done it. That Evan was dead because of him.

'You all right?' Jas asked, and I caught a glimpse of myself in the top corner of my phone screen, my face rigid. I moved my jaw from side to side, trying to release the tension.

'Fine.' I clicked on the first article and skimmed the opening paragraph.

Williams seems angry and hostile ... reluctantly cooperating with enquiries ... relationship with bandmate on the rocks ... bad-boy image proving less contrived than previously imagined ...

If it was me, I thought, I'd be angry and hostile, too. Angry, and hostile, and let down, and disappointed, and completely devastated. *God. He must be so scared.* I'd never been the biggest fan of the gossip press, but now the things they were writing filled me with rage. How could they be making this about Frankie's image when a human being was dead?

'So this press conference . . . are we going?'

Jas knew exactly when a silence had become too heavy; knew exactly when to break it. I closed the browser and turned back to my phone.

'Do you think we should?'

Reasons not to go to the press conference about the criminal investigation currently ongoing against a man you've never met, but have loved for a long time

1. There's very little chance they would even let us in.
2. It's October and it's cold, and travelling to London at 7 a.m. would be a brutal reminder of those things. This sounds like a terrible excuse and a classic case of avoidance. That's because it is.
3. If we're going to investigate this properly, it might be wise to keep a low profile at the beginning, so people don't get suspicious.
   – (By people, I mean police. Is this illegal? Note to self: must check.)
   – (In order to check, will actually need a proper plan.)
4. Inserting yourself into the middle of a murder investigation is almost never a wise move. I assume.
5. Because I want music management to be my career. Getting caught would definitely not help that, right?
6. Because I have no idea what I'm doing.
7. Because Jas has no idea what she's doing.

8. Because I'm scared.
9. What if we have to sit there and listen to them prove he did it?

Reasons to go to the press conference about the criminal investigation currently ongoing against a man you've never met, but have loved for a long time

1. Because it's Frankie.
2. Because we said *no matter what*.
3. Because those two reasons to do it overrule every single reason I can think of not to.

TRACK THREE

I tried to creep out quietly, forgetting that *graceful* was a word that had never been used to describe me. I had no idea how I managed to turn on the wrong light, illuminate the entire corridor, knock my half-full coffee cup from the work-top into the sink, cause a staggering amount of noise trying to close my bedroom door and still get out unquestioned, but I was thanking whichever God was responsible for student body clocks as I pulled my coat tighter against the frosty morning, stepped out on to the campus, and bumped face to arm (my face, his arm) into Stefan.

Of course.

A smile spread across his face, as if he'd caught me in a compromising position. Ironic, since he was the one clearly on his way home from wherever he'd spent the rest of last night.

'Going somewhere?' he asked, raising one dark eyebrow.

It would be so *easy*, I knew, if only I could make myself feel just a little bit more for him. I had wondered more than once, contemplative and alone in the dark, if it was the not-Frankie of him that was holding me back. It wasn't as though I'd ever really thought I'd end up with an international pop star I'd never met, but when you spend so long studying someone's (perfect) face, and falling for them more with every (perfect) thing they say, it's only natural that they become the benchmark for everyone else to measure up to, right?

'Harri?'

Oh. Right. Stef was waiting for an answer, and I briefly considered a flat-out lie. Given the dark circles under his eyes, I suspected he'd go upstairs in a few minutes and not emerge from his room until 5 p.m., by which point, I hoped, I'd be back and all this would be over. He'd never find out where I'd really been. His expectant expression and what-aren't-you-telling-me smile were a disarming combination, though, and since I didn't have time to come up with a fully formed alibi I decided to just go with the truth.

'I'm going to London. A friend is in trouble and just . . . needs someone, you know?'

All right, fine. A version of the truth. *The truth and a fact*, I reminded myself, *are not the same thing at all.*

'Good friend.'

'Yeah . . . a good friend,' I answered, and Stefan laughed. 'I meant you.'

'Oh. Right. Well, they've been there for me when I've needed it so . . .'

He reached out and brushed a hand against mine. 'See you when you get back? Want to watch films in my room tonight?'

I breathed out a laugh and closed my eyes.

'We'll see,' I promised as I turned to walk away. 'Go to bed, you dirty stop-out.'

He grinned at that, a grin that wouldn't have been out of place on a poster, adorning bedrooms the world over. 'Have fun with your friend.'

I nodded.

'Not sure if *fun* is the right word, but I'll try.'

The train was almost empty, just a few stray revellers and well-put-together women in activewear settling in with their coffees as we pulled out of Brighton station and headed towards London.

I'm on the train, I texted Jas as we picked up speed, and then immediately followed with: Is this a mistake?

Her reply took longer than usual so I was expecting one of those classic Jas messages that were somehow lyrical and perfectly crafted while also telling you, if not what you *wanted* to hear, then exactly what you *needed* to. I was surprised when all that came back was:

> I don't know. But think of the
> times and ways he's helped you.
> He needs us.

I was glad that at least she seemed to be fully onside this morning, and hoped the hesitation I'd sensed the night before was just my own paranoia. And she was, as always, completely right. Although I'd never counted, I suspected the times and ways were probably too many to keep track of.

Last year, for example, when my grandad was in hospital, I sat in the waiting room and listened to the live version of *Let There Be Light*, their perfect first album that had started everything. When they sang 'We'll come through this together', I believed them. It felt like they were singing just for me. Faced with literal mortality, I needed something to cling to that would stay the same, and they did. Through multiple image changes – even in the case of Frankie's awful blond hair and Jack's baggy hoodie phase – and every time their sound became, in their words, more mature, they had always kept the essence of Half Light. Everything was moving so fast it made me dizzy, and at the centre of the storm they remained perfectly still.

They'd given us exactly what we needed, and now we had to try to repay that.

He'd have the best team money could buy. That was a given. The best lawyers, the best publicists. Pure PR, the company set up just to handle the way the world saw Half Light, had dedicated years to curating and controlling an image of these boys, spinning stories that were more useful for 'the brand' than the truth could ever be. I'd always found the company name ironic. How could three boys as interesting as these ever be reduced to a word as boring and non-descriptive as *pure*?

I knew that as I sat here, my face pressed to the cool glass of the window, somewhere in London those sleek-haired, size-eight PR girls who could run after a boyband in six-inch heels, who I simultaneously hated and hoped to become some day, were being pulled from their beds. They'd be handed coffees, and bundled into waiting taxis that would take them to their offices with the big windows where they'd start working on getting Frankie out. He wasn't alone in this, I knew that.

But did those people notice when he forgot to wear his favourite necklace? Did they know that he rubbed the butterfly tattoo on his left wrist when he was nervous? Did they even stop to consider that, after so long, he still *got* nervous? Those people were probably so wrapped up in the version of him they'd decided was the truth that they'd stopped seeing the real Frankie at all. How were they going to help him, *really* help him, when they'd never taken the time to get to know him?

I sighed, and typed out a reply.

You're right. He really needs us.

I know. I always am.

Classic Jas.

Desperate for a distraction, I opened up Twitter, kidding myself that someone out there might be shouting into the void about anything other than what was happening to Frankie. No such luck. Practically my entire timeline was flooded with Phoebe Shaw's smiling face, head pressed close to Frankie's, a memory of happier times.

What has she got to say for herself? I wondered, clicking through to the original image on her Instagram.

I had nothing against Phoebe. Of all the many women Frankie had been linked with since the band made it big, she was probably the one I'd liked the most. A wannabe singer and influencer who was rarely out of a bikini, she seemed to have taken it pretty graciously when her boyfriend had broken up with her and immediately started dating his bandmate. *Respect*, I'd thought at the time. *Would I have been so calm? But, then again, Jack and Frankie are undeniable. Poor girl never really had a chance.*

Plus, Frankie had seemed to really care about her. I was grateful that he'd found people like Phoebe to carry him through those years before he realized he was allowed to love Jack; grateful that he'd had people who made him happy. In another life, I maybe could have even seen them lasting, two beautiful people just trying to navigate the apparent hardships that fame brought with it. But, if you placed a picture of them together beside an identically posed shot of Frankie with Jack, there could be no question that Phoebe had never been the one.

The picture on my screen now was new to me. Frankie and Phoebe's faces were both bare of make-up, and they were smiling at the camera on the phone Frankie was holding. I instinctively knew that it was a selfie never meant for anyone's eyes but their own. I tried to date it by the way Frankie's hair fell, but the complete lack of product in it meant I couldn't be sure. I loved him like this – private, and as close to relaxed as I'd ever seen him. I tried to ignore the tiny niggle that told me that I shouldn't be poring over shots he hadn't intended anyone to see.

Well, Phoebe posted it, I thought. *That justifies it, right?* I scrolled down to the caption.

You've probably all heard by now that my old friend Frankie is being held in connection with the tragic death of his beloved Evan. I'm certain the police are just doing their job and eliminating everyone systematically, but I could not stand by and say nothing. Frankie Williams is one of the gentlest, most loving men I have ever known, and yeah we all know he has his wild side, but to believe he could have had anything to do with this horrible accident is a stretch I can't make. Evan has been there for Frankie since they were four years old. They love each other so dearly. I don't know the facts, but the Frankie I know could never have done this. I know a lot of people are going to be hurting. I know this is hard, to see someone you love being accused of something so terrible. I'm feeling it too. So I just wanted to say that there's no shame at all if you need to take a step back while all this is going on. Frankie wouldn't want you to feel bad because of him, or for your own mental health to suffer. He cares so much about all of you. Do what you need to, please, and don't worry about him. The best people work with Half Light, and they're going to get him out of this. Until they do, though, my comments are open. If you need to talk, you can do it here. Take care of yourselves. Phoebe x

I closed Instagram and navigated straight to my texts with Jas.

Think we underestimated Phoebe Shaw, I tapped out.

> I know, right? What an absolute
> human angel.

I clicked back into the post and began to scroll through the comments.

Potentially a mistake, I thought as I tried to make my eyes go blurry over one that simply read, I always knew he was psychotic. I braced myself. *Carry on.* There were a couple of others along the same lines – questioning Phoebe's certainty, and Frankie's innocence, and as a result *Phoebe's innocence* – but eventually I found what I was looking for.

I'm scared, the first one began. I've loved Frankie for five years, and I know he wouldn't do this, and seeing people talk about him like this is making me feel awful. I'm really glad that, if this has to be happening, we're all in it together. Half Light have the best fans.

I was surprised to see Phoebe's name among the replies to the comment. *Not just lip service, then. She really is trying to be there for the people who love him.*

> I know it's hard, but please, please, put yourself first. Talk to other fans, talk about why you love him, talk about all the things he's going to do when he gets out to help find whoever is responsible for this. Take care, and remember I'm here.

I kept scrolling, and saw that Phoebe's name appeared beneath more comments than not. She shared memories, and tried to be comforting, and completely ignored anyone who was clearly trying to bait her into saying something she'd regret. Every comment ended the same way: *I'm here.* Although I hadn't known I'd needed it, I found myself feeling comforted by her presence. It meant a lot, that after everything that had happened between them Phoebe was still in Frankie's corner.

It's not just us, I thought. *This isn't one of those things where we're looking at him through rose-tinted fan glasses. He didn't do it. Even his ex is saying so.*

The morning was still misty as the train stuttered to a stop at Victoria Station, and I shoved my hands deep into my pockets in desperate search of some warmth as I half ran across the concourse. *Why were train stations always so cold?* It was one of those places that, on a weekday morning, would heave with commuters, but as I opened the door the cafe was almost empty. I glanced at the time on my phone as I silenced my music midway through 'Starlight', not my favourite of Half Light's songs, but a good one all the same. It was 8.20 a.m. Even London was mostly still sleeping this early on a Saturday.

Jas waved as she saw me walking over. I noticed the eyeliner was back, and wondered how she could get her hand steady enough to look so put together. I made a mental note to top up my make-up before we left. *If we have any chance at all of fitting in with the journalists and publicists today,* I thought, *we've got to look the part.* When you spend five years watching every move Half Light make, you learn a thing or two about acting the way you want the world to see you.

It was only as I reached the table and Jas stood up that I realized I'd forgotten to worry about what was about to happen.

Jas was bouncing from foot to foot as I reached out to her, and I immediately felt awkward. What was I going to do, shake her hand? She was the first person I wanted to tell all my news, and almost always the last one I spoke to before falling asleep. She'd talked me through grief and healing, and I'd guided her through many a family fight. We might never have met in person before, but Jas was my best friend. I couldn't just shake her hand. The look on her face in the moment before she hugged me told me she felt the same. It felt like coming home.

'Morning, sunshine,' she said. She smelled like clean washing and the Half Light perfume we'd all dutifully bought as soon as it was released. Its overly sweet scent was so familiar (I sprayed it on my pillows when I needed a little extra comfort) that I immediately felt safe. This girl was not a stranger. Screw anyone who said she was.

I was caught off guard, when I looked over her shoulder, to see Alex walking towards us from the counter, juggling three takeaway coffee cups.

'Alex is here?' I asked, and Jas nodded.

'Are you surprised?'

'Sort of.'

'She's weirdly cut up about it.' Jas lowered her voice as she spoke again. 'About Evan, I mean. Obviously, we're all upset, it's horrible, but I didn't know he meant that much to her.'

Maybe *surprised* was the wrong word, I conceded. It wasn't like I'd ever questioned Alex's devotion for a second, but, of all of us, it was she who had managed to make Half Light look like a sidenote to her real life, rather than the main attraction. She seemed older than the rest of us, I'd always thought, and had the kind of nonchalance you could not learn. If it wasn't in your bones, you were never going to come close. She had a sharp blond haircut, and a tall, willowy body, and every so often I still let myself be intimidated by that. But she was always there with a well-timed message if someone in our group chat couldn't sleep. She knew what to say if you were dumped, or drunk, or daydreaming. When to make you laugh, and when it was a little more serious than that. Why should I be surprised that she was here? When I thought about it, she always had been.

'How are you feeling?' she asked as I pulled out a chair and sat down, gratefully wrapping my cold hands round the coffee she handed me. No hello, no 'nice to meet you', but that seemed right. It felt more like picking up where we'd left off.

'Weird,' I admitted. 'Like . . . I'm not really feeling much at all, which is scaring me a little bit. It's going to absolutely blindside me when it hits, isn't it?'

'It might not hit,' Jas said, reaching over to rub my wrist. 'Maybe he'll be released this morning, and we'll get to pretend it didn't happen.'

'Or remember that it did happen and we went to battle for him,' Alex piped up.

'Evan will still be dead, though. Frankie will never get over that.' My voice was hoarse suddenly.

Alex looked down at her boots. 'That poor guy. He didn't do anything to deserve this.'

I reached across the table for her hand. 'I know, but he'll get out, Al.'

She looked at me like I'd descended from another planet. 'I meant Evan.'

Oh.

Was I an awful person? I wondered. Was it terrible that my first thought was still for Frankie? *Alive*, probably going to live a long and hopefully happy life Frankie, and not Evan? I felt completely racked with guilt, and wished I could take the comment back.

'Sorry. I just – I can't believe this is happening.'

Alex nodded. 'I know. I get it. Neither can I.'

I wasn't sure if it was the coffee or the nerves beginning to turn my stomach, but suddenly I desperately needed to get out of there. The cafe was starting to fill up now, the background buzz making it hard to focus, and I needed to keep a clear head if we were going to be of any help to Frankie at all.

I pushed back from the table and stood up. 'Shall we get out of here?'

Jas put out a hand to stop me.

'We're going to need all the help we can get to fit in at the press conference. Alex brought provisions.'

At that, Alex pulled a bulging carrier bag from underneath the table, and I didn't know whether to be scared or thankful when I saw what looked like a wig sticking out of the top.

'Disguises?' I asked, and Jas laughed out loud.

'If that's what you want to call it! But we look like students, H. We look like *fans*. Alex knows what people wear at these things. Think of it like –'

'Playing a character,' Alex interrupted. 'I do it all the time when I'm in situations where I'm not that comfortable. It's amazing the difference a costume can make.'

'*Costume?*' I asked, and this time the laughter came from both of them.

'Nothing drastic, I promise!' said Alex. 'Just a bit more make-up – maybe a blazer or something.'

'It'll be fun,' Jas chimed in, and I had to admit that I could use a helping hand. This might actually work.

The worst is already happening, I reminded myself. *We can't change that, but we can try to make what comes next for Frankie a little better. He needs us now. So suck it up, Harri.*

'Lead the way,' I said, and Alex clapped her hands together with joy as she walked ahead of us to the bathroom.

TRACK FOUR

'I look absolutely ridiculous.'

Even as I said it, I realized I didn't entirely hate the way Alex had painted her thick black-cat eyeliner on to my lids. It was way too much for a Saturday morning – probably way too much even for a Saturday night – but I knew that she wouldn't let me make a fool of myself.

'You look great,' she promised without fully looking up. 'Just don't smile like that.'

'Like what?'

'Like . . . whatever you're doing. It's intense.'

'That's my smile!' I looked in the mirror as I spoke, and had to admit that she was sort of right, even though I wasn't doing anything differently.

'Don't smile, then,' she concluded as the cubicle door behind us was unlocked, and Jas stepped – or more accurately wobbled – out.

'Do I really have to wear heels?' she asked, clinging to the doorframe like a lifeline.

I bit my lip to keep from cracking up. Alex was far less

35

restrained. She burst into laughter as Jas teetered towards the sinks, and reached out for Alex to stop herself falling.

'OK, let's rethink that!' said Alex. 'Take them off before you break your neck. I'll wear them. Let's swap.'

As Jas kicked off the shoes, Alex pulled the long red wig from her head and tossed it in Jas's general direction. Jas caught it, holding it at arm's length, her face screwed up in confusion.

'Al, nobody is going to believe that's my real hair colour.'

'Does it matter? You could've dyed it! That isn't anybody's real hair colour!'

'I thought the point was that we'd fit in,' I said. 'This is like . . . the opposite!'

Alex snatched the wig back out of Jas's hands, stuffing it back in her bag as she stepped into the heels. 'It is, but if we don't make any effort they'll be looking at us because we'll stand out anyway. Just *trust* me.'

I understood why she was stressed, but I knew that we needed her onside to have any chance of pulling this off.

'I'll wear it,' I said, reaching for the wig and wrestling it over my own hair. I hoped it would give off less of a Little Mermaid vibe on my head than it had in my hands.

Alex reached out and smoothed down a stray curl, and I had to admit that when I glanced back over my shoulder in the mirror I almost looked like I could belong.

Almost.

'Have you done this before?' I asked Alex as we rounded the corner and saw the hotel.

'No, but people on my course have. Sports journalism students mostly, wanting to be near footballers.'

'Not so different,' Jas said, and Alex pulled a face.

'Try telling them that. Being a fan is the most tragic thing they can possibly think of, unless you're a fan very specifically of the same thing as them. I've stopped even fighting it. What's the point?'

'I can imagine,' I said. 'I was so excited when the last World Cup came around and I thought I might actually have a way in with my dad. I was like, "You know how you feel about England now, and you really want them to win, even though you don't know any of the players personally and it won't affect your actual day-to-day life in any way? And all your friends feel the same so it's something that unites you? Well, imagine feeling like that about something for five years non-stop. Cos that's how I feel about Half Light." But apparently it's not the same thing at all. I don't think I stayed in the room long enough to find out *why* not.'

'Because boybands are for girls and football isn't?' Alex suggested, rolling her eyes.

'I don't think they'd admit to it in so many words, but yeah, probably. Anyway, what about us?' I asked. 'How are we going to get in?'

At this, Alex slowed ever so slightly, and turned to look at me as she spoke.

'It'll take a pretty massive leap of faith. I've got ID saying I'm a member of the press, and if you hold it in a certain way, and pray they're too busy to really care, they won't even notice that it says STUDENT. Then, if they ask,

37

you just say you're an intern. I'll almost definitely get away with saying one of you is my photographer. But – and it's a *huge* but – this all depends on how many other fans have had the same idea. If it's mobbed, we have no chance. We probably won't even get to the door. We're just going to have to play it by ear, ladies. Remember, though, we're doing it for Frankie. Even if we fail, we tried. That's got to count for something.'

I liked her confidence. Didn't mean for a second I thought her plan would work. For one thing, we'd heard the chatter of the waiting fans from a street away. They weren't screaming yet, which probably meant there hadn't been so much as a glimpse of the boys, but, as we approached, the girls were unmissable, held back from the entrance by a barrier, a security guard patrolling the line from one end to the other. And, if the guard wasn't intimidating enough, the hotel itself didn't feel particularly welcoming. The shallow steps up to the entrance were lined with grand marble pillars wrapped in slightly-too-early Christmas lights, and the traditionally dressed doorman, one hand on the gold handle, only further confirmed that we weren't getting in. Half Light were very good at making us feel part of their world, but there were plenty of places – the private clubs, the invite-only parties, the five-star hotels – where the fans could never go.

'Now what?' I asked, and Alex stopped.

'Honestly, Harri? I have no idea.'

'Should we just join them?' Jas pointed at the crowd. 'Try to catch a glimpse at least?'

She took a step, and Alex's hand flew out to pull her back.

'Absolutely *not*,' she hissed. 'I'm not giving up yet. I have one more *possible* plan, but if anyone sees us in that crowd it's over. Now act like you're looking for someone.' Then she began craning her neck, rising up on to her tiptoes, and scanned the crowd like she really was trying to spot a friend.

'Are we?' I asked as I mirrored her movements, and her nod was almost imperceptible.

'Even more of a long shot than the last plan, but yes. There's this one lecturer of mine who does a lot of work for entertainment magazines. She likes me because I'm not too high and mighty to admit I read them, unlike most of the snobs in her classes. Why you'd even study journalism if you can't appreciate there's a place for all of it – or at least most of it – I don't know. Anyway. This is exactly her bag. If she's here, she might be able to get us past that lot. Then it's back down to us, but it's a step in the right direction. OK, come on.'

Alex strode forward, barely giving me and Jas time to follow; we were almost running to keep up with her. She stopped when she reached a tall dark-haired woman, and it was obvious from the way the woman hugged her that she was pleased to see Alex, or at least going along with the plan.

'This is my lecturer, Anna,' Alex said quietly as we caught up. 'Look like we're all talking. Just some journalists having a chat!'

'Have you told her what we're really doing here?' Jas whispered.

Anna laughed. 'I can actually hear you. And she was just in the middle of explaining that. Alex, carry on.'

'So, like I was saying, we need to get into that press conference, Anna. Something's wrong, and we know enough about these boys to work out what, if only we can access the information. I know we can do it. And now you probably think I'm completely unprofessional and I'll fail your class – and even *then* I won't regret trying – because it's stupid Frankie Williams.'

Anna placed a hand on Alex's arm, and laughed again. 'If I thought it would be that easy, of course I'd help you. Do you know how many of us became entertainment journalists because we were fans? But these people see scenes like this every day. Maybe not on a Half Light scale, granted, but that isn't to say they won't be prepared. You think you're the only ones who'll be trying a stunt like this?'

I sort of had.

'So you're saying we have no chance at all?' Alex asked.

Anna's face became serious. 'I didn't say that. I said it wouldn't be as easy as the three of you just walking in.'

The way she emphasized the word *three* made my stomach drop. I feared I knew where this was going. At least one of us would be left out in the cold.

'So what do we do?' I said.

Anna thought for a second.

'Alex, you'll get in with your ID, I think. It's busy. These guys at least aren't checking against a list, although that may happen once you're through the door. It should be fine. Then one of the others as your photographer will probably work too.' Her eyes flitted to the camera bag slung over Jas's shoulder. 'And that leaves –'

'It leaves me, doesn't it?' I tried to keep my voice steady, but my panic levels were rising. I couldn't bear the thought of standing out here with these strangers while Alex and Jas got to be in the same room as Kyle and Jack.

Jas spun round to face me.

'Harri, no. We're not leaving anyone.' She reached out and squeezed my shoulder. 'One of us will just have to get in another way.'

Unsurprisingly, that didn't make me feel better.

'Anna, can you give us a second?' said Alex and, as Anna excused herself to make a phone call, Jas crouched down and started rifling through her bag, discarding random bits of make-up, receipts and sweet wrappers in a pile beside her.

'What are you looking for?' I asked.

She tilted her head up at me and grinned. 'I have no idea yet, but I will when I find it. Just something that will get us – yeah, that could work.' She held up a crumpled pharmacy bag as she spoke. 'OK, Harri –'

'Why me?' I interrupted. 'I'm terrible under pressure!'

'You have the best disguise,' she said. 'Once you get in there, you whip off the wig and they'll never recognize you.'

While I didn't like it one bit, I had to admit she had a point.

'Fine,' I said. 'What's the plan?'

Jas stood up and beckoned me closer as she handed me the bag.

'That's my girl. OK. Here's what we're going to do.'

I lingered at the back of the crowd until my phone vibrated in my hand. Jas's text told me everything I needed to put my part of the plan into action.

> Scarlett in the foyer with a guest
> list, no sign of any other Pure
> people so, if they ask, you're
> meeting her.

That meant they had at least made it through the door. Time to go.

I kept my head up against all my better instincts as I walked towards the service entrance, hands jammed firmly in my pockets to stop myself from running them through my hair, otherwise I'd end up pulling off the wig in front of the security guards right at the moment I needed them to take me seriously. Looking at the ground would have given them less time to memorize my features, but the kind of girl I was pretending to be would not have looked down, and so neither could I.

Eyes on the prize, I told myself as I went over the plan in my head. It was risky, I knew, but I couldn't let myself be the one that ruined it. If I got caught, it wouldn't be long before Jas and Alex came to look for me, and who knew what they'd do to us then? *Was it a crime to talk your way into a private event under false pretences?* Probably not, but I didn't want to find out. It definitely wouldn't *help*, that much I was sure of.

I started to smile as I got closer, the features on the guard's face coming into focus, then I remembered what Alex had said in the bathroom: *Don't smile.* I twisted my face back into what I hoped was a neutral expression, praying that he hadn't been paying enough attention to notice in the first place, but the way he seemed to be choking back a laugh suggested I was out of luck.

'Can I help you?' His voice was rough. I recoiled slightly as he shifted his weight from one foot to the other, blocking the door in a way that seemed more deliberate than before.

For Frankie, I reminded myself, and smiled again. This time I couldn't help it.

I lifted the pharmacy bag from where it was dangling at my side, my hand obscuring the label as I prayed the guard wouldn't take a closer look and ask who Jas Sidana was supposed to be.

'Kyle's medication,' I said, taking just a second of pride in the way my voice barely shook at all. 'It's been a bit of a chaotic morning, so it got missed, and it's important that he has it.'

I had no idea if the man now glaring at me in a way that was making me sweat a bit would even know who Half Light were. Perhaps he had no idea at all what I was talking about. From his unchanging expression, I couldn't tell.

'I can take that.'

He reached out a meaty hand and I recoiled, pulling the paper bag to my chest.

'Afraid not. Rich said I had to deliver it personally. Apparently, we've had problems before.'

There was a silence, the kind that had always made me feel as though it was my job to fill it, and I bit the inside of my lip to stop myself saying something that would give the whole game away.

'I can't just let you in here. You could be anyone.'

I sighed. We'd seen this coming.

'If he says no, blind him with science,' Jas had said. 'Just keep going, keep stating facts, make it as clear as day that you know what you're talking about and you're meant to be there. You can do this, H.'

I'd tried to argue; tried to make her see that she or Alex would have been much better suited to the role; that thinking on my feet and staying cool in the face of confrontation was not exactly my strong suit. Obviously it hadn't worked.

'I get it,' I said, smiling at the guard in a way I hoped was less manic. 'It's just that this has all been quite hard on the boys, you know? So it's really important I give him his medication, to stop it getting any harder.'

It had been headline news – or at least that's how it seemed from inside the Half Light bubble – when Kyle had told a journalist he was medicating his anxiety. I'd been proud of him. It had meant so much to see someone in his position saying, 'I'm making it a priority that I get better.' I hoped he knew how many fans it had pushed to get help,

44

too. It was the closest I had ever come myself, by a long shot.

'Who did you say sent you?' he asked, and I hoped it wasn't wishful thinking that made his features seem softer suddenly.

'Rich Charles? Half Light's manager?'

The guard considered this for a moment, then stepped, just slightly, to the side. 'Do you know where you're going?'

To lie and risk getting it wrong, or admit the truth? Both came with perils, I knew, but I suddenly had a new burst of confidence. I flicked my long red hair back over my shoulder, taking a second to appreciate how good that felt, and stepped into the doorway.

'No, but my colleague Scarlett is in the reception. I'll check in with her.'

Apparently, this was good enough. Tapping a pass against a card reader I hadn't noticed before, the guard pulled the door open and waved me through.

'Thank you!' I said breathlessly, and, if the gratitude in my voice gave me away, I was gone before he had a chance to comment.

The door clicked closed behind me, and I was halfway up the concrete staircase before I stopped to consider my surroundings. I couldn't tell, from the nondescript walls and complete lack of sound in the hallway, where in the hotel I was, but as I kept going towards the top, my boots clacking in a completely indiscreet fashion, I could just about pick out muffled chatter from behind the door at the end of the staircase. I straightened my wig and kept going.

The door was heavy but, mercifully, unlocked and, as I stepped from the top step on to a carpet so thick my heel sank into it, I felt as though I was stepping into their world. There was no time to stop and take it all in. I stuffed the empty pharmacy bag on to an unmanned room-service trolley as I passed, and pulled the frankly uncomfortable wig off and threw it into an open room, laughing out loud as I imagined the confusion of whoever found it. I was so busy marvelling at how light my head suddenly felt that I didn't even notice the striking Asian woman until she was mere steps away from me. *Damn these silent, rich-people carpets.*

Her heels were the thin kind that looked as if they defied the laws of gravity. Her eyelashes were longer than they seemed in photographs and, although she was around the same size as me, this woman was what I'd describe as curvy, a contrast to my muscular frame. She'd been the boys' publicist almost since the beginning. Everyone knew who Scarlett was.

She stopped in the middle of the corridor, looking down at her phone, and I slipped into an open doorway, crossing everything that I wouldn't be exposed by the housekeeping staff.

I flattened my back against the wall, close enough to the door to see if Scarlett passed, but hoping I wasn't *too* close that she'd notice me the moment she looked up. After a second, she began to speak. Peeking round the doorframe, I saw that she was pacing the corridor, phone to her ear. I quickly withdrew and tried to focus on what she was saying.

'I don't know how we can hide that they were in financial trouble, that's all. The spotlight on the inner workings of Half Light is the last thing any of us need, but that's what we've ended up with, so forgive me if I'm not really interested in your opinion, and need you to *do your job*.'

The boys were in financial trouble?

'No, I know the fact that we're haemorrhaging cash has nothing to do with Evan *falling off a roof*, but if they're looking into that they're going to find out, aren't they? Hang on –'

She fell silent, and I inched closer to the door to see what was going on. A flustered-looking girl I didn't recognize popped her head round the corner.

'We have to go – they're starting,' she said, and Scarlett nodded, holding up a finger.

'One second,' she said. Then, turning her attention back to the phone in her hand: 'Just keep your head down, and do what we ask you to. We don't have time for mistakes. We hired you because you said you were onboard with the narrative, Georgia. So prove it.'

Without another word, she began to stride down the corridor, the flustered girl hot on her heels. As soon as they disappeared from sight, I followed. *Georgia*. I knew exactly who Scarlett had been talking to. Georgia was a fan, or had been until she'd won one of Pure PR's ridiculously competitive internships and suddenly was far too good for the rest of us. The inner circle had swallowed her whole. We'd sort of been friends once, but it was like she'd completely disappeared. She and Alex used to hang out, I remembered suddenly. Two beautiful people right on the cusp of making it inside. Maybe she could help. Maybe she'd talk to Al. Surely her loyalty was still to Frankie, and not whatever Scarlett was so worried about?

I rounded the corner into the foyer, and immediately Alex was in front of me, a look of relief on her face.

'Oh, thank *God* you're all right. What took you so long?'

I shook my head. 'Tell you later. We need to speak to Georgia.'

'Georgia? Seriously?'

I nodded. 'Where's Jas?' I asked as Alex guided me towards the open doors of the conference room.

'Saving seats. Which is the opposite of blending in, but I couldn't talk her out of it.'

Classic Jas.

The long table at the front of the room was empty as we walked past rows of hovering journalists to where Jas was waiting, apart from three glasses of water, and three microphones.

Why do they need three if Frankie isn't here? I wondered, hope swelling for barely a second before I realized that one of them must be for Rich Charles, head of Half Light's management company and official spokesperson in circumstances where the boys could not be trusted to speak for themselves. I supposed that their bandmate being questioned in a murder case would count as one of those situations. The set-up was sparse compared to the hundreds just like it I had pored over videos of. Usually, there was something to let you know who was coming. I guessed it didn't work like that when you had no time to plan, though. Nobody had thought to print a banner emblazoned with Half Light's logo when one of their number was in police custody. They all had other things on their mind.

'Where are they?' I asked.

Jas looked up from where she was scrolling through her phone. 'Left Jack and Frankie's house about ten minutes ago, according to the girls waiting outside.'

'Both of them?'

'Yeah. Kyle and Rich picked Jack up.'

I rolled my eyes as I sat down beside her, and she passed the phone to me.

'Can't those girls give them *one day* without turning up outside their front door?' I said.

'Do you think it's that much worse than us having blagged our way in here?' Jas asked, and I nodded.

'Yeah, don't you? It's like . . . that's their *home*. I'd never cross that line.'

'I suppose,' Jas said, sounding somewhat unconvinced.

'You think it's bad that we're here?'

She shrugged. 'I don't know what I think any more, H.'

I looked down at the Insta post on her screen. It showed Jack and Kyle looking, if not *normal*, then at least more coiffed than they had since Evan's death. Someone had clearly caught them with a concealer brush because the dark circles were barely visible. They were even walking in step. The epitome of a united front.

I wondered what they were really thinking.

The boys are looking solemn but strong as they leave the house this morning, **the post began.** I know we'll be judged for coming here, but we just wanted them to know they still have our support, and that we're always on their side.

I could appreciate the sentiment, even if it wasn't the way I'd have shown it myself.

The chatter stopped abruptly as a portly man in police uniform strode down the centre aisle and took a seat behind the table. He tapped the microphone and shuffled the papers in front of him, then began to speak.

'Before we start and I'm joined by the members of Half Light and the head of their management, I'd like to update you on the criminal investigation into the death of Evan Byrd. As reported last night, police were called at five thirty-seven p.m. yesterday, Friday, October the twenty-fifth, to an address in Wembley following reports of a man falling from a building. The man, identified as Evan Byrd, was sadly pronounced dead at the scene. Unfortunately, this case is now being classed as a suspected homicide, and this morning Frankie Williams, who has been helping with our enquiries since the incident yesterday, was formally arrested in connection.'

It felt like all the blood in my body had rushed to my ears at once. I could barely hear what the police officer was saying, or the explosion of journalist chatter from the room. On my left, I felt Jas fold forward, as if to place her head between her knees, and Alex immediately reached across my lap and yanked her back upright.

'Professional, Jas,' she hissed.

I pinched my thigh to centre myself. *Stay in the room. You need to listen to this so you can work out what to do next.*

I forced myself to focus. The police officer was talking about an impending trial, and what would happen if Frankie was charged. *Arrested and charged are not the same thing*, I reminded myself. *This is not the worst it could be, not yet.* It helped, just slightly, but I still felt sick.

'I'm sure you have a lot of questions so I'm going to bring out the members of Half Light and head of their management, Richard Charles.'

The officer stood as the doors opened, and the boys and Rich walked straight down the aisle without looking at anyone.

It was the first time I'd been in the same room as them, unless you counted arenas so huge you could barely make out their faces. It was intoxicating. I bit the inside of my lip and hoped I wouldn't cry. A part of me had always imagined I would.

▶

How We Met – Kyle

We met in the queue for ice creams, golden hour, Tuesday afternoon, somewhere towards the end of summer. The beach was busy with teenage girls trying only to impress the boys they'd come with; so preoccupied that they didn't even notice the brooding beauty keeping mostly to himself; the drummer from their real favourite band, not the one they'd mention when they were trying to seem cool. You were hiding in plain sight. I, though, noticed you. I should have been quicker; should have known from the tattoo snaking above the waistband of your yellow swimming trunks that this was a body I was familiar with, but it's strange the way these things so rarely happen how you've imagined them. It wasn't until you spoke, a northern lilt asking softly for a Mint Choc Chip, that my thoughts began firing too fast for my brain to keep up with, and I realized it was you.

'Kyle.'

The sound that came out was more breath than voice, but you heard me, and you turned and smiled. It was only then that I considered that you might have come here not to be found. That I might have just ruined your plans.

'Hi,' you said, and your voice was quiet but so familiar. You'd never been my favourite – that crown had always been held by Mr Frankie Williams, but it was Half Light, not him, that was the making of me, and Half Light was not Half Light without you.

You asked my name and I told you. I asked what you were doing here, a million miles away from anywhere I'd expect to find you, and found that my first guess was right. You were hiding. I promised not to tell, even though you didn't ask me to.

To this day, we're the only ones who know about the golden hour where your skin was warm from the heat of the sun, and my glow was because of you.

*

We met in the crowd at a festival. Of all the people I expected to bump into, sticky with sweat and bleary-eyed from lack of sleep, you were low on the list. I thought at first that maybe I was hallucinating; that maybe I was so sun-tired that I was dreaming you into life. Shouldn't you be backstage, with the other stars? But you weren't. You were dancing with your eyes closed, more of your beer flying out of the cup and on to the ground, your shirt, other people than was actually going into your mouth. I think you could feel me watching, because you opened your eyes and smiled as you turned to me, and it felt like being caught red-handed.

'You all right?'

You knew I'd recognized you. That much was obvious. I nodded. 'I'm fine.'

'I'm Kyle.'

'I know.'

You laughed, and I realized that was a weird answer, even if it was true.

'Harri,' I said, and you held out a hand for me to shake.

'Nice to meet you, Harri.'

The music swelled and you closed your eyes again. There was no chance you'd remember this meeting in the morning, I realized, as you swayed unintentionally on your feet. I knew I couldn't take a photo; couldn't tell anyone this had happened.

'Nice to meet you, Kyle. I should . . . go.'

You waved without opening your eyes, but I'd like to think you knew I was doing it for your protection. That if it was up to me, nothing else considered, I would have stayed by your side all night. I turned back to see the crowd surge, and you disappear into it. Like the sand being swept away by a wave. Like blossom in the air, carried off by the wind. Like someone who was there, and then, just as quickly, was not.

We met in a music shop, the summer before I left for uni, when I was so desperate for some extra cash that I wasted my Saturdays behind the desk, flicking through records that nobody ever bought, CDs that nobody ever requested, and tapes that nobody even had the machines to play any more. It was the kind of shop that nobody ever came into, which made it even more remarkable when you did. On the other hand, I should not have been surprised. Of the three of you, you'd always been the one who was really in it for the love of music.

The bell above the door chimed, and I tried to remember what I was actually supposed to be doing there; how to talk to customers; any knowledge of music whatsoever in anticipation of what your question might be. And then I looked up. I think you saw the moment that I recognized you, because you smiled, and your whole face softened in a way I rarely saw in photographs. You were, after all, supposed to be the cool one.

'Can I help?' I asked, and my voice was hoarse, but I was feeling too many other things at once to make space for embarrassment.

'Just looking,' you said, and I nodded, permission for

you to look as long as you liked, as if you needed permission from me to do anything at all.

I watched you as you browsed, and I think you knew because every now and then you'd stop as you flicked through the boxes of vinyl, and smile in my direction. I tried to turn away, to go back to what I was doing before you walked in, but since that was absolutely nothing my eyes kept wandering back to you.

'Thanks for your help,' you said as you left without buying anything. It was a struggle to wait until you'd turned the corner, until the door had fully closed, before I crossed the shop and started flicking through the same vinyl, desperate for my hands to be where yours had been.

We met in the conference room of a fancy hotel, the morning after the police took Frankie. You swept past and your eyes met mine, just for a second. I smiled, to let you know we were still on your side. You didn't return it.

They took their seats behind the long table, the silence punctuated only by a few camera clicks, somewhere between awkward and respectful.

'Half Light and Richard Charles,' the police officer repeated, before standing aside, and gesturing for them to begin.

How can he call them Half Light when Frankie isn't here? I thought. *It looks incomplete without him. They're a unit. It doesn't work without all of them.*

Rich spoke first, reading from a single sheet of paper

that he held with both hands. *To stop it from shaking?* I wondered.

'As you've just heard, this morning Frankie Williams was arrested in connection with the death of our friend, Evan Byrd. We're helping the police with their enquiries in any way we can, but our position is that we support Frankie wholeheartedly, and believe he was not involved. We'll take questions, but please, guys, be respectful and understand there are some things we won't answer.'

His voice was rougher than I'd imagined in person, a strong Essex accent tinged with bravado and a little bit of defensiveness, but neither of those things could hide what sounded, to me at least, like genuine emotion. This was a man whose greatest achievement had been not just curating brand Half Light, but inventing it in the first place. So much of what they were was because Rich had made them that way.

Not really why we love them, though, I reminded myself. *The reason we paid attention in the first place maybe, but the things we adore about them now? That's entirely them.*

He must be terrified, I knew, that something none of us had seen coming could derail his whole masterpiece in a second. It was his job to anticipate the things that could break Half Light, and stop them from happening. And now Frankie was in jail. I thought that must count as a pretty big fail.

The silence seemed to last less than a second before the journalists were shouting over each other to be heard. Between questions about loyalty and the future of the band, it was Jack's name being hollered over and over and, when a woman I recognized from one of the major news shows finally shouted with enough clout to quieten down the rest of them, it was him she was zeroing in on.

'Jack, how do you feel about the fact that you were in a relationship with someone capable of murder and you didn't know? Or did you know?'

'Don't answer that!' Rich shouted in Jack's direction, at the same time that Jack said, 'Of *course* I didn't know.'

'So you *do* think he's capable of murder?' the woman continued, her tone even more accusatory than before. Jack's face went white.

'I didn't say that,' he whispered, but the microphone in front of him picked up every tremble in his voice. It felt like the way that people always describe a car crash – impossible to look away from, but horrifying to watch. Jack was a big guy, his shoulders broad and his whole body strong-looking. To see him this vulnerable, even when we knew he was gentle and loving and kind, a complete contrast to Frankie's magnetism and chaos – and that vulnerability was nothing new for him – made me feel physically sick.

'What does this mean for your relationship?' another woman in the front row piped up, jumping on the coat-tails of the previous journalist, her tone gentler but still probing.

'You all right?' Rich asked, and Jack nodded before he spoke.

'I'm standing by him until I have any reason at all not to. Which, right now, I don't. I'm just focusing on doing everything I can to get him out, and back where he belongs. With me.'

I closed my eyes and squeezed my hands into fists to stop myself applauding. He was nailing it. Wasn't he? I realized I had no idea what the right thing for him to say was in this situation.

'There must be evidence, no?' the gentler woman continued. I was starting to dislike her, too. 'I mean, they must have arrested him for a reason?'

Jack took a deep breath. 'I'm sure they have their reasons, but I'm not privy to them, I'm afraid. As far as I'm concerned, he was in the wrong place at the wrong time. Like I said, I'm sticking by him until I have a reason not to.'

'We all are,' Kyle interjected, taking Jack's hand where it rested on the table.

I covered my mouth to hide a smile. It must have been hard for Kyle when his bandmates hooked up. There was a not-that-small group of fans who thought that what Frankie and Jack had done was unfair; that Half Light had always been the three of them, and by falling in love (as if they could help it) they had ruined that, and shut Kyle out. Seeing them together, it was clear that wasn't true at *all*. What Kyle and Jack had was, obviously, completely different from what Jack had with Frankie, but that image – two hands clinging to each other – proved to me that their kind of love was no less special. They were still a trio. Their reasons may have been different, but they both *needed* to get their third member back.

'That's all we came to say,' Rich said as he stood. The

boys followed, a well-oiled machine. 'Take your photos, and we'll see you at the next press conference, once Frankie's back with us.'

It was the sound rather than the flashes that took me by surprise. The light I had expected, but the *click-click-click* of camera shutters was louder and altogether more overwhelming than I'd anticipated, and for a second I had to grab Alex's arm to steady myself as I stood up. Then Jas pulled out her camera, too, and I wasn't sure if she was just keeping up the pretence or if she genuinely wanted a souvenir of this bizarre morning.

Before I knew it, the boys were passing us again, not looking anyone in the face as they left the same way they'd come in. Up close, their concealer was streaky, as if it had been applied in a rush to reluctant skin. The dark circles under their eyes were creeping through. There were angry red rashes hiding just beneath their stubble, like they'd shaved too fast. I wanted to reach out, just skim my hand along Jack's forearm as he passed, and hope he'd feel that we were here for them. I wished I could meet Kyle's gaze again, or brush away the hair that was dangling over his eyes. I wanted a connection, but I didn't let myself move a muscle as they passed me.

The room began to empty, and we automatically hung back slightly, doing our best to stay out of the fray just in case anyone looked closely enough to realize that we didn't belong there. Jas was flicking through the pictures on her camera screen as we finally made our way out of the room. I averted my gaze – I didn't want to remember them like that, stuck posing for a crowd they wanted nothing more than to get away from.

Jas nudged the back of my ankle with her shoe, and I turned to see her gesturing at her camera.

'Look at this one,' she said. 'It's breaking my heart.'

'Jas, I really don't –'

'Just this one, H.'

Looking at the screen, I drew in a sharp breath. Jas had picked the right degree. She was a really excellent photographer. Only one end of the table, the one where Jack had been sitting, was in focus. The blurred outlines of Kyle and Rich were facing the gathered crowd, but Jack was looking away. The way Jas had framed it, you could see exactly what he was looking at – the end of the table where Frankie should have been, sitting beside him like he usually was. They had their order – Kyle on the left, then Jack and Frankie on the right. I could probably count on one hand the number of times they'd deviated from it. Today there was no chair, no microphone where their frontman normally sat. Instead, there was only *space*.

It was a really beautiful photo, but I couldn't look at it for too long.

'Turn it off,' I said, and she took my arm as she swung the camera strap back over her shoulder.

'All right,' she said. 'Let's do this. What next?'

TRACK FIVE

Half an hour later, the girls waiting outside Frankie and Jack's house in north London had posted that the whole convoy had returned and gone inside without saying a word. Yet we were reluctant to go home ourselves. How much good could we really do from my tiny bedroom, or Jas's kitchen table?

'Tell me again what Scarlett said to Georgia?' Jas asked over cups of chai in a cafe near the hotel that we'd seen the boys post pictures from.

'That they had to stick to the narrative, that the boys were in financial trouble, and that they didn't have time for mistakes,' I said, running through Scarlett's flustered words in my head. 'It makes no sense.'

'We should talk to her. I know it's been a while, but they do say tragedy brings people back together.' Jas pulled out her phone as she spoke.

Alex leaned across the table and placed her hand over the screen. 'Is that really a good idea?'

'Why not?' I asked. 'What's the worst she can say? Go away?'

'No, it's not that. I just don't think we should be telling a *Pure employee* what we're doing, even if it is Georgia.'

Jas pulled her phone slowly from under Alex's hand and put it away. I had to admit it was an excellent point.

Alex shrugged. 'I'm not saying never. I get that she could really help. Just not yet, OK?'

'You're right,' I said. 'We shouldn't tell her.'

Alex checked the time, picked up her bag and stood up. 'I'm really sorry, I have to go. I've got a study group that I can't miss.'

I wished I had her self-discipline. I thought of my own untouched essays waiting on my desk, and immediately pushed them to the back of my mind. I was sure this was more important. We said goodbye to Alex, all promising to keep in touch with even the tiniest updates. Then it was just me and Jas.

'Do you want to come back to mine?' she asked.

In so many ways, I wanted nothing more. It was strange to Jas, I knew, that I'd always had an excuse when she'd asked me to hang out before. It wasn't that I didn't want to see her, *so* far from that, but I was terrified that in person I wouldn't measure up. If I stayed away, I'd reasoned, it might take her longer to realize that I wasn't worthy of being her best friend.

'Won't your family mind?' I replied.

She laughed. 'God, no, they'll just be happy I'm actually engaging with a real-life person. We could probably even get away with not telling them we met on the internet – not that I think they'd ask. *A friend! What a novelty! Mustn't ask questions!*'

'You have loads of friends, Jas. You're . . . well, you're you.'

She linked her arm through mine as she began to guide me towards the Tube.

'I do have loads of friends obviously. And they live in Brighton, and Berlin, and like . . . wherever Gemma lives that she says is LA, but we all know isn't really. My friendships don't look like what they think friendships are supposed to look like, though, you know? I've sort of given up trying to explain to my parents. Doesn't matter anyway, does it? What they think?'

'Won't my actual human presence help, then?' I asked. 'Once they see that I'm a normal girl, and not some kind of internet catfish, maybe they'll start to get it.'

'You're like the opposite of a catfish,' she said, and I raised an eyebrow.

'How does that work?'

'You're way better in real life.'

I laughed, and tipped my head so it rested on her shoulder. 'I'd love to, but I think I should get back. I've got essays, too.'

It wasn't a lie, but the reality was that I was desperate to process everything that had happened. Frankie had been arrested, I'd met two of my closest friends in person for the first time, and my brain was firing in so many directions, and so quickly, that I was beginning to feel completely dazed by it.

Jas smiled. 'OK. I just want to say, though, that despite everything this has been one of my favourite days in ages.'

I grinned back at her. 'Me too.'

That part was entirely true.

I heard the creak of the floorboards on the first-floor landing as soon as I unlocked the front door. I knew from the weight of the steps that it would be Stefan, and the last thing I was in the mood for was trying not to be charmed by him. Before I could do anything about it, though, his head popped over the top of the banister, his ruffled hair suggesting he'd not long made it out of bed.

'I thought that was you.'

'What, you could tell by the way I unlocked the door?'

He grinned. 'Thought, hoped, same difference. Everything sorted with your friend?'

'Not so much. I think it will be, but ... no. Not so much.'

He cocked his head at me. 'Are you going to stand at the bottom of the stairs all day? Come on, I've just made some food. I'll let you share and you can tell me all about it. I'm actually quite helpful in a huge range of situations.'

I smiled. I doubted he could help with this one, but now he'd mentioned food I realized I was *starving*.

'What kind of food?' I asked as I started walking up to our landing.

'Chicken nuggets and chips. Nothing green in sight, I promise.'

I closed my eyes and groaned.

At that, Stef laughed out loud and said, 'I'll take that as a yes.'

I was right about him not being exactly helpful, but that was more because, once I'd finally finished the story, Stefan was the closest to speechless I'd ever seen another human.

'So . . . you're trying to get an international pop star cleared of a *major crime*?' he asked when he finally regained his ability to speak, and I nodded.

'Um. Yeah.'

He shook his head in disbelief.

'Do you think I'm crazy?'

We were sitting on the kitchen floor, where we'd settled when it became clear that this story was not a short one, our plates long since empty.

'*Yes*. I think that's absolute insanity, Harri. It's dangerous as *hell*. What are you thinking? You can't just wade right into the middle of this, thinking about Frankie, and completely neglect to think about yourself! Would he do the same for you?'

I made to stand up, but Stefan's raised eyebrow somehow held me in place.

'Harri, I'm only saying it because I care. You don't know this guy. You don't know what he's capable of. I also think –'

'All right, Stef, I get it – you think I'm stupid.'

'I never said that.'

'You didn't have to,' I huffed as I stood up, and suddenly Stefan was beside me, hands held up in surrender.

'If you'd let me finish, I was going to say that, *yes*, I think what you're doing is absolute insanity, but also *so badass*.'

'Really?' I asked, and he nodded.

'Yeah. I don't love the way you're going about it, but I think it's so cool that you love something enough to do that for it.'

'For him.'

'Yeah. Lucky him.'

'You really think that?' I asked.

'Course I do,' he answered, lingering in the doorway for a second as he turned to leave. 'Or am I saying it because I fancy you? Who can tell, Harriet Lodge? Who can tell . . .'

With that, he turned and left the kitchen, not looking back once. I choked out an unexpected laugh. *Who was this boy?* Suddenly I wanted him to turn round. Maybe it was just because I'd expected he would, but for the first time, as soon as his eyes weren't on me, I wished they were.

We don't have time for this, I scolded myself. *Let him walk away. You're exhausted and emotional and confused and you're looking for someone easy to cling to. Don't let this be something you'd regret.*

I stood in the kitchen until I was sure he was gone, and then reverted back to my original plan – completely overthinking the entire situation. Settling in bed with a steaming cup of tea, I pulled up Twitter on my phone. I wanted to see what the world was saying. I unfocused my eyes as I scrolled past journalists professing that they *'couldn't say'* whether he was guilty or not, and homophobic idiots with the audacity to call themselves fans claiming that:

> Everything went wrong when he broke up with Phoebe Shaw. Of course we don't think he did it, but this should be a lesson. When you've got a gorgeous woman who's perfect for you, you don't let her go.

'That makes literally no sense. Evan has been around since before Phoebe was born,' I said aloud as I carried on scrolling. I soon came across what I was actually looking for, and I snuggled further under my duvet as I read tweet after tweet, from friends and people who could be, all variations on the same theme: *We know you didn't do this. We're right here. We said no matter what.*

@GemmaJaneHomer
He doesn't know it, but Frankie has been there for me through a lot. That's why I have no choice. I've gotta be here for him now. #WeStandWithFrankie

@AlexHendrick19
Had the most surreal day, finally meeting @JasSidana and @HarriDaisy7 after all these years. Maybe the circumstances could have been better, but I hope FW knows we're here for him, and that in a very twisted way some good has come of all this.

67

I typed out one of my own.

@HarriDaisy7
1. The universe is really making us prove that when we said 'I'd do anything' we meant it.
2. It was so nice to be with @JasSidana and @AlexHendrick19 today.
3. #WeStandWithFrankie #WeStandWithFrankie #WeStandWithFrankie. And repeat. And repeat. And repeat.

Are there more of us than them? I wondered. I knew my timeline was an echo chamber mostly filled with voices just like mine who were completely on Frankie's side. Was that the general consensus, though? That he didn't do it? Or were there thousands of people out there who weren't surprised? Who were taking all this at face value – the police say he's guilty so he must be? Logically, I knew the answer. I knew how it looked from the outside. I couldn't quite bring myself to type his name into the search box, though; to see what the rest of the world was saying about *our Frankie.*

Not yet, I thought as I closed my eyes, my tea still steaming on the bedside table. *I'm just resting. I'll drink it in a second.*

I was well aware that by the next time I picked up that mug it would be stone cold.

I knew as soon as I woke that I'd slept longer than I had in ages. The sun streaming through my window told me it was at least mid-morning. I scrabbled for my phone and my glasses, and sat bolt upright when I saw the time. If I had any chance of making the one-off Sunday guest lecture I'd booked, I had to go *right now*. A huge part of me wanted to stay in bed, but I'd paid for the ticket. Plus, the lecturer had run the second biggest record company in the world for a decade. There was a reason I'd been willing to give up my day off to hear him speak.

However, as I ran across campus ten minutes later, hair still soaking wet and without a scrap of make-up on (but actually quite impressed by my own speed), I wondered whether there was even any point. It's not like I'd be able to concentrate on financial management and planning while Frankie was still locked up. By the time I skidded into the lecture hall just as the first slide was being projected on to the screen, I had resigned myself to using this hour to think about the next steps in our plan. *Difficult*, I thought, *when I have absolutely no idea where to start.*

My phone buzzed constantly in my pocket, but I didn't dare sneak a peek in case the light drew the lecturer's attention. I really did try to engage as he talked about financial predictions, and sources of income in a market where fewer and fewer people were paying for music, but my mind kept drifting back to Frankie.

There was another vibration in my pocket and, noticing the lecturer fiddling with his laptop, I decided to risk it. Sliding the phone on to my lap, I skimmed through the notifications on my home screen, most of them messages from Jas, itching to nail down our next move. I stopped at an email from a name I didn't know. Charlotte Macey. My eyes flitted down to the subject line: **Your internship application – Pure PR.**

Just what I need, I thought. In the middle of this media circus, how did anyone at Pure have time to be sending form rejection letters for a position that had closed months ago? I had made a habit of filing each rejection as it came through, which they had, like clockwork, ever since I'd started applying for these internships as soon as I turned sixteen. I thought they would be fun to look back on, on the off chance I was ever actually successful. *No luck yet*. My finger was already hovering over the MOVE TO FOLDER button when I glanced at the body of the email and almost threw my phone across the room. It was not a rejection at all.

I had to bite my lip to stop myself from screaming.

Hi Harriet,
I hope this email finds you well. When you have a moment, please could you give me a call on the number at the bottom of this email to talk about your recent internship application?

Thanks so much,
Charlotte Macey

HR Assistant
CharlotteMacey@purepr.co.uk
@PurePRTweets
02036698735

There was no way I'd got it. That was Georgia's job, I knew. *What could this woman possibly want?*

I quickly took a screenshot of the message and sent it to Jas, noticing with relief that she was online. Glancing up, I saw the slide at the front of the class change to one on how to adapt when your carefully laid planning went wrong. *That might actually be useful*, I thought, *but I really don't have time*. As the lecturer turned away again, I slid out of my seat and quickly made for the door.

My phone buzzed in my hand, Jas's response consisting of a string of question marks and exclamation marks. Seconds later, my phone was ringing.

'Hey.'

'Harri, *what* is that?'

I breathed out a long breath. 'I have no idea. I mean, obviously I didn't get the internship –'

'No, Georgia did. I know,' Jas interrupted.

'So what else could it be?'

'Well, have you called Charlotte Macey?' Jas asked impatiently.

'Not yet! I've only just read it and I wanted to talk to you first!'

'H, this could be it!' She sounded excited now. 'If you somehow get in with Pure, it'll be so much easier to prove Frankie's innocence! What are you waiting for? Call her, then call me straight back and tell me everything she said! Record it! Send it as a sound file! No details spared!'

'I will, I promise!' I said, laughing, and as we hung up I

71

almost believed I was the kind of person who could just ring up a world-famous PR agency with no hesitation at all. Sadly, that was not the reality. I wished I could be, but I was just not that girl.

I'll do it as soon as I get back to my room, I promised myself. *Or as soon as I've had a cup of tea*. But, as tea became toast, and toast became a long shower, I had to accept the fact that maybe I was looking for ways to avoid calling. It wasn't that I didn't want to, or that I was scared of what the elusive Charlotte Macey would say, but, when it came to phone calls to people I'd never spoken to before, something just blocked me. I couldn't bring myself to dial. Jas's texts demanding to know what Charlotte had said were descending from polite sentences, to just Harri? and finally to a single question mark. It was easy for her, I thought. I'd never known her to get nervous about anything.

'I can't do it,' I said aloud, and I must have been louder than I thought, because suddenly I heard Stefan's voice on the other side of my door.

'Can't do what?'

I flung the door open so quickly that he jumped back slightly, surprised.

'Whoa! You all right?'

'Were you just standing outside my door, listening like a creep, Stef?'

He rolled his eyes. 'No, Harriet, I was going to our shared kitchen, which as you know involves me walking *past* your slightly open door, and in doing so I heard you

72

talking to yourself, so I thought I'd stop and check if there was anything I could do to help.'

In the absence of a better plan, I decided to just tell him.

'Isn't that your dream internship?' he asked once he'd finished reading Charlotte's email.

'Well, yeah, but I didn't *get* the internship. It must be something else.'

'Harri, she wouldn't have sent you an email to tell you how laughable your application was, or that they think you're terrible. Trust me, I know nothing about this woman, but I know she doesn't have time.'

I had to admit that he was probably right.

'Why can't we do the whole thing by email, though?' I whined.

'Because it's quicker to pick up the phone and, as we *just* discussed, time is not on these people's side at the moment.'

'I just –'

'If you can't do it for you, do it for Frankie. Isn't that the whole point?'

I widened my eyes. He really had been listening last night.

'That's annoying,' I said.

'What is?' he asked.

'You. Being completely right.'

He grinned. 'I almost always am. As soon as you realize that, it's all over for you. Now make the call.'

I glared at his retreating back, hoping he could feel it, but I knew he had a point. This might be nothing, but it could also be the opportunity of a lifetime *and* a way to help Frankie.

'Screw you, Stef,' I mumbled as I dialled the number.

'Hello, Pure PR?'

The voice sounded harassed in a way that I associated with busy and important, and did nothing at all to calm my nerves.

'Hi, can I speak to Charlotte Macey, please?'

'You are.'

Oh.

'Hi, Charlotte, my name is Harri Lodge. I got an email about –'

'Your internship application?'

'Yeah . . .'

'Great. As you probably know, we don't usually take applications throughout the year, but we're in a bit of a spot at the moment and we need a lot of good people quickly. Your application was . . . well, you have at least what we need. Would you still be interested in helping us out on a short-term project, um . . . Harri?'

It sounded like she was trying to find my name on what was probably a very long list, but somehow I didn't mind. This was not the way it had gone in my many fantasies, but I'd take it.

'Definitely. Yes, I would.'

'Great.' I could hear the sigh of relief, and wondered just how desperate they were. I knew my CV was *fine*, considering I was actually studying music management and had been policing my public social-media feeds for

74

years in preparation for this exact moment, but this was far from my first application, and it had never got me through the door before. It had never even got me close to the door. What had changed?

What a stupid question, I thought immediately. *Absolutely everything has changed. They're in the middle of pretty much the biggest PR crisis imaginable.*

'How can I help?' I asked, and Charlotte laughed.

Not that funny, but OK.

'Well, I'm not sure if you can yet, Harri, but we'd certainly like you to try. As I'm sure you know, it's been a very busy time for us at Pure. Anyway, that means we're fielding a lot of press calls, and we simply don't have the manpower to deal with them all. We're taking on a lot more interns to help us cope with that, and we'll be looking to that pool when our regular internships open again in the summer.'

'I'm in, definitely,' I said.

She laughed again and I tried not to be offended.

'Well, not definitely,' she said. 'There's still an interview process with one of our more senior team members, just to make sure no crazy fans have slipped through the cracks. I'm not supposed to call them crazy, but . . . you know. Anyway, I can schedule that in for tomorrow if you're around?'

I thanked God that everyone at Pure was clearly far too busy to have found my private Twitter account – still under my real name, just a little more protected – as I skimmed through my mental calendar for no reason, knowing that it was completely empty. Let's face it, even if I'd had twelve lectures and three exams tomorrow, I'd miss them all for this.

Charlotte spoke again. 'If you're successful, your travel expenses will be reimbursed. You are London-based, aren't you?'

'Absolutely,' I lied effortlessly.

'Great, I'll shoot over the details in an email right now.'

'Thanks,' I said, but the tone on the end of the line told me she was already gone.

'What just happened?' I said out loud, half expecting Stefan to magically appear on his way past and demand all the details. When he didn't, well aware of the wrath I'd face for keeping her waiting, I called Jas.

'Took long enough.'

'Can I stay at your house tonight?' I began. 'I've got an interview at Pure PR tomorrow.'

I expected a stunned silence. She actually screamed so loudly I had to hold the phone away from my ear.

'Yes! Of course you can! Come now!'

'I don't need to come *now*,' I said, my mind frantically running through what I'd need to pack.

'Harri, you do. It's going to take that long for me to figure out what the hell you're going to wear!'

TRACK SIX

I arrived back in London as afternoon was drifting into evening, and Jas immediately set about the task of twisting and primping and transforming me until she thought I was worthy of walking through the doors of Pure's west London offices. She'd discarded almost all her dresses instantly, while warding off her mum, who kept appearing at the door with snacks and orange juice like she'd never known Jas to have company before. Jas lingered briefly on a navy jumpsuit, and landed eventually on a pair of cropped Burberry print trousers that I didn't dare ask the price of, and my own black jumper, thrown in my bag just in case I got cold, its wrinkles proof that I'd never planned to actually wear it.

'Really, Jas? That?'

'H, it screams confidence, I promise. Smart enough to show you care, but like . . . you're not walking in wearing the interview equivalent of a ballgown, or a Half Light hoodie, you know?'

'I'm scared.'

'I'll come with you,' she promised, and I smiled. I *needed* her there, to make sure I actually walked into the building, and to scrape me up off the pavement when I came out again, whatever the outcome. Anyway, it wasn't like she was giving me a choice.

So that was how we found ourselves, pre-10 a.m. on a cold and foggy October morning, meticulously following Google Maps to Pure HQ, not sure if our jitters were real or something to do with the three coffees we'd shared so far that morning just to keep warm.

'What are you going to do while I'm in there?' I asked, not for the first time, hoping by now she'd thought of a better answer than: *'Just see what happens.'*

'I'm just going to see what happens,' she said, and I tried not to panic at her lack of a plan. 'Stop panicking,' she added.

'I'm not.' I couldn't decide if I was grateful or irritated that she knew me so well.

'You are, and you have no reason to. I'm going to be fine. You're definitely not the only person they're interviewing, H. If anyone asks, I'll just lie and say I'm early for mine. Trust me, the communication in that place at a time like this will be nowhere near good enough that anyone will bother checking.'

'How can you be so sure?' I asked.

'Remember the other day when we infiltrated a massively confidential press conference before breakfast?'

All right. She had a point. I told her as much.

'I know,' she replied. 'I'm right, so shut up.'

*

Set back from the road, the building appeared empty, even on a weekday morning. The windows were dark from the outside, like they didn't want anyone to know what went on behind them, and looked imposing in contrast to the bright white pebbledashed walls. It was as if the place was confused about what it was – was it going for minimalist glamour or suburban family home? Ironic, I thought, since the whole point of Pure PR was to decide what people were supposed to be, and then make them that thing. I'd expected the headquarters of Half Light's management to be abuzz with activity, people rushing in and out, armed with the next strategy that was going to save Frankie, but that couldn't have been further from the reality. I wasn't sure if the calm made me feel more or less terrified as we walked up the path towards reception without speaking, our shoes loud on the concrete.

They've walked this path so many times, I thought. *Frankie's feet have been here, and Kyle's and Jack's. They were probably somewhere in this building when they finally put their foot down and said they refused to hide any more. Frankie and Jack probably walked right back down this path, and felt so relieved that the pretence was over, and they could tell the world after all this time. Maybe they were holding hands.*

Thinking about them here made me feel brave.

'Are you coming in?' I asked Jas as we reached the door.

'Yeah, I'm just going to sit in reception and wait for you, if they'll let me,' she said, twinkling somehow. Her smile gave her away.

'You're not, are you?'

'Of course I'm not,' she said. 'But that's not for you to worry about. You've got to smash this interview, H.'

For once, I thought, maybe I didn't need to have all the answers. Maybe we could both take our own lane, and do our own thing, and then come back together afterwards and work out how to make them fit. *She knows what she's doing*, I told myself.

The bored-looking receptionist barely glanced up as we approached.

'Interview?' she asked, tapping away at a keyboard with long neon-green nails.

'Yes, Harriet Lodge.'

'Great, take the lift to the second floor and they'll meet you. Conference room on the left when you get out.'

'Thanks,' I said.

As I walked off in the direction she'd pointed, I heard Jas say, 'I'm just going to wait here for her if that's OK? But do you have a bathroom I could use first?'

'Round this corner, up three stairs,' the receptionist said, and Jas glanced over her shoulder and smiled at me as she walked off in the opposite direction.

I barely had time to find the conference room when I stepped out of the lift. A delicate hand was reaching out to shake mine before the doors had even closed behind me, and I looked up to see Scarlett, who thankfully didn't seem to recognize me from the press conference. I tried to do something different with my face just in case, but her expression told me that was probably making it worse.

'Hi, I'm Scarlett. It was supposed to be Molly meeting you, but she's late so you get me for now. What's your name?' She shook my hand firmly.

'Harri Lodge.'

'Hi, Harri. Follow me.'

I trailed after her in silence, actually quite glad that it was Scarlett and not Molly leading me towards the conference room. Molly Jenkins was Half Light's strategy manager, but more accurately their confidante, leading lady, and always the answer they gave when they were asked who they trusted more than anyone, beyond each other. I actually felt starstruck by the idea of meeting her, which I knew was weird. It would feel, I thought, like a huge part of Half Light was standing in front of me, and I was scared I'd blow it by not knowing how to react.

'Sorry to throw you straight in,' Scarlett continued, 'but I'm sure you understand we've got a lot to get through here, and we need to find people to start as quickly as we can.'

'That's fine,' I said, and mentally congratulated my voice for coming out sounding surprisingly assured.

'Good. So I'm not sure how much you were told before, but essentially we're looking for people to field press calls. No comments required or, indeed, wanted. Basically, we need you to say nothing, pass on the people worth passing on, and politely get rid of the rest. There are scripts so don't worry. Anyway, we think the best way to test how you get on is to actually make you do it, so we're going to put you straight to work and just listen in, then once you're done with that there'll be a bit of a chat with Mol as soon as she's here, then we'll go from there. OK?'

'OK,' I said as we reached the door to the conference room, and she nudged it open with her hip to reveal a large round table with phones in front of every seat, some occupied by terrified-looking girls about my age, and others still waiting to be assigned.

'What is it you're studying?' she asked as she guided me towards one of the empty seats, and gestured for me to sit.

'Music management.'

'I like it. Starting early! I wish I'd known at your age that this job was even a thing.'

She leaned over me and pressed a few buttons on the phone as she spoke, one eye on the door the whole time. Probably waiting for her next candidate, I thought. Although she was friendly, she seemed on edge. This must be the last thing she needed.

'Stick to the script and you'll be fine,' she assured me. 'All the instructions are there, but national press are put through to Pure staff – just press two and hang up. Locals, you can take their details and say we'll call them back, which we might, and bloggers ... candidly, I wouldn't really care if you just hung up on them, but I'm not allowed to say that, so just say no comment, but that you'll add them to our press list for when there's an update. You good?'

I nodded. 'I think so.'

'It's easy, I promise. That's Jen.' She pointed to a

stressed-looking woman in the corner of the room, who was currently tapping at one of the phones but looked up when she heard her name, and waved in my general direction. 'She's listening to see how you're all getting on, but she's also here to help if you need it.'

I picked up the printed script they'd left me. 'Thank you. I'll be fine.'

'Thank *you*. And good luck!'

She was back through the door before I could say another word. The phone started ringing on the desk in front of me. Jen looked over pointedly and I took the hint.

'Hello, Pure PR?'

'Hi, it's Nick Middleton calling from *The Times* for Rich,' the voice on the end of the line said. I breathed a sigh of relief. An easy one.

'Let me put you right through to his office,' I said, pressing 2 as instructed and hanging up before the reporter could say anything else. I felt victorious for a second. If they were all like this, I'd be *fine*.

In the hour that followed, I promised local journalists that they'd get a call back as soon as someone was available, added blogger after blogger to the press list, which seemed to be all they actually wanted anyway, and put through more members of the national press than I even knew existed. I was on an absolute roll.

Every now and then, Jen would hover behind me for a second, listening without intruding. She seemed irritated with the whole set-up, I thought, huffing away whenever she was asked a question with a more complicated answer than yes or no. 'I hope he knows what he's putting us all through,' I heard her say to another of the publicists who came in with the latest interviewee.

Like any of this is actually Frankie's fault, I thought. *Surely they don't believe that?*

The phone rang again, and my index finger flew out to press the accept button.

'Hello, Pure PR?' There was a crackling on the line, but nobody spoke. 'Hello?' I waited. 'Hello? You're through to Harri at Pure PR. Are you there?'

'Hello.'

The voice was quiet – I guessed around my age – but the speaker sounded nervous, which I thought might be making her seem younger than she was.

'Hi. How can I help?'

Probably a blogger trying her luck, I thought, or a fan with a Twitter account dedicated to the boys wondering if that means she can call herself press. *Quite clever actually.*

'I don't know if I should . . .'

'Don't know if you should what?' I asked, instinctively turning my body so Jen couldn't read my lips. Something told me I didn't want her to hear this. I was completely off script already.

'I heard something. About Frankie . . . and Jack. I recorded something.'

I felt sick. *Please let this be a hoax*, I thought. *Please* don't *let this be a hoax.*

'What did you record?' I asked, gentle but terrified.

'I wasn't going to tell anyone. I would never do anything to hurt them. I *love* them. That's why I was listening in the first place. But now . . . it's wrong not to tell, isn't it?'

I wished the phone was cordless so I could get up and leave the room, screw the consequences, and have this conversation properly. I wished Jen would just leave, or one of the others would mess up so badly that they needed her full attention, just for as long as it took me to work out what this poor girl was talking about. None of those things happened, though. I just had to carry on.

'Hey, listen.' I dropped my voice so it was barely above a whisper. 'I'm a fan, too, and we all just want to help Frankie, don't we? So why don't you tell me what you know and we can work it out, I promise?'

'It won't help Frankie.' Her voice cracked, and I gripped the edge of the desk in panic. I couldn't lose her now.

'Come on. Anything we can find out will help more than you know. What did you hear? What was it you recorded?'

'I can't,' she said, and the line went dead.

I slammed the receiver on the desk hard, and Jen looked over sharply.

'I'm fine,' I promised. 'Just a rude blogger who wouldn't take no for an answer.'

She walked over and rested a hand on my shoulder. 'You're good, don't worry. And, on that note, follow me. You've flown through this bit. I think it's high time for your chat.'

I stood up. 'Can I use the bathroom first?'

Jen smiled. 'Of course. It's not prison. Oh crap, that was bad taste, wasn't it?'

I grinned. I was a fan of dark humour. 'It's fine. It was funny.'

'Well, humour seems fitting since this entire thing is a *complete joke*,' she said, pointing out the bathroom door as we left the conference room.

'What do you think happened?' I knew asking her was a risk, but while I had Jen onside it felt like an opportunity I couldn't pass up.

'I have no idea, but I'll tell you one thing: Frankie Williams is always getting himself involved in ridiculous situations and expecting the rest of us to get him out of them. Well, he's gone too far this time.'

'Do you think he did it?'

Her laugh was short and harsh. 'No way. He's not that clever. If Frankie had anything to do with it, they'd have sentenced him by now because he would have left all kinds of stupid clues. The boy doesn't know how to go unnoticed. It's one of the most infuriating things about him when you just want him to keep his head down, but – fingers crossed – this time it might just save him.'

'I hope so.'

'I'll wait out here.' She gestured again to the bathroom door, and I took my cue. Ducking inside, I ran the tap as I pulled my phone out of my pocket and began to type a Tumblr post. I couldn't be sure, of course, but something told me the person I needed to see it would be watching.

Hi Half-Lighters,

I'm interning for Pure PR today, just as a temporary thing as part of my uni course (I know! Lucky me!) and I took a phone call earlier from a lovely fan who got cut off before we could finish chatting. I'd love to know more about what we were talking about, but I didn't get your name! If you check out my blog, you'll see I love the boys just as much as you do, and I think what you were saying could help a lot of people right now. It's been hard on us all, you know? Message me, please! You know who you are.

Love Harri x

I used every Half Light-related tag I could think of, hoping to hell that everyone at Pure was too busy to be keeping on top of social-media posts for at least as long as it took me to get out of the building. I barely had time to register the fact that there were no texts from Jas before I heard voices in the corridor. I washed my hands, despite the fact that all I'd been doing was typing, and when I walked back into the corridor it wasn't Jen or Scarlett who greeted me but Molly Jenkins. I tried to breathe steadily.

Like most of the people who surrounded Half Light, Molly had become something of a celebrity herself. Brands selling fake tan, expensive make-up and premium hair extensions paid her to be photographed in their products, and as she stood before me, in the flesh for the first time, the woody, almost masculine, smell of her perfume and the perfect messy curls in the long blond hair I knew was not entirely hers made me want to shrink inside my own skin, intimidated by how *deliberate* everything about her was.

She was dressed simply, in jeans that probably used to be black, but now were more of a dark grey, and a T-shirt with the sleeves cut off, a seventies band I had only vaguely heard of emblazoned across her chest, and what looked like a bandage peeking out from where her hair fell over the top of her arm. *Perhaps a new tattoo?* I thought. She would not have looked out of place on the cover of any cool indie magazine. Even with one of her closest friends in prison, she was so *perfectly* put together.

Imagine, I thought, *being lucky enough to be friends with Half Light and inherently stylish enough that, even when you're going through what must be the worst time of your life, you can look like that.*

'Hey, I'm Molly,' she said, and I tried to stop myself answering with, '*I know.*'

'Harri.'

'Sorry I wasn't here when you arrived, Harri. Bus hit a motorcyclist at the end of my street this morning. Total chaos – nobody was getting in or out.' She pulled a face. 'And sorry about the asshole gossip bloggers,' she added, walking down the corridor and gesturing for me to follow.

'Oh, it's fine.'

'It's not. They're idiots who hinder more than they help, but Jen said you handled it brilliantly so it was a good test of that, at least.'

She guided me into a small office and closed the door. A pull-up banner with the Half Light logo and the boys' smiling faces stood in front of the only window. They looked so young. It was during Jack's platinum-blond phase – they'd all had one – that, thankfully, had been short-lived. Looking at the photo now made me smile. *Simpler times.* I looked up at Molly as she took a seat opposite me and noticed in the light that her face was puffy and red. Had she been crying?

'Are you OK?' I asked, and she looked embarrassed.

'Ugh, yes, sorry. I'm fine. It just keeps hitting me, you know? My best friend has been arrested for murder and none of us have really had a second to stop and process that. Hence crying in the toilets in every five-minute break we get! It's fine! Really . . . let's talk about something else. Let's talk about you! Why do you want to work in music?'

Her energy was wild, as though she might burst into tears again at any moment. There was something about how vulnerable she had made herself to me, a complete stranger, that convinced me I should be honest.

'Because of them.'

I wasn't entirely sure I was going to say it until I did.

She looked up sharply. 'Because of what?'

I knew immediately it had been a mistake. There was a split second where *maybe* I could have backtracked. Maybe I could have convinced her that she'd misheard, or that I'd misspoken and hadn't meant that at all. Not the way it sounded. The moment was so fleeting, existing only in the time it took for our eyes to meet, and for me to decide how to arrange my face so that it seemed like there was nothing wrong at all.

I missed it.

'Because of what?' she asked again, sinking her head into her hands. 'Because, if you mean what I think you do, that's a hell of a long game. It's almost respectable if what you're saying is that you went to university and are spending all that money on getting this degree because you think one day it might get you in the same room as Half Light. That's dedication. You know there are easier ways to meet them, don't you?'

'It's not that,' I said quickly.

'Really?'

'Well, it is *sort of* that. But not how you said it. I'm not doing it in the hope of meeting them; I know you guys are a completely closed shop. It's more like . . . I want to be part of something like that, you know? I'm doing it because of them, but not *for* them.'

'God, that's irritating,' she mumbled into her hands.

'Um . . . what is?' I asked.

Molly lifted her head and looked straight at me.

'You were good, Harri. Jen said you aced the trial, but you know I can't hire you now, don't you?'

Surprisingly, the thought hadn't actually occurred to me. As much as I'd always tried to stay realistic, and promised anyone who asked that I wasn't doing it all with the dream of working at Pure one day, I felt something sputter out inside me when I heard it said aloud.

'Right,' I said. 'Should I just –'

She didn't let me finish before she was speaking again, quickly now.

'Do you have any idea how hard it is to find good people who aren't here because they want to run away with the circus? Or because they're hoping to catch a glimpse and then Kyle will fall in love with them or something? It's *hard*, and between trying to staff this beast and the police trying to convince us Frankie is a killer, and has killed *Evan*, of all people, it's –'

She cut herself off, wincing as if she thought she had already said too much. Now that she knew I was a fan, every word was guarded; every gesture just a little more closed off than it had been before.

I'd ruined it. The world looked dark from inside these tinted windows, too, I noticed. I'd imagined that the effect would only go one way, that from in here the outside would look as sharp and shiny as ever, that being cocooned behind the glass would feel no different at all. It wasn't true, I thought as I leaned closer. Their world was not as bright as they'd made it out to be.

'Listen, Molly, I get it –' I began, and she cut me off with a wave of her hand.

'You don't. You couldn't possibly, and trust me when I say you should be so pleased about that. You don't want to learn how this world works, Harri. It ruins it.'

'We just want to help Frankie,' I said, my voice soft, and she huffed out a laugh as she smiled.

'We all just want to help Frankie. It's why all of us are here, darling. I'll tell you one thing, though: he doesn't make it easy.'

'But I think we could do it. The fans could, I mean. We

91

know him in a different way from everyone else. We've spent a long time watching him. I think we could help. We're trying to.'

I had no idea what it was about her that rendered me completely incapable of keeping my mouth shut. Literally, this time. It was like I was so desperate to impress her that I'd stopped thinking logically at all, and instead was speaking every thought I had out loud the second it entered my head. I sat there just *gaping* at her for a moment, with no idea at all how I was going to get out of this one.

'This just gets better and better – by which I obviously mean worse and worse. You can't go digging around in this, Harri. It's a police investigation, not a game! He has the best legal team going. If he actually didn't do it, they *will* get him off, I swear, but they wouldn't arrest him if they didn't have evidence. I'm sorry.'

'What *is* the evidence, Molly?' I asked. I desperately wanted to turn my head, to look through the office window for Jas, but I couldn't risk losing Molly's attention for even a second. Where the hell was my best friend? She was the one people told things to. Probably because they were slightly scared of her, but even so. It was a skill. I decided to try a different tack.

'Look, it isn't in my interest to tell anyone, is it? That would just make it worse for him. It's the opposite of what we're trying to achieve.'

She smiled, and shook her head. 'You've got to understand that I've been doing this for a while, Harri. This is not my first batch of overgrown teenagers and it probably won't be the last. I know that information is power for you lot. You say you love them and wouldn't do anything to deliberately hurt them, and that's probably true, but then you go and post something on the internet that hurts them in ways you'd never even imagined. Sometimes what you think is helping isn't at all. I'm really sorry, I know you're trying, but I can't do it. You've gotta go, Harri. Like *now*.'

I nodded sadly, and smiled at her. 'They're really lucky to have you,' I said as I stood, and held out my hand for her to shake.

'Oh, for God's sake,' she said, and I saw tears rising in her eyes again. 'Likewise, sweetheart. And listen, you girls are terrifying to me, in so many ways, because I know that if anyone *could* do it – could clear him – it's you.'

'We'll try,' I promised.

'Please don't,' Molly said.

I was halfway down the corridor to the exit when a hand flew out of a door I hadn't even noticed was ajar and pulled me in. I could tell by the abundance of Half Light perfume that it was Jas. We probably should have considered how wise it was for her to wear that in the one building where most of the employees would recognize the scent, but you live and learn.

'What are you doing?' I hissed, and she clamped a hand over my mouth, spinning me to face her. I could just about make out her features in the dark.

'Are we in a cupboard?' I whispered when she pulled her hand away.

'Yes, we're in a cupboard, but only because Scarlett is on the other side of that wall and from here you can hear *everything* she's saying.'

She pointed to the blank wall at the back of the cupboard and, as I turned to look, I stumbled backwards. Standing in the corner was a life-size cut-out of Frankie. I burst out laughing and immediately clapped my hands over my mouth.

'Oh my GOD!' I hissed through my fingers. 'What is that doing here?'

'Oh yeah, forgot to say he's here, too.'

'Jas, this is ridiculous. What are we going to do? Stay here till she says something incriminating?'

Jas smiled, the sort of smile that told me she knew something I didn't. 'Yes. Which is about to happen. About two seconds before you got here, she told Rich as he walked past that Molly was back, and as soon as Molly was done with your interview she was coming to tell Scarlett about the latest evidence. I thought you might want to hear that.'

My knees started to buckle, but I stiffened just in time. Of course I wanted to hear it, but having seen first hand how upset Molly had been I knew it couldn't be good.

'Oh, and I got their alibis,' Jas continued. 'Scarlett and Rich's, I mean. They were here, in a meeting, at the time Evan died.'

I hadn't thought of Scarlett and Rich needing alibis. My focus had been so firmly on getting Frankie cleared that it hadn't even crossed my mind.

'How did you find that out?'

'Scarlett said it. That she couldn't believe they were

94

here, holed up in a frustrating meeting about international tour dates, with no idea that all this was happening.'

'Good intel.'

'And that made me think to check Molly, too. She's clear as well – she posted an Insta selfie from a bar on the other side of London just a few minutes before the call to the police. I'm pretty sure it's Georgia with her from the rings.' She turned her phone round to show me the perfectly framed shot of Molly, tagged at a bar I'd never heard of. Jas was right: the chunky rings in the corner of the shot did look like Georgia's.

None of this helped Frankie, though.

My thoughts were interrupted by Scarlett's voice on the other side of the wall.

'Finally! What took you so long?'

I moved closer, and pressed my ear against the wall. Jas followed just as Molly answered.

'Sorry.'

'Mol, what's happened? Have you been crying?'

'She has,' I whispered, and Jas held a finger to her lips.

'Shh. Listen.'

'I spoke to the detective,' Molly said, her voice watery and weak. I wished I could see them. It was almost impossible to get a proper grip on the situation with our ears to the cold wall.

'And?'

Instead of answering, Molly burst into tears.

We stood there, frozen, as Scarlett tried to calm Molly down.

'You can't help him like this, babe. How do you think he'd feel knowing you're this upset over it all?' Her voice was patient and kind, and I thought that if it was me the frustration at not knowing would be creeping in. Was that something that came from working in PR? Did they teach you how to reframe everything – pretend it was all OK? If so, I had a lot to learn.

'Come on, babe. He needs us.'

At this, it was as if Molly's hesitance disappeared entirely. Her voice was clear and unwavering when she spoke again.

'There's new evidence. We know they formally arrested him on Saturday because they found out that Frankie and Evan had planned to meet at Albany Road the day Evan died. I stand by that being flimsy reasoning: they were best friends, for God's sake; they planned to meet up all the time – but now there's more. They did a second search of the roof this morning because the alarms were triggered, and found Frankie's T-shirt. It has Evan's DNA on it. Blood, too, but they don't know if that's his yet. Doesn't matter if I'm crying or not – maybe we just can't help him.'

Jas's sudden grip was vice-like on my arm. It was one of the many ways in which we were opposites – in times of stress or trauma, she reached out for human contact, whereas my first instinct was to shrink into myself. I didn't want to be touched. I barely stopped to think about the fact that they'd planned to meet; that Frankie had been arrested because the police had found this out. The situation was escalating so fast. The reason for his arrest paled in comparison to the fact that they'd found *blood*. I shuddered.

'How do they know it's Frankie's shirt?' I whispered, and it was as if Molly could hear me.

'It's the one with the stupid pretentious Keats quote stitched on the hem. One of a kind, and it belongs to Frankie. It's definitely his.'

Heard melodies are sweet, but those unheard are sweeter.

I knew exactly which T-shirt she meant. Any fan of Half Light would. I loved that shirt. We'd always thought it was a thinly veiled reference to his relationship with Jack. Sure, what he got to show the world was sweet enough, but the secret they were keeping? Their hidden love? That was the *sweetest*.

Molly started crying again, and Scarlett didn't miss a beat. 'Tell me exactly what the detective said, Mol.'

'Just that. There's DNA on it that's a match to Evan, and a spot of fresh blood, but that's so small they haven't been able to match it yet. Frankie told the police he hadn't seen Evan that day, so now we know he's lying about that at least. What else is he not telling us, Scar? Are we all wasting our time here because he actually did it?'

'We need to tell Rich.' Scarlett's voice wobbled, then there was some shuffling, followed by stark silence. Wherever they'd gone, we could no longer hear them.

'What are we going to do?' I asked, and Jas shrugged her shoulders.

'Harri, I have no idea.'

The clacking of heels along the corridor pulled me back

to the reality of the situation. We were hiding in a cupboard with a life-size Frankie Williams, and we absolutely had to get out of there without being seen. I tiptoed towards the door, and pressed one eye to the crack where it was still ajar. I recognized the petite blond girl walking towards us straight away.

'It's Georgia!'

Jas was by my side immediately, her chin hooked over my shoulder as we watched Georgia stride along the corridor with a confidence I envied. Of *course* they'd hired her. She was born to be here.

'We have to talk to her!'

'Jas, we can't just pop out of a cupboard in the middle of her workplace and shout, "Surprise!" We're not meant to be here, remember? We need a better plan!'

'You're right,' Jas said, but as she spoke she was squeezing past me, positioning herself right behind the door.

'What the hell are you doing?'

The moment Georgia passed, Jas grabbed my hand and pulled me behind her into the corridor. I didn't say a word. Were we still supposed to be keeping quiet? I looked at Jas in a way I hoped said, *If you have a plan, now would be the time to put it into action*, and it seemed to work.

'Georgia?'

Georgia turned to face us, her smile turning to confusion once she realized who we were.

'Hi?' She phrased it as a question, and I knew what she really meant was, *You'd better have a good reason for being here. Where you're definitely not supposed to be.*

'I totally forgot you work here!' Jas was half skipping along the corridor now, as if she'd just bumped into a long-lost friend and not someone we had only known briefly, and a while ago at that.

'Um. Yeah. I do. But what are you doing here?'

I followed behind Jas, hoping my smile was putting Georgia at ease rather than making her think she should probably call security. *Did they have security?* I couldn't remember seeing any, but surely Pure wouldn't leave themselves exposed like that? *Focus, Harri.*

'We had interviews!' I piped up, and immediately Georgia's face softened.

'Oh thank God. I thought you'd like . . . broken in or something.' Her voice was light now, in a way that seemed entirely false to me. I forced myself to laugh along with her.

'Ha! No! Of course we didn't *break in*. So how are you? You must be stressed what with . . . everything that's going on.'

Georgia placed a perfectly manicured hand on my arm, and smiled in a way that was definitely patronizing, but I hoped she meant to be sweet. 'It's so kind of you to ask. I'm rushed off my feet here, babe. Just trying to get him cleared, you know? Get everything back to normal.'

Well, you're an intern, so I don't think getting him cleared is going to be up to you, I thought, returning her sickly smile.

'We want to help,' Jas said suddenly and, while I didn't

99

take my eyes off Georgia to acknowledge that she'd spoken, I hoped she knew that, if I had, I'd be glaring.

'What?' Georgia lifted her hand from my arm. 'Help with . . . what?'

'With the investigation,' Jas continued, and, *oh*, she was making it so much worse. I had no choice but to go along with it now. I should have warned her that this tack wasn't going down well with the Pure staff.

'We know there's evidence against him,' Jas said, and Georgia shook her head.

'You know what? You actually know *nothing*. You have no idea what's going on here.'

'Then tell us,' I said, apparently regaining my ability to speak. 'You know better than anyone what the fandom is like. Give us the information. We'll figure it out; you know we will, Georgia. We just need to know what's going on.'

Georgia shook her head.

'I worked *so* hard to get through this door and I'm not giving it up that easily. If you want in, you're going to have to get your intel from someone else. I'm sorry. I have nothing to tell.'

'Not even for Frankie?' Jas asked, and Georgia lifted a hand.

'Let me stop you there. This is not about me giving up on Frankie; it's about me getting to keep my job. I won't let you make me feel guilty about that, Jas.'

'Then what are we supposed to *do*?' My voice came out sounding more like a whine than I'd intended.

'Talk to Alex.'

What?

'What . . . has Alex . . . got to do with this?' Jas spoke slowly, as if trying to put the pieces together before she reached the end of the sentence, and failing.

Georgia shrugged as she began walking away, her reflective silver boots loud on the tiles. 'You want information? Ask her. And you really need to leave before anyone finds you. The interviews are over.'

She was right, I thought as I watched her walk away. The interviews were over, but it felt like something far more complicated had just begun.

TRACK SEVEN

Something wasn't sitting right. I thought it might have been the fact that Alex, who usually had her phone surgically attached to her hand, had ignored every one of our calls and texts since we'd left the Pure offices and headed back to Jas's place. I couldn't be sure, but my stomach was in knots.

Jas and I went to ground in the conservatory as soon as we got back. I had always known – sort of – that her family had money, but I'd never considered before the last few days that it was 'essentially give your teenage daughter her own conservatory' sort of money. The panoramic windows opened on to a garden that must have been *regularly* pruned by a professional. Jas's parents kept popping in, but I thought I'd probably be able to cope with what basically amounted to parental spying if I got to spend my days hanging out in this room.

'Honestly, it's just lovely to see Jas spending time with a real person, and not people inside her computer,' Jas's dad said as he brought us more snacks.

'Yeah, thanks, Dad. You were right. Real friends are the best, aren't they?' Her voice was dripping with completely unsubtle sarcasm, but he didn't seem to notice.

'Just let me know if you need anything else,' he said as he left, and Jas rolled her eyes at his retreating back.

'See what I mean? They're obsessed with me hanging out with people I didn't meet on the internet.' We'd decided to tell them that we were friends from uni, purely to buy ourselves a little more privacy.

'They're sweet,' I said. 'Listen, what the hell are we going to do about Frankie?'

'God, Harri, I don't know.' Jas put down her phone as another call to Alex went unanswered.

'I wish we knew what kind of DNA we were dealing with here,' I said. I was hugely out of practice with science stuff, but I could remember enough to know that a stray hair was usually far more innocent than, say . . . a piece of bone. I winced. I didn't want to think about that.

'Why? Are some better than others?'

I nodded.

'A hair could have got there if they'd hugged, or even just if Evan had been standing close enough to Frankie last time he wore the shirt. Skin cells are also not *awful*, because really all he'd have to do was touch it. If Evan ever actually *wore* the shirt and it hadn't been washed yet, skin cells are a given. It's when we get to things like saliva, or body tissue, that we're really in trouble. You never really hear of innocent ways they end up at crime scenes, do you? I'm not sure if there are any.'

'God, how did you stop finding all this *fascinating*?' Jas asked.

'I'm not sure I stopped exactly. More that I found something I loved more, and that I might actually be good at. Plus, the thought of bone fragments on Frankie's T-shirt makes me feel physically sick. I couldn't have hacked it.'

'So we hope for a hair and wait to be proven wrong.'

'I just wish that girl from the phone call had messaged back,' I said. I had filled Jas in the moment we'd left the building. 'She sounded so distraught about whatever she knew and, let's face it, we need all the information we can get right now.'

'We don't even know if she's seen it, do we?' Jas asked, and I shook my head.

'We don't even know if, when she says she's a fan, she means she'd recognize the boys in the street and casually likes their music or if she means she knows where all their tattoos are and what they did for Christmas three years ago.'

'I don't know what any of them did for Christmas three years ago,' Jas said.

'No, but you probably did at the time.'

She laughed. 'All right, I get the point.'

Giggling coming from behind the conservatory door pulled our attention from the mysterious fan for a second.

'Oi, twins! Stop hiding and come in if you want!' Jas bellowed, her voice far too loud for the echoing room, and the door squeaked open as two small figures walked tentatively in.

'Arjun, Padma, this is my friend Harri.'

The little girl stepped forward first, her maverick bravery clearly impressing her brother who followed instantly, if less confidently.

'Are you Jas's girlfriend?' Padma asked, not looking directly at me.

I smiled. 'No, we're just best friends.'

The girl sighed impatiently. 'But Jas *always* says that when she has a girlfriend they'll have to be her best friend, too.'

'Too wise for an eight-year-old,' Jas muttered. 'Listens at the exact time you don't really want her to.'

'You never have friends over,' Arjun piped up, and Jas rose from where she'd been curled up on the floor and began shepherding the twins towards the door.

'So every member of this family keeps telling me, pal. And now I do, so maybe you should all be happy and let me hang out with her.'

The twins looked at each other in a way that I couldn't decide if I found disconcerting or cute. Padma screwed up her adorable little face as if she was thinking, then turned to Jas.

'Fine. But later you have to play whatever we want.'

'We will, promise,' Jas said as she closed the door on the twins and turned back to where I was still sat.

'So.' She looked at the ground as she spoke.

'You're gay – or at least not straight – and I just found out from your tiny sibling about ten seconds after meeting her, and not you after years of friendship?'

'Ouch,' Jas said, looking up, and I grimaced.

'Sorry. That came out way harsher than I meant it to.'

'I know. Don't worry.'

Jas settled back into her spot on the floor, sighed in a way I knew meant she'd known this conversation was inevitable, pulled a cushion from the sofa to rest her feet on and turned to me.

'So it's something I've been figuring out, but, yeah, I think I'm gay. It's entirely theoretical right now, though, so I didn't feel like I needed some big *coming out* moment, you know? I'm in no rush to solidify . . . that . . . but I'm pretty sure that, when I do meet someone, it'll be a girl, and then I'll shout it from the rooftops. Nothing has actually changed about what I *do*, which is still *nothing*. All that's changed is what I call it – call myself – and I didn't really feel it warranted a big announcement. Does that make sense?'

I nodded. 'It *does*, of course, and I'm not saying you owe me anything or whatever; I just didn't realize there were big things like that we didn't know about each other. Like, I feel as if I know you really well so it's weird for me to think that maybe I don't?'

'You do, though. Like, you know *me* even if you don't know all the facts about me.'

'So what about Frankie? All the boys actually. You fancy them, right?'

'I can appreciate that they're gorgeous and I feel very connected to them so, in a sense, yes,' Jas answered. 'It's not really sexual attraction as such, though. It's more that

I want to snuggle them tight and make sure nobody hurts them. I'm fascinated by them more than I fancy them, I'd say.'

'Wait, so you don't want to have sex with Frankie?' I asked, half joking but intrigued now.

Jas shook her head. 'Not really, not in that animalistic "he's hot so I want to sleep with him" kinda way. I mean, actually that's a lie. I do very much want to have sex with Frankie, but more because I adore him as a person.'

'Despite not *actually* knowing him as a person?' I asked.

'Yeah . . . it's complicated, because I feel like I do know him as a person, obviously, and I guess the bit of my brain that connects that deep "I know you and I love you" feeling to sex doesn't know how to differentiate between, say, Frankie and, like . . . the metaphorical cute girl next door.'

'God, how do you get your head around it?' I said. 'Is that ignorant to ask?'

'No. It's a fair question. I suppose I don't really need to get my head around it as much as everyone else does, because I actually feel it. And that's usually enough . . . It was harder at first, I suppose, when I was first trying to work out what it all meant, if anything. Like, do I just think Emma Watson is beautiful because she *is* or because I want her to be my girlfriend?'

'A hard dilemma if ever I heard one,' I said, smiling.

'But it sort of came down to the fact that I was spending so much time trying to analyse it and, like . . . predict what it was going to mean for my future, and eventually I realized all that thinking wasn't actually going to change a thing. I could think about it forever, but how I felt would stay the same, so I decided to just start getting on with it.'

'Fair enough,' I said. 'Sorry for, like, interrogating you.'

'Don't be. Sorry I didn't tell you before.'

'You're right, though. It doesn't actually change anything, does it?'

'No,' Jas said. 'And it doesn't matter – I don't think, anyway – that there are things we don't know about each other because we don't see each other every day, cos there are parts of me that *only* you lot get to see. We can't be all things to all people at all times, you know? Doesn't make it any less real cos you'd never met my family.'

'And now I have,' I said, stretching out and nudging Jas's ankle with my toes.

'Yeah. Maybe one day we'll even tell them the truth about how we met!'

We stayed in the conservatory for hours, talking past and over and around what I'd started to think of as the Boyband Murder Mystery. We ordered Chinese. Every now and then, Jas would try Alex again, but at this point we were going straight through to voicemail. By the time my own phone chimed, still nestled in my jacket pocket on the other side of the room where I'd left it when we came in, I was so mellowed by warmth and spring rolls that I almost ignored it.

'Ugh, tell them I don't care,' I said, and Jas laughed, grabbing her own phone.

'It's probably just the group chat wanting to know the latest – which is obviously nothing.'

She held the phone up as I spoke, and I saw that the screen was free of notifications.

'Not the group. Whoever it is only wants you this time.'

'Nobody who isn't my parents ever texts *just me*,' I said.

'Well, there you go, then. It's your parents.'

I groaned as I pulled myself to my feet and shuffled across the room to get my phone, my socks sliding on the laminate floor. I hadn't messaged either of them all day, which was not normal for us. That had been my mum's only rule when I'd left for uni: one text a day. Just to let them know I was OK. I know a lot of people would have found it annoying, having to check in like that. To me it felt more like an anchor: a reminder of where I'd come from – that, no matter what, I would always have somewhere to go home to. I smiled as I looked down at the screen.

The first message I saw had come in forty-seven minutes earlier. I tried to ignore the way my cheeks grew warm when I saw it was from Stefan. That was new. I skimmed it quickly (Hope the interview went well! Know you smashed it!) and decided to reply later. The chime I'd just heard, though, had not been my parents at all. It was a Tumblr message from a user I didn't recognize calling themselves Beck83757. Not their real account, I knew immediately. In a world where social-media popularity was currency, nobody would call themselves something so impossible to remember.

'All right?' Jas asked, handing me a gin and tonic when

I returned, before lying on the floor in what looked like a pretty blissful food coma.

'Tumblr message from what looks like a bot,' I said as I opened the app. And then I gasped, gripping on to the table to stop my legs from giving way.

'What?'

'It's her. The girl who called.'

'Read it to me.' Jas's voice was serious immediately, her whole demeanour growing tense in the time it took me to turn up the brightness on my screen. 'What's her story? What did she hear?'

I breathed deeply and read the message aloud.

Hi Harri,

Thanks for being so kind to me when I called today, and sorry I hung up on you. I freaked out, I guess, and didn't want to get anyone in trouble. But not telling anyone is stressing me out and I know now that you only want the best for Frankie, and for all of them, so I'm going to tell you. I just don't know what's going to happen once I do.

A few days ago, I was in a bar in London with my aunt. I was bored as hell, but then this couple (or I thought it was a couple) sat down next to me. I recognized Molly first, because obviously she wasn't trying to disguise herself, and only realized it was Frankie she was with when their friend walked in and I heard him speak. Evan. He – Frankie – was wearing a baseball cap and a hoodie – imagine the least Frankie outfit you can, and it was something like that. Hiding

110

in plain sight, except it didn't work because he was with the two most Frankie-related people in the world, apart from Jack and Kyle obviously. Anyway, course I didn't know what they were about to say, but I thought it would be a cool thing to take back to the fandom. I hoped they might mention a tour or something. So I put the phone as close to the edge of the table as I could, and pressed record.

That . . . isn't what they were talking about. I still don't know if I can trust you, but at this point what have I actually got to lose?

I've attached the recording. I can't tell you what they said. I can't be the person who ruins it all for you. Just listen. And don't share this with anyone.

Becca x

'Oh my God,' I said, clicking on to the attachment.

'Tell one of us, you tell all of us,' Jas said, and I nodded.

'What the hell could it be?' I asked. 'What could have her so scared? Surely, whatever they were talking about has nothing to do with what happened to Evan?'

I didn't wait for her answer before I pressed play, and the crackle of the kind of bar I had never stepped inside blared tinny and distorted out of my phone speaker.

'Let's find out.'

TRACK EIGHT

'We'll get through this, Mol. We always do.'

I closed my eyes as Frankie's voice filled the room. Hearing it like this was visceral to me. The sound of him speaking made me feel thrilled and sick all at once. That had never happened before.

'It's never been this bad,' Molly said. 'We've never actually lost sales from year to year. It's meant to keep getting better until we decide we want it to stop – and we haven't decided. The last single only just scraped the top ten, Frank. I know I don't need to tell you that is not good. We need a better plan.'

'That's not on him, Mol. It's not on any of them to figure this out.' Evan spoke calmly, but hearing his voice, knowing what had happened since, made me feel anything but.

Concentrate, I urged myself. I know it's weird, but you can't change what happened to him, and listening to what he has to say might just help free Frankie. The thought didn't reduce the sick feeling in the pit of my stomach at all. I sensed an edge to his voice that made me smile. He was always so protective of Frankie.

'No offence to either of you, but I'd never ask him to. If I can't figure this out, and if Rich can't, and Scar can't, then Frankie definitely can't. I know it's your life, but let's be honest: we did basically create it.'

'Well, why does he feel like he has to, then? Why is he risking everything to try to make this situation better with no regard at all for who it's going to hurt, himself included?'

'Evan, stop.' Frankie's voice sounded ominous.

Molly laughed and not kindly. 'Sorry, but what on earth is he risking? He has everything he could ever want and he's barely lifted a finger for any of it. And you should be more grateful, too. Brands basically pay you to be seen with him. Hard life, isn't it? Frank, tell your friend to stop talking crap.'

I guessed that, at this point, Becca had somehow moved her phone closer, because, although their voices lowered, the background chatter all but disappeared. It was just Molly, Evan and Frankie, with Becca's quiet breathing acting as punctuation. I wondered how on earth she had managed not to get caught. When Frankie spoke again, his voice was somewhere between remorseful and resigned to what came next.

'Evan, I really wish you hadn't done that. I trusted you, mate.'

'I can't just watch you destroy lives for your career any more. You've done it. You made it. It happened.

113

Don't you think that rather than throwing yourself under the bus for it to carry on it might be time to just . . . move on?'

'*Can someone tell me what the hell is going on?*' Molly raised her voice in a way I guessed she'd become accustomed to when strangers started eavesdropping on everything she said – it was authoritative and silenced everyone around her, but was somehow still quiet enough not to draw attention. Frankie sighed. It still surprised me that I could recognize the sound without even seeing him, but I didn't know why. That had been the case for years.

'*Fine. He's talking about me and Jack. That's what the fans have wanted forever, isn't it? So I decided to give them what they want.*'

'*Give* us?' Jas asked. 'Why don't I like the sound of that?'

'*Yeah, nice try, but you can't call that a plan when it was happening anyway. You don't get to take the credit for that just cos your actual life lines up with what the fans want for once.*' Molly's voice cut across Jas's.

'See?' I said. 'It's totally fine.' I took a sip of my gin and tonic. It had grown warm, but the burn was still satisfying.

Jas raised an eyebrow. 'Either it's totally fine, or we're getting totally played.'

'*Frankie, tell her.*' Evan's voice was urgent now, in a way I didn't want to comprehend. Until I heard Frankie say it, I could pretend nothing out of the ordinary was happening here.

'*It wasn't happening anyway,*' Frankie whispered.

I tried to ignore Jas muttering, 'Knew it.' This all felt so surreal suddenly.

'*What are you talking about?*' When Molly spoke now, she was more tentative. Maybe, I thought, it was one of those moments where *before* and *after* can be clearly defined, even as it's happening. She was toeing the line gently, knowing full well that she had to listen to what he had to say, but not sure that she wanted to hear it.

'*It wasn't happening anyway. We only started . . . after we knew the sales were down. After we knew we were in trouble. Because we knew we were in trouble.*'

'*Frankie. Are you telling me it isn't real?*'

It was a surprise to me that my first thought was for Becca. That poor girl had become the fourth person in a whispered conversation between three friends, and had held what she'd heard close, and tight, and heavy. And then that thought passed, and I just felt sick. I pushed away my glass. I didn't need that burn any more. What I was hearing burned enough.

'*Frankie?*'

He stayed quiet. I imagined him nodding, or lowering his eyes to the table in a way that answered the question for her, because she said, '*Shit.*' Then her tone changed completely. '*All right. You're going to tell me everything. Not a choice, Frank. Do you know how bad it will be if this ever gets out? They'll crucify you! Both of you. Start talking.*'

'*I overheard you guys – you and Rich – at that party with the massive beer-pong table. I can't remember where it was.*'

I could have told him the answer. The pictures from that party were famous in the Half Light fandom. It was so nice to see them looking so relaxed, dressed like the twenty-something guys they were rather than the catwalk mannequins we'd become used to. It was at the house of one of the record-company execs, after one of the big summer radio concerts. Highgate maybe, or Hampstead. Were they the same place? Did it even matter any more?

'Anyway, I knew that if you were talking about it at a party it must be bad, so I listened. You said something about how we all knew this album wasn't going to do as well as the others, and that everyone had to step up. So I decided to step up.'

'And what?' she asked. 'Got Jack onboard, dragged him into the bathroom, snogged his face off and made sure someone took a picture?'

'No!' Frankie protested, and for a moment I let myself believe that this wasn't as catastrophic as it seemed. Because it sort of felt like the world was ending.

'I didn't do anything that night. That bathroom picture . . . he'd been crying because he was drunk and I was helping him. Nothing happened, but that picture of us walking out . . . well, by the time it came out, there was this whole narrative, and it worked. So . . . we just never corrected them. I talked to him the next afternoon. Thought about it overnight, and the next morning, and then went to him and . . . we talked about it.'

'Frank, he's been in love with you forever. We all know that. How on earth did you get him to agree?'

'*Yeah, Frank. How did you get him to agree?*' Evan sounded spiteful now, a complete about-turn from the defensive Frankie-protector I'd always known him to be.

I wished I could have stopped listening there. All that I'd already heard, I probably could have found a way to deal with. Probably could have reconciled it in my mind; probably could have convinced myself that Frankie and Jack were actually only looking out for us, giving us what we'd always asked for.

Was this *our* fault? I pushed the thought far enough back so that all the others couldn't snag on it. I'd come back to it later, I told myself. Once I'd had time to really think. Once I'd decided if I really wanted to know the answer.

'*He didn't,*' Frankie said, and I could barely make out Molly's voice when she replied, it was so quiet and defeated.

'*You forced him to pretend?*'

'*No. Of course not. I didn't force him to do anything.*'

'*Then what?*'

I was sure that whatever Frankie was about to say couldn't ruin it any more than he already had, but still I was scared.

'*He didn't know we were pretending.*'

And, oh, that was so much worse.

'*What the hell do you mean, Frank?*'

Please let me be confused. He can't be saying what I think he's saying. Can he?

'*He thought it was real,*' Frankie admitted.

Yeah. That was what I feared.

117

The questions I didn't want to answer came back with a vengeance. Had we done this? Were the fans to blame? Had we shouted about how much we wanted this so loudly, and for so long, that we made it come true in the worst possible way?

'Harri, be quiet,' Jas said, reaching across me to pause the recording, my phone still in my hand. I hadn't even realized I was speaking out loud. I made a zipping motion across my lips.

'Ready to carry on?'

No, I thought.

'Yes,' I said.

She pressed play.

'*Tell me what happened.*' Molly was back in manager mode with what seemed like no effort at all, considering she'd just been told the love between two of her closest friends was a total lie. Frankie began to speak.

'*You know I love him, Mol. Obviously I love him. Just . . . never really like that. But then I thought,* Well, what difference does it make *how* I love him? *I still do.*'

'*Um, quite a big difference,*' Molly interrupted.

'*See? She thinks it's complete madness, too, Frank!*'

Poor Evan. Even without what had come next, I would have felt sorry for him in this situation. He was just trying to help, as he always did. Molly was right. Frankie really didn't make things easy.

'*I just thought . . . this makes everyone happy, right? Jack's happy because he gets to be with me. The fans are happy because this is what they've always wanted –*'

'What about you? Were you happy with this idiotic little arrangement?'

'Of course he isn't happy! That's my point! It's destroying him. It's destroying all of us.'

When Molly spoke again, she sounded furious.

'Evan, shut up. You're not helping. I'm trying to figure out what the hell is going on here and how we're going to get them out of it. I really don't need your input right now. Frankie, carry on.'

'Mol, you know this band is everything to me. I was happy because everyone else was. Because we get to keep doing what we love if everyone else is happy.'

'That's stupid. Did you sleep with him?'

Jas spat the sip of gin she'd just taken right across the table.

'If he says no to this, everything we thought we knew was a lie. I mean, look at them, H. That's a couple having a lot of hot sex, right?'

'Well, I would have said that was a couple madly in love,' I said, 'but I guess you live and learn.'

There was a long pause before Frankie answered, 'Yeah, we did.'

'Told ya.'

'Shh, Jas, stop interrupting.'

'How?' Molly asked, and I took brief pleasure in the way Frankie sounded like he was choking. Good.

'Come on, Mol. Biology. It's pretty easy, isn't it? He's hot. I'm human. We just did.'

'So, what? When did you tell him it wasn't real?'

There was a brief moment of quiet. I knew before Frankie spoke that he *hadn't* told Jack. That Jack probably *still* thought it was real, and was pining for the love of his life, who was locked up in a prison cell somewhere knowing that it was all a lie. Molly must have been able to tell from his face.

'*You haven't, have you? God, Frank. You idiot.*'

'*Have I ruined everything?*' Frankie asked.

She didn't answer. I couldn't imagine her expression. How could she possibly answer that?

'*Does anyone else know?*' Molly's tone was growing surer, I thought. Frankie needed her so she was there for him. It was her job to get him out of this, and I knew I was projecting, but I thought I could hear in her voice that she was well aware of that. She'd had her moment of shock, and now it was back to business.

'*Know what?*'

'*That none of this is real . . . Jesus, Frankie, what were you thinking?*'

'*Just Evan. And now, I guess, you.*'

The sound of chair legs scraping along the floor cut through Frankie's sentence, and Evan's voice sounded further away than before when he said, '*I can't listen to any more of this. I'm getting some drinks. Change the subject before I get back.*' Footsteps on what sounded like marble told me he had walked away. It was just Molly and Frankie now.

'*All right. Me and Evan. It could be worse,*' Molly said, defiant but resigned.

'*Are you going to tell Jack?*'

For the first time, it sounded as though Frankie was realizing the magnitude of what he'd done.

'*That can only come from you, Frank. You dragged him into it, and now you have to get him out. But I'm deadly serious when I say nobody else can find out about this. It's bad enough that you've implicated me, the one person who, may I remind you, is meant to be aware of your every move before it happens. God, how did I not see this coming?*'

'Mol, I'm sorry.' To his credit, Frankie's voice was full of what sounded like genuine guilt.

'*For which part?*'

'*All of it. That Evan just spilled it like that. I would have told Jack soon, Mol. I would have ended it.*'

'*Well, your masterplan has imploded, Frankie. What's the contingency? Didn't think of one because you're a singer and not a strategy manager? What a surprise.*'

I almost laughed out loud at that part. She had a point.

'*What do we do?*'

'*No. There's no "we" here, Frank. I have to try to find any angle at all that makes this not* completely *devastating, and you need to stay out of it before you make things even worse. All you can do right now is convince Evan not to say anything until we have a proper plan. I'll work it out. It'll be fine, no thanks to you.*'

'*Ask Georgia to keep an eye on him,*' Frankie said.

I turned to Jas and raised an eyebrow.

'*Well, that sounds like a terrible idea. We can't tell an intern, Frank.*'

'*Not tell her,*' Frankie clarified. '*Just . . . ask her to keep*

121

an eye. Swoop in if she sees Evan talking to anyone. That kind of thing.'

'And give her what reason?'

'She won't ask. She'll do anything you tell her to, Mol.'

'She's loyal, Frankie, not stupid. Anyway, let's just hope it doesn't come to that.'

There was the screech of a chair on the floor, and then silence.

Suddenly I desperately needed to get out. The room was swimming and my eyes were blurring. I felt sick. I pushed open the French doors and only when the cold air hit me did I remember I was wearing a T-shirt. I was freezing, and the chill on my skin hurt, but I sat down on the decking anyway, my back against the cold brick wall, forcing myself to count the seconds as I breathed in and out to stop this from turning into a full-blown panic attack.

Calm down, Harri, I told myself. *You know how to fight this.*

Well, theoretically that was true. I chose not to linger on the fact that none of the coping strategies had ever *really* worked. It had also never been anywhere near this bad before.

All right. Breathe. Remember how you twist your way out of this. You're here, remember? What does it start with? Five things you can see . . .

It was pitch-black. I could hardly see anything. Whoever thought of these anxiety exercises hadn't considered that.

Come on, I urged myself. *Five things.*

My fingers. I held them out in front of me and tried to

ignore the way that they were shaking. I clasped them together like I was somebody I loved, somebody whose hand I wanted to hold. I used to imagine it was Frankie's hand that I was clinging to in these moments. Unsurprisingly, that didn't help this time around.

OK. Next.

My shoes, still bright white in the black of the garden. Was I supposed to go into detail about all the sights I was listing? I didn't think so. Surely I wasn't the only person to have anxiety about the fact that I didn't know if I was doing the anxiety exercises right? I felt untethered, as if I was watching myself from afar. I forced myself to carry on.

The huge round table on the grass. The lamps hanging in the bushes that were glowing dimly. They charged up on the sun, I knew, and when it got dark they took all that harnessed energy and lit up. It was kind of beautiful, I thought. Was this helping? I couldn't really tell.

I didn't turn round when I heard Jas step out of the conservatory. It wasn't like she'd never seen me fall apart before, at least as pixels on an iPhone screen, but her mind had sensible-person coping mechanisms, like wanting to *talk about it*, and that was the last thing I felt ready to do.

One more thing, I forced myself. *You're doing great. Just find one more thing you can see.* I tilted my head backwards and made myself exhale the breath deeply.

Stars.

I could see stars.

'You OK?' Jas asked as she sank down beside me. She must be freezing, too, I thought.

123

'You must be freezing,' I said, and she scooted closer and linked her arm through mine.

'I'm fine. Body heat.'

We were silent for a moment. It was so quiet I could hear her heartbeat, slow and steady beside the erratic rush in my own chest.

'What just happened?' she asked.

'There are so many stars,' I answered. A non-answer really, but the only one I felt like I could give.

Jas pulled her phone from her pocket, and I was so grateful that she was letting this go that I almost wanted to backtrack and answer her honestly – give her the truth she deserved. That, yes, she'd walked into the middle of what was probably about to become my first full-blown panic attack about one of the people who was supposed to be my respite from all that.

'I have an app,' she said, 'for the stars. Can I tell you about it?'

'Jas, I know how *stars* work.' I tried to make my voice sound light, but it was laced with tension, and she laughed.

'Please.'

I sank lower so I was almost vertical, closed my eyes, listened to her talk.

'The thing about stars is that even when they're visible, which is rare in itself relatively speaking, you can never know what's happening with them right now. Open your eyes,' she said, and I blinked and complied.

'All right, take that one.' Jas pointed at one of the

brightest and held up her phone. 'According to this app, that star is twenty-six million light years away.'

'Meaning?' I asked, tilting my head back further to get a better look at the particular twinkle she was pointing at.

'Meaning that light we're seeing was generated twenty-six million years ago. Anything could have happened in that time. That star could have exploded under the pressure, or one day just died out, and we'd have no idea. We'd still be here, looking up at it exactly as we are, and thinking we're seeing something magic. Like . . . a right-now light. We won't know for another twenty-six million years what really happened in that corner of the sky.'

'I know that, Jas. I meant . . . what's your point?'

She wriggled until she was sitting up straight, then took my hand and pulled me up with her.

'It's like Frankie, isn't it?'

'Is it?'

'He's a star, too. And what we see isn't actually what's going on, not really. He's all twinkle and right-now glow . . . but twenty-six million years ago he could have murdered his best friend to stop him from exposing his fake boyfriend. That light just hasn't reached us yet.'

I was glad it was dark. I couldn't really make out her face, which meant, I hoped, that the features of mine were blurry, too, and that she might miss the few stray tears I let fall. We were quiet. It was a comment that needed space – to settle into the air and hang there, where we'd have to face it.

'Is that what you really think?' I asked.

'Maybe. Do you?'

'No. I don't know,' I admitted. 'Do you want to give up?'

She was quiet for a while.

'I sort of wish I *did* want to give up,' she said finally. 'If I could just walk away, and accept that it's not my place to interfere, and that we'll probably *never* know what happened, wouldn't that be easier?'

We sat there quietly for a moment, and then Jas continued.

'So many people have been hurt because of this, H, and more are probably going to, and I think we just have to ask ourselves if we're missing something. If we have to consider that he isn't the person we thought he was. But no. Even taking all that into account, I *still* don't want to give up on Frankie.'

I reached for her hand again, and the rustle must have tipped her off because she was immediately reaching back. We sat there like that for a while, fingers clasped, not looking at each other, our eyes on the stars even knowing what we knew; even knowing that the thing we were looking at probably didn't exist any more, and maybe hadn't for a long time. It may have been artificial light, but it was still light. *Frankie* was still our light.

One of the lamps hanging in the bushes flashed dark for a moment, then shone brighter than before.

'Is that a firefly?' I asked, and Jas laughed.

'No, it was a moth on the glass.'

Not the same thing at all.

TRACK NINE

'Alex is on her way over.'

Jas was waiting by the door, phone in hand, when I joined her back inside, my face cold and my mind only slightly less foggy than when I'd left.

'Oh, *finally*. Where the hell has she been? Did you tell her what Georgia said? Did you tell her about Becca?'

'Not yet. Thought we should do it in person.'

She was quiet for a few moments before she spoke again. 'Do you think this is our fault?'

'Do I think what is?' I could guess where she was going with this. It was the same question I'd pushed to the back of my mind multiple times since we'd heard Frankie's confession.

'All this. Jack and Frankie. Is it . . . I don't know . . . unethical, the way we love them?'

She looked at me, waiting for an answer, but I just nodded at her to carry on.

'I wonder if we loved them too loudly. If we wanted this

too much, you know? Would Frankie have faked it if we hadn't basically asked him to?'

'I don't think we did ask him to,' I said, but I knew she had a point. 'We were saying it about them, not to them, so I think it's fine?'

'Yeah, *we* were, but not everyone was, H. Some people were definitely saying it to them. I guess it doesn't matter now, though. We can't know if it would have been any different.'

She was quiet for a moment, but I could tell she wasn't finished.

'Do you think Evan's dead because of Frankie? Even if Frankie didn't kill him, I mean?' She didn't leave enough space for me to answer before she was speaking again. 'It's something I've been thinking about, you know? The way we only ever think of Evan in relation to the boys. As a sidekick. But he was a person in his own right, too, wasn't he? He had a whole life that had nothing to do with Half Light. And it would be easier for me to think that this isn't happening because of Frankie and Jack – that it's actually nothing to do with them at all. Think of how many things we just don't know about Evan. It *could* be anything. But . . . it always comes back to them, doesn't it? All roads lead back to Frankie Williams. And especially now that we've heard that recording.'

It was unlike Jas to talk in circles. That was usually my territory.

'There's nothing to say that what happened to Evan has anything to do with that recording. Not necessarily.'

Jas looked at me. 'Harri, coincidences like that don't just happen. They said what they said, and it looks *bad*. I know you don't want to hear it, and I don't want to say it, but they've got to be related.'

'So what? You're saying he killed his best friend now?'

She put her head in her hands, and held it there for a moment before she spoke. 'That's absolutely not what I said, Harri. Don't be indignant – we don't have time. But you don't think it's weird that this evidence shows up – Evan's blood on Frankie's T-shirt, remember? – and now this recording, *and* he's been arrested? As much as we want it not to be true, the police aren't completely incompetent. They must have *something* on him to be holding him this long.'

'We don't know that it's Evan's –'

'Of course it's his blood.'

'You just said outside that you didn't want to give up on Frankie. Now you think he's involved?' I knew I was beginning to sound irate, but I couldn't help it.

A dark look crossed her face and she slammed her glass down on the table. 'Yeah, I do. Is that what you want me to say?'

It was the *opposite* of what I wanted her to say.

The sound of the doorbell interrupted us before I could respond, and relief washed over me. I didn't want to keep doing this. I didn't want to believe she *could* think that.

Alex looked flushed as Jas's dad showed her into the conservatory, hands jammed in her pockets awkwardly. 'What?' she asked when she saw our faces.

'Shouldn't we be asking you that?' I said. Her expression barely changed, but I saw a slight twitch in her cheek.

'Jack and Frankie aren't real,' Jas snapped, and the look of defeat that crossed Alex's face gave me total clarity, while at the same time making no sense at all.

'Alex, why do you look like you knew?'

She covered her eyes with her hand. It felt as if everything I thought I understood was hanging in the balance; like whatever happened next would either convince me that we hadn't been living a lie, or blow it all wide open. The moment lingered. Jas took a step towards me, so close we were almost touching. Alex dropped her hand from her face and looked at us.

'I knew.'

The world fell apart.

TRACK TEN

'Can I please just explain?' Alex asked as she sank down on to the sofa.

'I don't know, can you?' I said, staring hard at her.

'Harri, let her try,' Jas said. *Since when was she so forgiving?*

'Fine.' I sounded angry. *Good.* I was.

'Guys, I really don't want you to be mad about this –'

'Well, right now we are, so start talking,' Jas interrupted, and I bit back a smile. *There she is.*

'I didn't tell you because I knew it meant everything would change. I was trying to protect you, I promise, and then Frankie was arrested and what was already quite bad became a million times worse and I – just didn't know what to say.'

'Who did you hear it from?' I asked. 'Georgia?'

Alex shook her head slowly, a movement that told me I definitely wasn't going to like the answer.

'No. She was there, but no.'

'Alex, the time for being cryptic is long gone. Answer the –'

'Evan told me.' Alex looked down as she cut Jas off, and I felt my eyes widen.

'*What?*' I was glad Jas asked, since it seemed I was rendered completely speechless.

'I heard it from Evan.'

'Yes, Alex, I got that bit.'

'Please will you just *let me explain*.' Alex raised her voice, and Jas crossed the room, closed the door to the rest of the house and turned, hands on hips, to Alex.

'OK. Explain.'

'We met at the after-party of an awards show about two weeks ago. The ILovePop Awards. The boys weren't even nominated. I had no idea Evan was going to be there.'

'You went to a party with Georgia, met Evan and didn't tell us?' I interrupted.

Alex held up a hand. 'Just let me speak, Harri. No, I didn't go with Georgia. I haven't talked to Georgia in months, not since she started the internship. I went with people from uni who were covering the awards, but Georgia was there, and so was Evan, and *obviously* I wanted to talk to him. So I went over.

'He'd clearly been drinking, and I didn't want him to know that I'd only approached him because of the boys, so I just made small talk about the awards and the party. I guess I kind of let him think I didn't know who he was. We had a laugh. He was nice. I didn't even realize at first, when he brought it up, that he was talking about Frankie.'

'What did he say?' Jas asked.

'He told me he was worried about his best friend. That

he – the friend – was hurting everyone around him because he only ever thought of himself, and his career.'

'How could you *not* know he was talking about Frankie?' Jas asked.

'I don't know. What if he had this other best friend that none of us knew about? We didn't *know him*, remember?'

I thought back to what Jas had said. Evan had had a life outside Frankie and the band, too. 'So how did you realize he was?'

'He said this friend was in a relationship to make other people happy, and that it wasn't real at all. He said the other person didn't know it was fake, and that he'd just come from trying to convince his friend to end it, but it hadn't worked. And then he slipped up. He said, "Poor Jack."'

As angry as I was that she'd kept it to herself, that must have been awful for Alex to hear.

'I was basically in shock, but trying not to let him see. That was when Georgia came over.'

I could just imagine Georgia sweeping in on a cloud of perfume, steady even in ridiculous heels, refusing to be far from the centre of the action. She would have hated seeing Alex talking to Evan, I thought.

'She said that Frankie had asked her to check that Evan was OK – we all know Frankie doesn't text interns, so I assume it was Molly or Rich or someone – and that seemed to bring him back to his senses. He said it was nice to meet me and walked off.'

'Frankie did say he wanted to get Georgia to keep an

eye,' Jas reminded me. 'Maybe he actually did ask Molly to step in.'

'And Georgia? What did she do?' I didn't for a second believe she would have left without asking Alex what they'd been talking about.

'She followed him.'

'She didn't say anything at all?' From the incredulous tone of Jas's voice, I knew that we were on the same page.

Alex shook her head. 'Not really. Well, she told me that, whatever he'd said, it was best I forget about it.'

'That's not *nothing*,' I half shouted. 'That means she knew that whatever he said would cause problems!'

'Al, you know not telling us this was the *dumbest* plan in the world, right?'

Alex rolled her eyes as she turned to Jas. 'I didn't tell you because I knew you'd react like this. I didn't *tell you* because I couldn't bear for it to be true. I couldn't deal with the idea of this awful truth existing in the world, and me knowing, but that was easier than it existing and me having to be the one to tell you. If it had to be me, out of all the fans, who knew, I wanted it to be *only* me.'

'You couldn't cope with anyone else knowing?' I asked.

Alex shook her head. Clearly, she didn't see where I was going with this.

Where am I going with this?

'So you got rid of the only other person who knew?'

Oh. I'm going there.

Jas's head snapped round to face me. 'Harri, what are you doing?'

'I'm asking a question.'

Alex was pale. 'Are you asking me if I killed Evan to make sure nobody ever found out the truth about Jack and Frankie?'

Was I? Really?

'Harri?'

'All right, fine,' I said. 'Yes, maybe I am.'

Alex stood up, shaking her head. 'I can't believe you actually just said that out loud. No, Harri, I didn't. I'm *sorry* you think I should have told you, but I'm not sorry that I didn't and this has just proved why. Jas, she's all yours.'

'Alex, you can't just walk away!' I called as she made for the door.

She turned and looked at me. 'Actually, I can. Good luck. I'm out.'

I didn't move until I heard the front door close, then I turned to Jas. She was uncharacteristically quiet.

'So we need to talk to Georgia *now*,' I said.

'Harri, don't you think you're taking this too far?'

'What are you talking about?'

'H. You just as good as accused Alex – our *really good friend* Alex – of killing Evan.'

'I didn't acc–'

'Yes, you did.'

'You don't know what I was going to say next!' I protested, but she did. She always did.

135

'You were going to say you didn't accuse her, because now you're realizing maybe that wasn't a very wise move. But you kinda did, Harri. And it wasn't fair.'

'All right. Fine. Maybe I shouldn't have accused her. It's just . . . I know it can't be Frankie. It has to be *anyone* but Frankie.'

'Even if that anyone is *Alex*? Why is it so hard for you to admit that Frankie might not be who we thought he was, H? I love him, too, and I desperately want there to be another answer, but even if there is, it isn't *Alex*.'

'It's just . . . Half Light are what gave me my identity, you know?' It wasn't what I'd planned to say, but it was what came out. Jas raised an eyebrow and I felt myself tense. 'Well, no, I don't suppose you do know. You've never had to worry about that, have you?'

Her head snapped up and, as our eyes met, I realized I'd known that would rile her, somewhere deep within. I was surprised to find, though, that what I'd expected – wanted even – was anger. What I saw on Jas's face was unmistakably sadness.

'Are you joking?'

She spoke quietly, and not in her usual dramatic, every-cadence-planned kind of way. I'd messed up big time, I could tell, and it worried me that I wasn't quite sure how. I hadn't meant for what I'd said to be the fatal blow. I had a feeling we weren't talking about Alex any more, so I said nothing, waiting for her to carry on. She took a deep breath and closed her eyes. When she opened them again, she looked utterly defeated. I'd done that, I realized. It felt terrible.

'I don't know what it's like to build an identity round them?' she asked.

I stayed silent.

'Harri, I'm an Indian Christian who has never been to India and doesn't believe in God. *Nothing* people think I am when they look at me represents *Jas*, you know? I have my family and my upbringing and I'm grateful for that, but I didn't know who *I* was, without all that stuff that never quite felt like the bones of me, until I heard those boys sing, and more than that until I started talking to other people who felt the same. They're why I can say I'm a gay woman. They're how I made friends I could show *myself* to instead of the facade. How do you not get that, H?'

I moved closer and reached out for her arm, and actually gasped when she pulled back before my hand could touch her sleeve.

'Don't, Harri. It's a *joke*. Your love always has to be more valid, doesn't it? But you've always had a choice about who you were going to be. I just wish it would cross your mind for *one second* sometimes that it isn't as easy as that for some of us.'

'Jas, that isn't what I meant. Is that really what you think of me? That my love always has to be more valid?' I was mortified. My voice shook.

Jas sighed. 'I know it isn't what you meant, H, but it's what you said. That's kind of the point. You don't even have to think about that stuff.'

'Jas, you're being ridiculous!' I said, reaching out again for her arm. As I touched her, she stiffened.

'*I'm* being ridiculous?'

'Jas, that's not –'

'Not what you meant, I know.'

I was quiet, partly because I had no idea what I wanted to say, partly because I knew exactly what I wanted to say, but feared it was wrong. I should apologize, but all the versions of *sorry* I rehearsed in my head sounded empty. I just knew I didn't want to make things any worse.

'I'm going to go to bed,' she said eventually, 'and I think . . . you should go home, H.'

I nodded. I suspected I had long since missed the last train back to uni, and it didn't seem the right time to pull out my phone and check. Maybe I'd be forced to call my parents. I loved them both dearly, but explaining what was going on with Frankie to two people who'd never been quite onboard with the ways that I loved Half Light didn't sound like my idea of fun tonight.

'Can you get back this late?' she asked, and it felt like my heart was being squeezed. Even when we were fighting, she still cared about me more than anyone else.

'Yes,' I lied.

'You're lying.'

'All right, I haven't checked, but if I can't I'll call my dad. He has a lot of work events in London. He might be able to drive me back.'

Jas laughed. 'Oh God, don't do that. Last thing you need is to have to explain all this to them right now.' She pulled out her phone, tapped the screen. 'You're fine. Just. My dad will drive you to the station.'

'Your dad thinks we're friends from uni, Jas.'

She huffed. Sighed. 'God, Harri, even fighting with you is complicated.'

I didn't dare ask what she meant by that. *Even?*

'We'll tell him you had a family emergency, and you need to go home,' she continued, making her way to the door.

'Dad!' she called softly, and I heard his footsteps padding towards the conservatory almost immediately.

'Are we OK?' I forced myself to ask, desperate to fix this before he arrived at the door and we had to start pretending. It felt, in some ways, like this was the first time she'd actually been honest with me. Like everything that had come before had been sanitized somehow. Like a surface-level friendship where we didn't fight because it just wasn't that deep. Had we been wrong, all along, about everything this meant?

I made myself look up from the floor. My eyes met hers and my stomach flipped. No. We hadn't been wrong. Jas was my best friend and I'd completely blown it.

'Right now? No. But we're us, Harri. We'll have to find a way to be, won't we?'

'Jas, I'm sorry,' I said, but the words sounded hollow and I felt it, too.

'I know.' Her voice was resigned.

'How can I fix it?' I asked as she walked into the hallway.

'I don't know yet.'

Jas picked up my bag and handed it to me. She took a deep breath. I reached out for her again, and she was slower to back away this time, but she still didn't let me touch her.

'Harri, seriously, don't,' she said. 'It's not you. Or at least it's not *all* you. But you've gotta just let me feel this for a little while, OK?'

I nodded.

'Don't call me, please. I'm just . . . I'm so tired, H.'

'You'll call me?' I asked. I wanted her to promise. I'd been so angry, running on so much adrenaline and rage that she thought Frankie could possibly be a part of this, that now it was gone it was like I'd deflated, a shrivelled-up balloon at the end of a party.

She smiled. 'Of course I will.'

'OK.'

'And you need to apologize to Al.'

'I know. I will.'

'Dad, will you drive Harri to the station?' she called, and his head popped round the corner, where he must have been waiting. More than anything else, I was so embarrassed. Jas's dad nodded and quickly disappeared in the direction of the front door. I picked up my bag and began to make my way down the hallway.

'Harri?'

I turned, my eyes a question.

'Of course I don't think Frankie killed him. There's no way.'

That, at least, was something.

TRACK ELEVEN

Campus was dark and quiet by the time I arrived, heading for home before I turned into a pumpkin and could never go back to before. *I can't anyway*, I thought as I neared the front door and began digging through my bag for my keys. *Not knowing what we know. The change has already happened. This is just how we live now.*

I rooted deeper through my things, becoming more frustrated the longer it took to hear the clink of metal on metal. 'Where the hell are they?' I crouched on the doorstep and unpacked, trying to remember the last time I'd seen them. Had I left in such a rush to get to London that they were still somewhere in my room? Or had I taken them out for some reason at Jas's and now they lay forgotten in her conservatory, or her garden? I supposed it didn't really matter – they weren't here.

I sighed, and pulled out my phone. I knew at least one person in the building would be awake. I'd never known him to fall asleep the right side of midnight.

He'll never let me live this down, I thought as I listened to the dialling tone.

'Hello?'

'Stef,' I said. 'I need your help.'

To his credit, he didn't laugh at me. He did, however, insist on waiting in the corridor as the caretaker unlocked my door, and then in my doorway as I searched for my keys, finally finding them flung on my window ledge behind a plant I hadn't watered in weeks.

'You can go, you know,' I said multiple times, hoping it was coming across more as an instruction than an option.

But each time he just replied, 'I'm fine.' Eventually, I stopped hinting.

'Are you going to tell me what's going on now?' he asked when I'd finally finished putting the pieces of my ransacked room back in their rightful places. 'Or, like . . . invite me in?'

'Do I have to?'

He laughed. 'No. But I totally saved your ass, Lodge. Spill. What's got you all in a tizz?'

'Am I in a tizz?'

'Yes, and now you're trying to avoid the question. Come on . . . what happened in London?'

I sat down on the bed, and patted the empty space next to me. Maybe saying it aloud to someone who wasn't as immersed in it as we all were would bring some clarity.

'So, first of all, the interview was a complete bust.

Actually, that isn't true. It went great until I admitted that I was a massive fan of Half Light and said we were basically the only people who could get Frankie cleared.'

I hadn't found it even remotely funny until Stefan laughed so loud that it was as if the sound was reverberating off all four walls of my bedroom. I allowed myself a chuckle, too. I had to admit that, if it wasn't happening to me, I would have found the whole thing surreal, and probably hilarious.

'Anyway,' I continued once he'd got his hysterics under control, 'that isn't even the most interesting part. You think that's insane? Just you wait.'

'Tell me then . . .'

So I did.

Night had become early morning by the time we finished talking, but it was nowhere near getting light. I was glad. It felt like the kind of conversation that had to happen in darkness.

'Well. That isn't what I expected . . .' His voice was thick with tiredness, which made me feel my own exhaustion that bit more. I stretched out along the bed where we were both still sitting, and closed my eyes.

'You asked . . .'

'I know, I'm not judging. I think it's pretty cool. Not the part where you accused Alex of murder, that was completely out of order, but I think you know that. And what you said to Jas was far from your finest moment too. The rest of it, though. Cool.'

I opened one eye and looked at him. 'Is it?'

'Yeah . . . in that it's totally the opposite of cool and you don't care. You just do it anyway because you love that band so much. You know how I feel about the not-putting-yourself-in-danger bit, but as long as you're not . . . I'm into it. And I don't think you need to worry about your friends. We all make mistakes, Harri.'

His northern accent became stronger when he was tired, I noticed. It was kind of endearing. Satisfied with his answer, I closed my eyes.

'Yeah, I do love it. And them. So much.'

I felt him shift, and could sense him leaning over, so I opened my eyes again. He was propped up on one elbow, kind of looming above me. When he saw my eyes were open, he began to lean in.

'Stef, what are you doing?'

'What do you think I'm doing?'

I stretched out an arm to stop him, and he retreated.

'I'm not saying never, and I really do mean that. Just . . . not yet, OK?'

He nodded, and stretched out beside me.

'I guess not-never is a concession, at least.'

I meant what I said, too. The more time I spent with him, the more I was coming round to the idea that maybe this was something we should try, but I still couldn't quite let myself go.

'Yeah. Are you staying here?'

I knew I was giving him mixed messages, but selfishly I was desperate for the company. Usually, I would have been texting Jas until one of us couldn't stay awake.

'Do you want me to?'

'Do what you want,' I said, closing my eyes again. 'I'm going to sleep, though.'

'Me too,' I think he said, but I was already drifting.

The next time I woke, it was light and he was gone, but when I rolled into the space where he'd been it was still just a little bit warm.

TRACK TWELVE

I tried to put whatever-that-was with Stefan out of my mind when I finally emerged from underneath my duvet, ready to face the day. My parents were expecting me for lunch, Tuesday being the day they took off together once a fortnight in a truly sickening display of enduring love, as well as my only day without lectures. Although the last thing I wanted was to have to discuss the case with them, I knew they'd be upset if I cancelled. Besides, I thought, I could delve into the Half Light scrapbooks I'd been meaning to revisit for months. It had been ages since I'd looked at them, but all this stuff with Frankie was making me nostalgic for the days when cutting out their pictures and sticking them to the page was as complicated as it got.

I pulled up Instagram as the bus rolled along the streets I'd grown up on. I smiled sadly as Phoebe Shaw's pouting face filled my screen: another photo cuddled up to Frankie, but this time with Evan on her other side. She was fully made up in this one, her public face well and truly painted on, but the way both guys were looking at her was so genuine that I could tell straight away they saw right through the thick eyeliner, and almost-purple lips. Was she good friends with Evan? I wondered. I'd never really noticed them together, but then again I'd never really paid attention to other people when Frankie was in the frame. I scrolled down to the caption.

Still in total shock that our friend Evan is gone. When you become friends with Frankie Williams, you become friends with his friends, because he has his circle that he keeps close. These two lovely men were inseparable, but beyond that I saw a lot of myself in Evan. We cared for Frankie in a very similar way, and both wanted what was best for him, and it was so nice to find that kindred spirit who just got it. When you love someone like Frankie, it can be hard, because they're sharing themselves with so many people, so Evan and I became pretty tight in our own right, because we knew how the other was feeling. I still can't believe for a second that anyone who saw them together would think Frankie could have anything to do with this. It feels like I've lost both of them, and I'm heartbroken. Just wanted to check in and say that I might be off social media for a little while – so many people are saying so many lovely things about my friends, but for the hundreds of supportive comments there's one so spiteful that it breaks my heart, and I think it's only human for my brain to stick on those ones. It's a lot to cope with right now. I'll be back soon, but for now look after each other, and keep Frankie in your thoughts.

Phoebe x

Her support for him had not gone unnoted. Lines were starting to pop up in the many news articles I skimmed, the journalists seemingly incredulous that Frankie could still count Phoebe among his supporters after 'what he'd done to her', by which I assumed they meant ending his relationship with her and then, admittedly quickly, starting one with Jack.

Good for her, I thought as I liked the post and closed the app. Once she and Frankie had finished, Phoebe had retreated to Instagram-star levels of celebrity, which was a whole universe away from Half Light levels. It must have been hard being catapulted back into that world now, and having to defend Frankie, while grieving for Evan and trying to keep her own mental health intact. *Who'd want it?* I wondered.

I stepped inside my childhood home and my dad stuck his head round the living-room door, teacup steaming in his hand. *Great timing*, I thought. I wouldn't even have to reboil the kettle.

'Hello, darling. Wasn't expecting you so early. How's your week going? What have you been up to?'

I decided not to lie. 'I was with Jas yesterday.'

I half hoped that, in typical Dad fashion, he'd have forgotten who Jas was and would decide not to ask. I also hoped he'd recognize that I was exhausted and on the verge of gunning for a fight. *Well, it's inevitably going to happen. Might as well start early.*

'Is she a friend from uni?'

'No, um . . . I know her through the boys.'

To his credit, he tried really hard not to let me notice as his face fell.

'Did you have a nice time?'

'Frankie's been arrested,' I said, sweeping past him into the living room and sinking on to the sofa.

'I saw something about that.'

'Yeah, bet you loved it.'

I knew I shouldn't have said that, but the thought of them seeing it all unfold on the news, feeling smug that they were right, made me angry suddenly, in a way I hadn't been yet. I thought of the stages of grief. *One of those is anger, right?* It was kind of ridiculous that I was equating this to grief, I knew, but that was what it felt like.

'What do you mean?'

He looked confused in a way that would probably have been endearing to an outsider, but was *intensely* irritating to me, his forehead wrinkling as his brain ticked through all the possible interpretations of what I'd said, trying, I knew, in his kind-hearted way, to find one that wasn't confrontational. Failing, of course. I was all in, it seemed, and that irritated me, too. Anyone else would have backed off, admitting that he'd done absolutely nothing wrong, but apparently I could not be that person today.

'Oh, come on, Dad. You've been trying to tell me he's bad news since I first ripped his face out of your newspaper and stuck it on my wall. Don't pretend you're not a little bit smug at being right.'

'That isn't what I was thinking at *all*.'

I tipped my head back to look at what we'd always affectionately referred to as the Hall of Fame – a whole wall filled with framed photos, the best bits of our lives as seen by Mum and Dad. I could barely make out the images from that angle, the bottoms of the frames cutting us off at the waist, or the neck, but I'd looked at them enough to know that there were far fewer pictures of me as I hit my teenage years. My sister Rachel's med-school graduation was there, but there was no room for Harriet hanging out with her friends from the internet. No space on their walls for things they didn't even try to understand.

I hadn't turned out the way they wanted, or expected, I knew. My whole childhood had been spent doing kitchen-table science experiments with my dad, which was probably dangerous in retrospect, but had made both of us so happy. Dad was an immunologist, and there had been talk of a biochemistry degree for me, of top universities with funding for female scientists, of the wonderful life I would have in labs and lecture theatres for as long as I wanted.

Except I hadn't wanted. It had just taken Half Light coming along, and making me realize what passion was actually supposed to feel like, to give me the guts to say so. That, predictably, had not gone down well.

'I just need to get a scrapbook from upstairs so I'll be out of your way for a bit,' I said, scooping the cat into my arms as I stood. If retreating to my bedroom was the only way to avoid saying something I'd regret, that's what I'd do.

'Are you hungover?' Dad asked, and *oh*, if that didn't just make it a million times worse.

'No, I'm *exhausted*, Dad. This whole thing has just got me so *tired*. I know you don't mean it, I know you're just wired in a way that means I make no sense to you, but honestly? I could do without your judgement today, because I know you can't possibly understand why, but this is actually pretty hard for me. So *please*, just let me go and look for my scrapbook, then I'll leave if that's what you want.'

I felt so childish as I stomped out of the room and up the stairs, my socks not making as much sound on the wooden floor as I'd hoped they would, the punctuation to my point.

It was only as I sat down on my bed, cold to the touch and unslept in since the end of the summer, and lowered the cat down beside me, that I realized my dad had not deserved that at all.

'Frankie Williams, you're turning me into a monster,' I said out loud as I reached under my bed for the first scrapbook. I wasn't sure if I was looking for a specific piece of evidence or just a feeling, but something told me I'd find whatever I needed in these pages. I always had before. I leaned back on the stack of pillows propped against the headboard, and flipped to the first page. The boys looked *so young*.

'Literally children,' I mumbled, even though all three of them were older than me. It was strange the kind of love we felt for them. At any given moment, I couldn't decide if I wanted to kiss them or wrap them all in blankets and make sure they never came to any harm. Looking at them like this – so young, so completely clueless about everything that was about to happen, and all the ways their lives were about to change – I just wanted to tell them everything was going to be OK. *Just look at their hopeful little faces*, I thought. *If you'd told those boys it was all going to end up like this, they wouldn't have believed you for a second.*

There they were, silhouetted against stage lights at the end of their first concert, a small venue in Manchester that these days they'd fill ten times over, captured by someone I'd never met, her only acknowledgement for this photo a credit so small it was almost illegible in the corner of the frame. Flipping the page, I came to their first printed interviews where they were so nervous, so fresh out of media training that their answers barely read like human speech at all.

And yet we fell for it anyway, I thought. *We saw something underneath that veneer that was interesting. Not the polished, teen-idol parts they wanted us to see. No, we fell for them when they were being weird, and messy, and completely contradicting everything that the marketing teams in their glass-fronted offices were telling them to do and say. And then they started doing that more. Just being who they were. And more and more people started listening.*

The pages were annotated, the notes made by my fourteen-year-old self written in one of those scented purple gel pens. I lifted the paper to my nose and sniffed, but the smell had faded. The words, though, seemed to be pretty timeless. I laughed as I scanned the underlinings, exclamation marks noting the things Frankie had said that I'd believed to be particularly profound or important, my own EVERYTHING HE SAYS IS MAGIC scribbled in the margins like I'd be tested on it later.

I reached down again and pulled out the next volume, thanking past-me for her insistence on everything being in order. I still wasn't searching for anything specific – more, I thought, a sign that this was worth it. That we were doing the right thing, trying to prove that the police were wrong.

We'd be able to tell, after all this time, if he was guilty, right? I typed out the thought exactly as it came and texted it to Ruby in Berlin. I knew that Jas had filled her and Gemma in on everything that had happened, and hoped that Ruby didn't think I was treating her as a replacement best friend. It wasn't that at all, I told myself, but part of me wished I could have sent the message to Jas.

The third book was my favourite. The internet had made my collection pretty redundant as the quickest way to find a picture, or a clipping, but of the whole collection that book was definitely the most well thumbed. *This one starts just as Jack came out*, I remembered. There had been a cheap interview in a trashy tabloid that smacked of damage control; of Jack saying, '*Fine. I'll tell it my way because otherwise you'll tell it yours.*' The words were empty, and in the accompanying photo, posed moodily against an exposed-brick wall, his eyes were empty, too. We didn't mind, though. That article, we knew, wasn't for us. It was for the casual fans; the onlookers; the people who may have known his name, but otherwise couldn't have told you a single thing about him. It ended with the line, '*Our fans know who I really am. I don't think who I choose to date will change that.*'

But it did change it. It changed everything, because what we got was a man who was suddenly allowed to be himself. It was like he was suddenly living in the way he was always supposed to – as loud and offbeat and extraordinary as he wanted, finally. He knew we'd notice; knew we didn't need an interview printed on paper so disposable it would end up in the recycling bin by the time the week was out.

This book was full of *those* moments. Of Jack leaving a club hand in hand with a man we'd never seen before. Of interviews where he talked about the things he *really* looked for in a partner, finally not imprisoned by the words *woman* or *girlfriend*. I flipped the page to one of my favourite photos, taken from the wings of a TV set where Jack was being interviewed, Molly watching from the sidelines with a look in her eyes that could have warmed the very coldest night as she smiled at him. *God*, I thought. *They had all been so proud.*

And then, of course, came the Frankie Stuff.

They'd always been tactile. It was such a given, right from day one, that I don't think any of us even noticed when it first became . . . well, more than that. I smiled as I flicked through, past pictures of them arm in arm that we thought nothing of at the time, of them whispering in each other's ears onstage, and then, eventually, offstage, when they thought no one was watching, at least as much as the world's most-watched band could ever think that.

I glanced up as I heard the door open, and smiled at the arm curled round the frame, face not visible, holding a cup of what smelled like chai. A peace offering. *I don't deserve that*, I thought, but I reached out anyway, my heart fit to burst as I registered the fact that neither of my parents drank chai, but they always kept some in the cupboard for me.

'I should come home more,' I said as I took the cup from my dad's hand, pulling the door back with my toes so we were facing each other. I hoped he knew that was my way of saying sorry.

'You should,' he agreed, walking into my room. 'How are you holding up?'

'What do you mean?'

I took a sip of my tea to avoid looking at him. The milk to chai ratio was almost perfect. *Exactly how you liked it when you lived here*, I reminded myself. *He doesn't know you prefer it a little less tame now. A little more spice.*

'It must be hard, love. Seeing what everyone's saying about him, after you girls have given him so much of your energy. I just wanted to check you were doing OK.'

'He didn't do it,' I said, which was not an answer and the only answer all at once.

My dad hesitated before he spoke. 'Well. You seem sure.'

'Are you not?' I tried to keep the edge out of my voice this time.

'I can't be, love. I don't know enough to think anything much about it, full stop. But you'd think, after all this time, you fans of all people would be able to tell if he was lying.'

I stared down into my cup as if that might stop the choking feeling in my throat. I decided not to tell him about Jack.

'Yeah. That's our theory, too. We're going to prove he didn't do it.'

He took his hand from where it had been resting on the doorframe, and stepped closer. 'From afar and only theoretically?'

'Of course . . .'

'Harri, please don't do anything stupid for this boy.'

'I promise I won't,' I said, finally looking up, and hoping he didn't remember what I'd always said about rules, and resolutions, and promises. *I think they're made to be broken.*

'Well, you're an adult now. I can't stop you. Just . . . stay aware, sweetheart.'

'I will, Dad.'

I nodded to where the discarded scrapbooks lay on my bed.

'Let me just find what I need, then I'll be down. We can talk about something else, all right?'

He took the hint. I couldn't quite put my finger on why the slap of his feet against the floorboards as he walked down the stairs made me want to cry. I suspected that, by the time I made it back down, Mum would have had our conversation recounted word for word, which didn't make me want to rush.

I picked up the third scrapbook again, and softened when I saw the page it was open at. Frankie's hand on the small of Jack's back as they left the first venue on the Home Again tour, comfortable enough at their own shows to let their guard slip, just a little. Jack's coat wrapped round Frankie's much smaller frame leaving a private club in King's Cross on a Saturday night turned Sunday morning that they'd thought was just for them. Beside the photographs, the first articles asking *Are we missing something here?*

They hadn't said a word about the rumours for months.

One morning, I woke up to a picture of them kissing.

It was stuck in the scrapbook on its own page. I wasn't surprised to find it still gave me butterflies.

I hadn't looked at this one for ages, spoiled for choice as we now were by a relationship lived largely in public, where it seemed they couldn't keep their hands off each other for longer than five minutes at a time. This one was like costume jewellery compared to some of the solid-gold glimpses of the love story we'd been treated to since, but it was still one of my favourites. It was so grainy you could be forgiven, at first, for not noticing it was even them. On closer inspection, though, there was no question. The butterfly tattoo on Frankie's left wrist where his hand curled round the back of Jack's neck. Jack's distinctive rings on the fingers gripping Frankie's waist. They were standing in the gateway of their old apartment complex, Frankie's face to the camera in a way that made me wonder if he knew they were being watched. I'd never thought too hard about it before, but, knowing what I did now, the cynic in me suspected he'd positioned them in just the right spot on purpose.

Funnily enough, I remembered that it was Georgia who had sent it to us all, completely without comment, because what could she even say that would begin to be enough?

Finally, I'd thought, then. *Finally*.

Every paper, magazine, random blog that had sprung up just in the nick of time seemed to have a *source close to the boys* waxing lyrical about how they'd tried to keep it secret, but just couldn't any more, and how this had been a long time coming, but Frankie and Jack themselves never said a word. They didn't need to. It was not some publicity stunt they needed to talk about. It was *real* for them.

I tried not to linger too long on what I'd learned since. My phone chimed. Ruby.

> Well, we couldn't tell he was
> lying about his entire
> relationship, could we? So
> honestly who knows at this
> point. How's home? Also you
> need to talk to Jas.

Well, I thought. *I've so far lashed out at my dad for absolutely no reason and I still can't put my finger on what I came here for, so it could definitely be better.*

158

Fine. And it's Jas who doesn't
want to talk to me.

One more page, I told myself and, by the time my mum's
voice called up the stairs to tell me there was cake, I had
devoured another four pages of letters from the girls, of
more blurry photos from the back of slightly bigger arenas,
of lives lived so *loudly* if the pages of these scrapbooks
were to be believed. *It's time*, I thought, replacing all the
books under the bed and making my way down to the
living room. *We did this in secret long enough, and now
the whole world is talking about him. Time to tell them
what we know.*

'How are you doing, darling?' my mum asked as she
handed me a slice of cake the moment I walked into the
room.

'He hasn't *died*, Mum,' I said through my first mouthful.
'I'm doing all right. Tired. Over it. You know?'

'Yeah. Well, no, I don't know, but I can imagine.'

We sat in companionable silence for a second, the cat
rubbing against my ankles, listening to Dad pottering
about in the kitchen.

'Your dad mentioned that you're trying to prove he's
innocent,' Mum said finally, and a little warily.

'Prove Dad's innocent?' My attempt at a joke didn't
make her laugh.

'Harri, I really don't think this is a good idea.'

Of course she didn't.

'We're being careful. We can't get close enough to be in

any real danger, I promise. He's literally locked away and the rest of them are being so closely guarded that right now our "investigation" is messages on the internet and seriously overanalysing old photos. No different from any other day in a lot of ways.'

She didn't look at me as she took a bite of cake, and kept her eyes averted as she swallowed. 'It won't look good if your name gets dragged into this, darling. For your career, I mean. Nobody will want to hire you if they think you're going to cause trouble.'

'I don't think it's that black and white, Mum.'

'I'm just looking out for you, Harri. And what about uni? You're not doing anything that could get you into trouble there, are you?'

I took advantage of the second she looked down at her plate to roll my eyes.

'Honestly, Mum, I'm not doing anything that could get me into trouble. All we're doing is trying to support him, and using the things we know about him to try and work out what happened.'

'All right,' she said, her voice still dubious. 'I just worry about you, you know? It's my job. I'm your mother.'

'And looking after Frankie is my job,' I said and, although I tried to pass it off as a joke, it came out sounding very close to serious. Her expression was something between fear and dismay, so I took a risk on a change of subject.

'So what's the latest with Rachel's boyfriend?'

My mum pursed her lips and sat back in her chair. If

there was one thing she liked talking about more than my questionable decisions when it came to Half Light, it was my sister's terrible taste in men.

'Well,' she began, and I let my mind go fuzzy as she spoke. Score one for Harri.

'You promise me you'll be careful,' my mum said, handing me a bag laden with food as I got into a waiting taxi.

'I will,' I called from the window as the car carried me towards campus. I pulled my phone from my bag, and still felt the sting when there was nothing from Jas. There was, however, a text from Ruby.

> She doesn't not want to speak to
> you, she wants what happened
> to not have happened, we all
> do, but it has, so the two of you
> and Alex have to find a way
> through it. For Frankie, if not
> yourselves.

I put my phone away, and rested my head on the window of the taxi.

Later, I thought.

TRACK THIRTEEN

I was in quite a fatalistic mood anyway, so it wasn't too surprising to me that when Stefan walked into the kitchen a few days later, where I was washing up plates that didn't belong to me, I was thinking about what I'd do if Frankie died.

Would it have been easier? I was wondering. It would almost be the opposite of this. People would be talking about all the lives he changed, and all the things he stood for, and all the love he gave. People would feel sorry for us. They'd tiptoe around, offering to bring us tea, or something altogether stronger, and tell us it was fine if we wanted to cry; if we needed to be alone; if we were too tired to know what we needed at all. *I could do with all that right now.*

It would be strange to know that his funeral was happening and not be among the mourners, I thought. So many of the people who loved him the most would not be involved in the official goodbyes at all. We'd be left to fend for ourselves, to organize our own memorials, our own celebrations of all that he had been, while the people who spent day after day with him were allowed to express their grief in public, thinking that proximity equalled validity. That wasn't true. *We love him just as much. Just in a way that's harder for them to understand.*

I wondered when Evan's funeral would be. They'd have to come to some kind of concrete conclusion about what had happened first, I assumed.

I wouldn't wear black. That was not Frankie; that was the *opposite* of Frankie. Yes, he himself wore black all the time, but the whole point for us was that he brought colour. He was the one saying, 'Come out of the darkness,' and we had. My mourning would be yellow, and scarlet, and royal blue. I looked down at the white T-shirt I was wearing and laughed. Why wait? I'd change as soon as I got back to my room, I decided.

I was deep into this fantasy, imagining a scenario where Jack would have to identify the body by the placement of the tattoos, when I heard the kitchen door swing open. I didn't turn round, but carried on in my daydream. I wondered what songs his family would play; if they'd say goodbye in a church, despite Frankie being famously atheist. If Jack would hold hands with his would-be mother-in-law in the front row. I pondered whether I'd be able to bear the sight of Jack's puffy, tear-streaked face. If they'd burn Frankie or bury him. I supposed it didn't really matter. Everything that he had been would be gone. It would be up to us to carry round the things he left behind; to keep slipping them into the way we lived, so that a part of him might get to stay.

'What are you thinking about?'

I knew he was there, but Stef's voice still made me jump.

'If I'd still recognize Frankie's body if he didn't have a face any more.'

'And would you?'

I couldn't decide if the lack of judgement in his voice was endearing or cause for concern.

'Definitely, yes.'

I turned to him, and his lazy smile and hooded, hungover eyes made me feel, if not sleepy, like I wanted to crawl into bed beside him and just lie there, relaxed in the light of that not-quite grin. I shook my shoulders.

Really, Harri? Where did that come from?

Stefan stepped towards me. 'Well, as weird and therefore fascinating to me as that is, I actually didn't come to talk about the decomposing body of your prison boy.'

'Oh no?' I couldn't help smiling.

'Surprisingly not. I was actually going to ask if you wanted to go to a party tonight.'

It had been days since I'd spoken to Jas, and I'd kept my promise – I didn't text, or call, and resisted all my urges to comment on her photos, or her tweets. I sat with my thoughts and accepted I'd been completely out of line, and I rehearsed my apology over and over, ready for when the time came. I left her alone, and the longer I did, the more I expected it to become normal. It didn't. What did, though, was the amount of time I was spending with Stefan: drinking tea, actually working on essays, watching films until one of us fell asleep and the other sneaked back to their own room, feeling strangely like something was beginning. Everything was changing. I could let it happen *to* me, or I could take control of it.

Carrying the spirit of Frankie with me, I remembered.

'Harri?' Stef asked.

'Yes. I want to go to a party.'

Maybe nothing will happen, I thought as I loosely curled my hair, then immediately pulled a brush through it, wondering why my results were always frizzier than the girls I'd watched do exactly that on YouTube over and over.

Maybe he just feels sorry for me, because of Jas. He's probably just being nice. The memory of his hand, warm on the small of my back as I'd left the kitchen that morning, told me that was almost definitely untrue.

Even if he does like me, maybe it just isn't that kind of party, I pondered as I ran my mascara brush through my lashes. I knew that wasn't true, either. These kitchen-floor nights were notorious for hook-ups, when everyone else was too busy to be watching, and two people found each other in a corner and let themselves fall into something. I knew that if I wanted to, I could make that happen with Stef tonight. It would take little more than the right look at the right time. It would be easy.

You really don't have to do this, I told myself as I pressed my lips together, setting the almost-purple lipstick that was bolder than I'd usually go for. I felt like being someone else, though. I sort of felt like being Phoebe.

I think I want to.

165

I headed down the corridor, the music growing louder. People were standing around in clusters, drinking vodka and gin and cans of craft beer. It wasn't like I'd avoided these nights completely before. That would have been almost impossible. But before I had always had my phone in hand, Jas, or Alex, or Ruby at the end of it if I needed backup, which I'd always told myself I did. I may have lived these nights in body, but my spirit had always been elsewhere. It was as if, I realized, I hadn't been there at all. Maybe that was why most of these people looked like strangers to me. I felt a twinge of something – a feeling at the intersection of guilt and sadness that I couldn't quite name. Was it my fault uni hadn't been what everyone promised? Had I been shutting myself off?

Stefan had disappeared a few minutes ago, but I was surprised to find I was happy perched on the edge of the kitchen table, sipping on the cava I'd brought with me, surrounded by people I didn't know. *He'll be back*, I told myself. *For some reason, this social butterfly of a boy thinks I'm interesting.*

It was almost midnight, but for once my spirit was far from winding down for the night. I was wired. I didn't know if it was the cava, or the company, or something else entirely. All I knew was that it felt good.

'What're you drinking?' Stefan asked, hooking his chin over my shoulder as he came up behind me. I felt the scratch of stubble against my skin. I had to admit I actually sort of liked it.

'Cava,' I told him, and he laughed as he nuzzled his nose against my neck.

'What student drinks cava?' he asked.

'What? Cava's nice!'

He took the half-full glass from my hand and more gulped than sipped before reaching towards the worktop behind him and putting it down.

'Yeah, it's OK,' he said, and I didn't notice how close he'd got until he was kissing me.

At first it felt mechanical, like something that had been choreographed, but I'd forgotten the steps. It wasn't my first kiss, but it was like my body was trying to remember how to move in a way it hadn't for a while. Which, to be fair, was pretty accurate.

Relax, I urged myself. *This is meant to feel nice and, if it doesn't, you shouldn't be doing it.*

It did feel nice, though. More than nice. I slid my hands, still cold from the glass, up the back of his neck to tangle my fingers in his just-too-short hair and – *Whoa. Where had that come from? How had my hands known to do that?* He pulled back, his eyes hooded and dark, and smiled at me.

'Is this OK?' he asked, and I grinned, nodded, tried to pull him back. He extended an arm to hold me still. 'Then stop thinking so hard.'

'OK,' I said, and surprised myself when I actually did.

The thing about kissing is that, unless you want to stay alive through incredibly unattractive nose breathing alone, you eventually have to come up for air. The longer we

167

kissed, the drunker I began to feel, although I knew that it wasn't alcohol bubbling beneath the surface of my skin, making me burn from the inside out like this. When he finally pulled back, I was surprised at how I didn't really feel changed at all. It sort of felt like we'd been doing this the whole time. I could hardly remember why we hadn't.

'Drink?' he asked.

I shook my head.

'You tired?'

I shook my head again.

'Do you want to come back to my room?' he said, and it was like I could feel a line being drawn beneath my feet. I was standing on one side, the *before* side, and, if I shuffled forward the slightest bit, I'd be on the other. *After.* Not the kind of place you can come back from, so you'd better be sure you want to go.

Why do you want me? I thought, not unkindly towards myself at all but genuinely questioning. *You're beautiful. You could have any of those pretty girls, and for some reason you still want me.* I thought of Alex and her no-big-deal attitude; the way I'd wished so often I could be more like her. I thought of Jack, giving himself over to someone he trusted unconditionally, and wondered if he'd found out yet that none of it was real. I thought of Jas, and the way she'd always said she *could* wait, but wasn't actively. She was just going with the flow. The only thing she hadn't planned down to the last second.

What am I supposed to do? I asked the ever-present version of Jas in my head, but I knew what she'd say.

This one is all on you.

I'd have to work it out another way.

Reasons to go back to Stefan's room, knowing what that means, and aware that it would change everything

1. Stef is kind. For some reason, he seems to really like me.
2. He's pretty funny, too.
3. Not to mention he's gorgeous and I'm beginning to *really* fancy him.
4. I don't feel rushed or pressured. I trust him. He makes me feel safe.
5. I . . . think I really want to do this.

Reasons not to go back to Stefan's room, knowing what that means, and aware that it would change everything

1.
2.
3. Oh, come on, Harri. Admit that you can't think of any. Stop stalling. You should –

'Harri?' Stefan broke into my thoughts, smiling, so close to my face that if I stuck out my tongue I could lick his lips. I'd never had a thought like that before. It was unnerving, in a way I sort of liked.

'Let's go,' I told him.

TRACK FOURTEEN

It was still dark when I woke up, and cold, too. A quick glance around told me we'd forgotten to close the window. I moved my legs tentatively, the dull, heavy ache satisfying in the strangest way. *I didn't know it made your legs hurt*, I thought, and immediately felt incredibly naive and exposed, even though I was the only one awake.

I twisted my head to look at Stef, sleeping and still. He wasn't feeling strange at all, I knew. He'd done this before. He was fine. I, however, was sort of spinning out. I put my head in my hands and rubbed my eyes. It wasn't that I regretted it. I'd been so sure. It was just . . . not the way I'd imagined. In my head, it was in a hotel room, with the curtains fluttering in the breeze from the open balcony doors. In my head, there were flowers, and white sheets, and I was wearing a ridiculous floaty nightdress. *Would rip as soon as you looked at it*, I thought, glancing around for my own top where Stefan had thrown it. I couldn't find it in the darkness. I pulled the duvet tighter about my shoulders. In my head, it wasn't like this at all. In my head, it was someone I really loved. Had done for a

170

long time. In my head, as much as I had known forever that it wouldn't be, couldn't be . . . it had always been Frankie.

I sighed, and Stefan stirred beside me.

'Watching me sleep?' he murmured, and I laughed. He took my hand and pulled me back down until I was lying flat again, facing him. 'What time is it?'

'Like, four a.m. I need water.'

'Do you want me to get it?' he asked, but I could tell from his voice that he was already slipping back into unconsciousness.

'No, I'm all right.' I pulled myself upright and scrambled around on the floor for my clothes. I pulled on my jeans. 'Where's my top?'

'Dunno,' he mumbled without looking. 'Wear mine.'

I picked up the first piece of fabric I touched, and squinted in the dark to check it was a top at all.

'This one?'

He opened one eye. 'Wear that one if you want, but it's Darren's. We sort of just share clothes.'

I threw it back on to the pile. 'I'm not wearing Darren's clothes. That's weird.'

'I do.'

'Yeah, but he's your best friend. Best friends share clothes,' I said, picking up another.

It was like a lightning bolt. I couldn't believe I hadn't thought of it before. I gasped aloud.

'What?' he asked.

I threw the shirt over my head, no longer caring which boy it belonged to.

'I've gotta go.' I didn't bother looking for the rest of my things. I'd be back.

'Is this a boyband thing?' he asked as I flung open the door and let the light, and the reality of what had just happened, into the dark room. The last stragglers were chattering away in the kitchen. How could they not feel how much had changed since we'd walked out of the party a few hours before?

'Yeah.'

'Can you tell me?'

I crossed the room quickly so I was standing over the bed, then leaned down and kissed him. He grinned.

'I can. I will. I just need to tell Jas first.'

I had to check that I was right. I was almost certain, but I had to get rid of the *almost* before I opened a can of worms I could not close again. It didn't take long. Less than five seconds' flicking through my message history gave me all the evidence I needed.

I wondered briefly if it was OK to call someone you weren't technically speaking to at 4 a.m., and decided that it was fine in real emergencies, of which this was one.

Still, I thought, *I should probably text first to see if she's up.*

I was going to lead with an apology. I was going to come right out and say it. I typed and deleted and typed and deleted and eventually decided Are you up? would work. I had to stop myself from pacing the room while I waited for her reply. Luckily, this was Jas. I didn't have to wait long.

No, I wasn't. It's 4.13 a.m., Harri.

172

Well. She was now. I dialled, and prayed she'd answer. It took her until the third ring.

'*What?*'

'They wear each other's clothes, Jas.'

There would be time for apologies and *I missed you*'s later.

'You didn't call me at four a.m. to tell me something we've all known for years, H.'

'No, Jas, listen to me. They *wear each other's clothes.*'

'You're just saying the same words with different intonation.' She sounded exasperated now, but me? I was almost vibrating with anticipation. 'What are you actually trying to tell me, Harri?'

'Frankie was taken into custody on Friday, right?'

'Yes . . .'

'And the police found his Keats shirt on the roof of the studio on Monday morning?'

'Harri, come *on.*'

'Someone's setting him up. He can't have killed Evan wearing the Keats shirt. That can't be real evidence,' I blurted out, and I heard Jas shuffle. I imagined her sitting up.

'Tell me why.' Her tone was irate, but I knew she was really listening now.

'Because he was taken into custody on Friday.'

'Yes?'

'Look at your photos from the press conference, Jas. Look at the bottom of Jack's hoodie. You can see it, just the hem poking out. Jack was wearing the Keats shirt on Saturday morning.'

173

TRACK FIFTEEN

I had barely slept once Jas and I had hung up, both too tired and far too awake.

You're not coming back, are you? Stefan had texted somewhere around six, and I couldn't think of a single reason not to tiptoe back along the hallway, and knock on his door, and fall back into his bed until the sun came up, so I did exactly that.

What a brilliant way to pass the time, I thought, and I didn't know if that was the kind of thing a boy would be offended by if you said it out loud. *I can't believe I've been missing this for so long*, I thought, and that time I said it and he laughed and pulled me closer.

'Too busy playing boyband detective,' he said. 'Are you going to tell me why you ran out of here like the place was on fire earlier, by the way?'

And so, although I knew he might not understand, I did.

'They share clothes all the time, right? And the new bit of evidence that they're all saying is going to tie up the case is this shirt they all share, which was found on the roof of the studio on Monday morning, with Evan's DNA and some blood on it. I guess the police's theory was that whoever killed Evan had been wearing it, and to be fair it does actually belong to Frankie, so I can see how they've made that leap. They're wrong, though. Frankie was taken in on Friday night, within minutes of Evan being found. Jack was wearing that shirt when we saw him on Saturday morning. Whoever is behind this went back to the studio at some point to plant it. Frankie's being set up.'

'You're terrifying,' Stef whispered as he pulled me closer and wrapped his arms round me. I took that as a compliment.

I went back to my room when I heard the flat begin to wake up. This time I didn't feel the need to sneak past the bedrooms where I could hear movement. They'd all seen us leave the party together. I was surprised by my own ability to act so casually about it. I knew it was a big deal – this night would be a part of my story forever, for so many reasons – but it was nice to realize I didn't care what anyone else thought.

There seemed little point in trying to doze any more, so I drank a cup of coffee to keep me awake as I listened to Half Light's second album, and waited. Jas would be here soon.

'I'm going to come over,' she'd said almost immediately on hearing the news. 'We can talk about what happened between us later. This is more important right now, isn't it? We've lost time.'

'It isn't more important,' I said, and I'd heard Jas sigh softly.

'No. It isn't. I didn't mean that. I meant more time-sensitive, I suppose.'

'Missed you,' I told her as we said goodbye.

'Harri. Shut up and I'll see you in a few hours.'

I knew then we'd be fine.

I didn't question how she'd got past the locked door to my building when she began pounding on my bedroom door around nine thirty.

'Late night?' she asked as I opened the door, raising her eyebrows. I must have blushed because she grabbed my arm and screeched, 'Tell me everything!'

'How do you even know there's anything to tell?'

'Harri, you called me at four a.m.! It's all over your face! Also your lips are swollen! You've been kissing!'

'Later,' I promised, touching a finger to my admittedly tender mouth. 'Shall we try and figure out what the hell is going on with Frankie first?'

'We can, but don't think you're getting out of talking about it,' she said, finally loosening her grip.

'I didn't imagine you'd let me for a second.'

Jas reached over to my dressing table where my laptop was charging and pulled it on to her lap. I couldn't see the screen as she started to type.

'What are you doing?'

'Tumblr post,' she said.

'About?'

Her fingers flew across the keys at speed. 'Hang on.'

Neither of us spoke until she'd finished. It was probably less than two minutes, but the quiet made me restless, and I was relieved when she spun the laptop to face me.

'Read before I press post.'

Hi Half-Lighters,

Jas and Harri here, coming at you live from a university bedroom where someone (it's Harri) looks like she didn't get much sleep last night. Can't wait to hear all about that when we've finished the task at hand, i.e. saving boy wonder Frankie Williams from a life in prison. Which is where we need your help. (Why am I talking like Gossip Girl? I don't know. I'm going to stop.)

Anyway. We think maybe we've found something that proves Frankie is being set up. I don't want to say what, because y'know . . . this is the internet and the person setting him up may well be watching. The goal here is not to make it all worse. We'll tell you if we're right, I promise, but right now we need info that we don't have to figure out if we are. This is what I'm asking – no judgement – did any of you go to Jack and Frankie's house at any point in the few days after Frankie was arrested? We're looking specifically at Saturday afternoon to early Monday, but anything at all that whole week could possibly be useful. We know the boys were coming and going, but who else? Who went in, who came out, and when? If you could tell us, you'd be helping. We'll keep it discreet, too. We all want the same thing here, don't we?

Thank you. We love you, and we really hope we're getting close.

Jas & Harri x

'Did that just come out of your brain as you typed it?' I asked, amazed.

Jas shrugged. 'I was thinking about it on the train here, but mostly.'

I pressed my face into her shoulder, my best friend back where she belonged. 'You're a genius.'

'Yeah, I know.'

'Take out the bit about me not getting much sleep,' I said, and watched in only half-horror as she ignored me and pressed the post button.

'Oops.'

'I hate you.'

'You don't.'

Of course I didn't. I couldn't. The thing about Jas knowing me so well was that she *knew me so well*. She knew I wasn't really angry. She knew how happy I was to have her here.

'So what's the theory?' I asked once her words were out in the ether. 'Are we assuming that whoever did this found out about Frankie's lie? Wanted to send a message that he wouldn't get away with it?'

'Well, maybe, but killing his best friend and framing him for it seems like an extreme way to, as you put it, *send a message*, doesn't it?'

'I suppose.'

'Maybe it wasn't about Frankie at all,' said Jas, frowning. 'I know I said I thought it had to be, but . . . It's like Alex said. Evan had this whole life outside of the boys that we don't know about. It could be nothing to do with Frankie.'

'But, if it's nothing to do with Frankie, why take Frankie's shirt back to the scene and plant it there?' I pointed out. 'It *has* to be related to him, Jas.'

My thoughts had snagged on something else she'd said. *Alex.* I couldn't help feeling guilty suddenly. I'd all but accused her of being involved and, while I still couldn't quite get my head round why she hadn't told us about Evan, I was certain – or at least almost certain – that it hadn't been malicious.

'Does Al hate me?'

Jas sighed as she pushed my laptop aside and gestured for me to snuggle up to her. 'I doubt it, H. It's an emotional time. We're all stressed.'

'Yeah, but we didn't *all* accuse her of being involved, did we?'

Jas choked back a laugh. 'Fine, she's probably a bit pissed off with you *now*, but you'll be all right. We'll all be all right. What choice have we got?'

'Jas, I'm sorry.'

She shook her head, waved her hand to silence me, but I carried on regardless.

'No, listen. I was really ignorant. I should never have assumed our experiences have been the same. I shouldn't have even thought those things, let alone tried to defend myself when you told me I was wrong. I'm sorry. I'll do better.'

Jas reached out her hand and took mine.

'Apology appreciated. And accepted. Now can we talk about something else while we're waiting for the girls on Tumblr to reply?'

'What do you want to talk about?' Even as I said it, I could predict her answer from the glint in her eye.

'I want you to tell me about last night,' she said and, although I rolled my eyes, I pulled the duvet up round us and did not spare a single detail.

TRACK SIXTEEN

I was nearing the end of the story when my phone chimed, and Jas's vibrated at the same moment, which always meant that something was happening in our Half Light group chat.

'It's Gem,' I said, reaching for mine first. 'She says – oh my God. She says she thinks she might have found a way to hack the CCTV cameras at Albany Road.'

'As in the place Evan died?' Jas sat bolt upright. I couldn't tell from her tone if she was open to the idea or not.

'Yeah. That place.'

Another message appeared on my screen. 'Turns out in theory it's quite easy and not even *that* illegal.'

Now that it had happened, I had no idea why we hadn't thought of it before. Gemma had never met a piece of technology she didn't immediately want to pick apart. She was studying computer science and killing it. *Of course* she'd been looking at ways to hack the CCTV.

'Are we scary people?' Jas asked, and I couldn't help the way I beamed at her.

'No. We just want to get a pop star out of prison. That makes us a force for good, right?'

Jas returned my smile. 'All right.'

'She wants to FaceTime,' I said, reading Gemma's next message as it came in and grabbing my laptop.

'Wait, she's doing this *right now*?'

I shrugged. 'Shall we find out?'

'I have no idea if this is going to work,' Gemma said as soon as her face filled my laptop screen, before even hello. 'I'm literally getting this from internet articles and YouTube videos. I've never hacked anything before in my life.'

I didn't *quite* believe that.

'Hi, Gem, nice to speak to you, too,' I said, and she laughed, showing her perfect American-girl teeth.

'Have you looked yet?' Jas asked. 'Can you tell how hard it's going to be?'

Gemma spun her phone so the camera faced her laptop, where a password screen was open in the browser, as well as, I noticed, multiple tabs that seemed to be giving instructions on what we were about to try.

'So we just have to guess the password?' I asked.

'Yes,' Gemma's disembodied voice said, 'but the chances of doing that are pretty much impossible, so I'm going to see if I can find a way to bypass it. As far as I understand it, we basically need to hack into the camera feed itself rather than this interface.'

'*As far as you understand it?* Gem, have you really just taught yourself all of this in the *hour* since you first had the idea?' For Jas to sound so impressed, I knew what Gemma had done couldn't have been easy.

She turned the phone back on her own face and grinned. I wished I could smile like that without feeling self-conscious about my teeth.

'Wouldn't be the first thing I'd taught myself because of Half Light,' she said. 'Probably the most spontaneous, and definitely the most complicated, but the actual act of teaching myself stuff because it relates to them? Babe, I'm an old hand at that. Plus, I know my way round a piece of software. That made it kinda easy.'

She rested the phone against the screen of her computer as she began to type. Middle-aged white men in suits who worked in tech were always being quoted on the news saying they wished they could find more female talent interested in this stuff, if only they knew where to look. *Look at our fandom*, I thought. *We could change entire industries with the things we know because we loved a band.*

'So what we essentially need to do is work out the IP address for the studio. That's easy enough – them having a website is half the battle. Then there's software that'll do a lot of the rest of the work for us. The next problem will be how they store their old footage. It probably hasn't been deleted yet, but the question is where do they keep it? If it isn't online, we're screwed. There's nothing we can do.'

'Gemma, you're scary,' Jas said.

'Thank you.'

She tapped away at her keyboard, the screen not visible

to us, but I could tell by the way her brow furrowed that she was concentrating hard.

'What's happening?' I asked.

'Hang . . . on. I'm scanning IP addresses in the range of their website to see what cameras it brings up.'

'Of course you are,' Jas said drily, and I felt a bubble of excitement rise in my chest. There was no feeling I'd come across yet that compared to banding together with these girls in Half Light's name. We'd defended them against internet trolls, and bitchy journalists who just didn't get it, and now we were going into battle for them again, arming ourselves with the information we'd need to protect them, just like we always had.

I let myself feel it for just a second before I realized something like doubt was tugging at my stomach. 'Guys. I don't want to see him fall.'

Gemma stopped typing and looked straight at the camera.

'Harri, of *course*. No matter what happens, no matter what these cameras show, we'll stop it before then, OK? I promise. We won't go any further than we need to.'

Jas reached out to touch my arm, and I gave her a weak smile.

'All right,' I said. 'Cool.'

I saw Gemma's expression change, a flash of triumph across her face.

'What?' I asked quickly, and she spun the phone to face her laptop screen.

'We're in.'

'What am I looking at?' I asked.

'Albany Road,' Gem said. 'Live.'

The screen was full of squares, each representing a room or corridor, most of which were black. I recognized what I was seeing as a low-quality camera feed, but I couldn't make out the detail. Gemma clicked around, going in and out of each individual square to find whatever it was she was looking for.

'Bad news is that a lot of these cameras aren't switched on, or don't work. Looks like they haven't for ages. You'd think Pure would be more security-conscious given how anal they are about literally everything else, but we can thank them for this lapse because at least we don't have to trawl through a million hours of nothingness. I've got one of the entrances, which I suppose is good, but it won't help us clear him. We already know he was there – we're not trying to disprove that. Anyway. It doesn't look like the roof was covered by cameras, but fingers crossed we'll get something. And, hey, if not, maybe we get to watch Frankie mooch round a studio on his own for a little while. A reward for our efforts.'

Gemma clicked again, and an empty studio filled the screen.

'So can we rewind and watch the footage from Friday?' Jas asked.

'I'm not a hundred per cent sure ... Each of these cameras has a whole list of files, so I guess we just start somewhere and try to work out what these filenames mean?'

She wiggled the mouse, and a time marker appeared at the bottom of the shot. Gemma dragged her cursor to the left, and the screen sped up, nondescript people coming and going, walking and running backwards out of shot, ticking ever closer to the day we knew Frankie had been there.

'There!' Jas shouted, as a figure in a beanie walked into the shot. I would have recognized his stance anywhere.

'He's alone,' I breathed, not realizing until I said it aloud that I'd been worried he wouldn't be. Seeing him with Evan in this context – I didn't know how I would have computed that in my mind. Gemma stopped dragging the cursor, letting the scene play out in real time. The date and time bar at the bottom of the screen read 16:27, Friday 25 October.

Screen-Frankie stood in front of the mirrored walls for just a second before he started dancing, his movements jerky on the seemingly ancient camera.

'Oh, look at him,' Jas said as Gemma fumbled to zoom in. 'I haven't seen him look that free for ages.'

I knew what she meant. Even with the time lag, I could tell the way he was dancing was almost completely devoid of inhibition. I knew straight away that it was not Half Light choreography; it was more elegant and lyrical than anything I'd seen him do before. He seemed . . . peaceful.

'What do we do now?' Jas asked.

'Just enjoy this until something happens,' Gemma replied dreamily.

He stayed like that for a while, just dancing in the

mirror like a boy with no cares, but after a few minutes he looked over his shoulder, and I thought I made out a smile as he stopped dancing and moved out of shot.

'Zoom out! Zoom out!' Jas cried as Gemma scrambled to keep up with screen-Frankie.

'I think someone just came in,' she said as she zoomed out once and then again, still not quite getting the whole room in shot.

'Evan, surely?' I said. 'Switch cameras, Gem! Is there one facing the other way?'

As I spoke, Frankie backed into the shot, still smiling, gesturing at whoever had joined him to follow. I braced myself to see Evan's stocky frame trailing after him.

'Wait, what?'

Gemma paused the camera, and Jas somehow crowded even closer to the screen.

'Don't pause it!' I said, and Gem pressed play.

I wanted to be sure of what I was seeing before I said it out loud, but Jas beat me to it, her tone somewhere between confused and horrified when she said, 'Guys. Is that Phoebe Shaw?'

TRACK SEVENTEEN

We rewatched the same five-second segment of tape over and over, as if repeating it might change something, but obviously it didn't. Every time, Frankie stopped dancing to smile at the figure in the doorway and, every time, that figure stepped further into the studio and revealed herself as Phoebe. They seemed to chat for a while, Phoebe with her back to the camera and Frankie looking almost directly at it, then Phoebe put her bags down at the edge of the shot, and Frankie resumed his place in front of the mirror.

'Shall I carry on?' Gemma asked after the fifth time we'd watched the sequence, and didn't wait for us to answer before she pressed play.

'What are we actually watching here?' Jas asked. 'Are we really meant to believe Frankie and Phoebe have plotted to throw Evan off the roof, but they're stopping for a little dance first? What's she doing here anyway?'

'She's not a dancer, is she?' Gemma asked.

'No, I think he's teaching her.' I imagined what it must

be like to have Frankie as your teacher; to have all his attention focused so intently on you.

They danced to the silent music for what felt like forever, but the time bar at the bottom of the screen told me had only been twenty minutes. We were quiet as we watched them, hyperalert for anything that could be considered a clue – anything that could prove Frankie had nothing to do with what happened to Evan because he was here, three floors below, dancing.

Somewhere around the thirty-minute mark, Phoebe picked up her things, hugged Frankie and disappeared quickly out of shot the way she'd come in.

'Where's she going?' My voice was more urgent than I intended. 'Gem, can we tell what time this was? I can't make it out.'

Gemma spun the phone screen so her face was in focus again, and my stomach dropped at the thought of no longer having eyes on them both. As long as they were there, faces reflected back at us in a mirrored wall, they were safe. As long as they didn't leave that room, they were both innocent.

As long as Phoebe was with Frankie, he had an alibi.

'Five twelve p.m. according to the time bar. The call to the police was made at five thirty-seven, right? So that's twenty-five minutes where she can do whatever she's doing – grabbing a quick coffee maybe? – and get back in this room, with Frankie, before anything happens to Evan.'

A niggling voice in my head was saying, *If she was just grabbing a quick coffee, she wouldn't have taken all her bags with her. If she was Frankie's alibi, she'd have told the police.*

'She'll be back in a second, right?' I said hopefully at the same time Jas was saying, 'Switch cameras. See how far we can follow her.'

Gemma clicked back out of the close-up, and began to drag the cursor along the time bar at the bottom of the screen. Once again the screen was filled with grainy squares, some of them in total darkness, but others showing movement. Frankie was in one corner, still dancing; Phoebe was a corridor away in a square two rows below, on her way out of the building the same way we had watched Frankie come in.

Gemma let the cameras keep playing. 'I want to see if she left the building or just the room,' she said. 'If she came out of that studio, walked outside and got in her car, then she's not involved. Evan isn't even there yet, as far as we've seen.'

I had to admit it was a wise idea. I probably would have chosen to watch every frame of Frankie doing whatever he was doing inside, but we had to see what Phoebe did next.

Gemma scrolled forward so fast that I almost missed it when a man walked into the frame, appearing in another square entirely, an exterior view of the building right at the edge of the monitor, as if he'd walked straight off the street on to Gemma's screen. Jas gave a sharp gasp, eyes trained on the camera as if she'd be tested on it later.

'Who's that?' My question was met with silence. It was as if nobody wanted to be the one to say it.

'You know who that is,' Jas conceded eventually – and, yeah, I did. He'd appeared by Frankie's side enough times that I'd recognize Evan Byrd anywhere.

'Crap.' Gemma's voice sounded like a hiss, and I knew how she felt. When it had just been Frankie alone, this had seemed more like a treat than a trial. Even when Phoebe showed up, it had been easy enough to ignore the reason we were doing it in the first place. But now Evan had entered the picture, literally, it all came rushing back in clear focus: the man we were about to watch walk into this building would never walk out again.

Except . . . he wasn't walking in.

I let my eyes widen as Evan carried on straight past the studio doors and continued round the side of the building.

'What's round there?' I asked. I didn't expect Jas or Gemma to know any better than I did, but I needed to ask anyway. It turned out, though, that Gemma had pre-empted my question. Never one to take on a role by halves, she paused the feed for a second as she clicked into another tab in her browser, switching to what looked like a floor plan.

'How did you get that?' Jas asked.

'Wasn't even hard. They have a whole page on their website about hiring the studios. It's just one of the attachments.'

Gemma zoomed in. I saw Studio 3, where Frankie had been, and the corridor we had just watched Phoebe walk down.

'Well? What's it showing us?'

'There are stairs on the outside of the building round that corner, where Evan just went.'

'So?' I asked.

'Stairs to the roof,' Gemma said.

191

Oh.

She kept the screen paused for a while, none of us quite sure what to say. I'd been clear that I hadn't wanted to watch him fall, but seeing Evan go round the corner, knowing that he was about to take those stairs, was not much easier.

'Look, we know how it ends for him,' Jas said eventually. 'I know it sounds really harsh, but we can't change that. What we can change is whether or not Frankie goes down for it. So. Shall we carry on?'

'Yeah,' Gemma said as she pressed play, and the way that nothing happened for a while after Evan had left the shot made it feel like even the cameras were hesitating over discovering what came next.

A creak from the bedroom door pulled my attention away from the screen, and I turned to see Stefan peeking round the frame.

Hi, I thought, cheeks warming, and then immediately changed my mind. A part of me wanted nothing more than to feel Stef's arm round my shoulders as I introduced him to Jas; to spend an afternoon watching them learn the bits of each other that I liked the most. *No.* I shook it off. We didn't have time. We had to focus, and I couldn't do that with him around. *That's new.*

I tried to smile in a way that conveyed *I have no regrets about what happened last night, but I really need you to leave.* Unsurprisingly, he didn't take the hint.

'What you up to?' he asked from the doorway, and Jas turned round and shot him a look of intrigue mixed with irritation.

'Currently? Hacking the security cameras at a rehearsal studio to try to get a pop star cleared of murder. Do you want to help?'

I couldn't help laughing at Jas's comeback. 'I don't think that'll scare him,' I said, and Stefan held his hands up in surrender.

'Don't be so sure. I'll leave you to it. Hello, I'm Stefan, by the way.'

'I guessed that,' Jas said. 'I'm Jas.'

'Um, guys?' Gemma's tinny voice through my laptop speakers pulled me back to the task at hand.

'We'll see you later, OK?' I asked, and Stefan nodded, taking his cue to leave.

'He's cute,' Jas said, loud enough that Stef could hear, which I knew was her intention. I felt my cheeks flush even hotter.

'Yeah. He's all right.'

Gemma cleared her throat. 'If you've quite finished, I've had this feed on pause for at least twenty seconds so we can all see at the same time where Phoebe went when she left that studio.'

Gemma pressed play as Phoebe walked through the studio doors, making no effort to hide her face, or check her surroundings, or anything else commonly associated with a guilty party. She walked quickly to the road.

I expected her to cross out of shot and return to her own life – yet I was also hoping she'd turn round and walk back inside the building.

She did neither of those things. Instead, she took a right,

disappearing round the same corner of the building where Evan had stepped out of sight just minutes before.

'No. Way.' My voice was thick with shock. 'There's a camera round there, right?'

Somehow I knew even as I asked that there wasn't. Gemma shook her head, confirming my fears, and I realized that, as much as I didn't want Frankie to be guilty, I didn't want Phoebe to be, either. *It's still only five sixteen*, I told myself, glancing at the time bar on the screen. *She still has time to come back.*

'I don't get it. Why have they arrested Frankie when he hasn't left that little studio? Why not Phoebe when we've as good as watched her walk up there? The police must have seen this, right?' asked Jas.

She was right, I realized. We'd just watched Evan essentially walk to his death, and Phoebe follow straight after. With every second that passed, I felt surer and surer that I didn't want Phoebe Shaw to be responsible for his death – but it wasn't looking good for her, based on this footage. I knew, though, that we must still be missing something. The police would just have arrested Phoebe if this evidence was as damning as it seemed. Something was off.

'Zoom back in on Frankie,' I said, and Jas looked at me quizzically.

'Why?'

'If the CCTV has him dancing in front of that bloody mirror until after the time of Evan's death, that does it, yeah? He's clear.'

'She's right,' Gemma said, clicking back into the original camera feed. My whole body relaxed when I saw Frankie still standing there. As long as he didn't move in the next twenty-one minutes, we were fine. It reminded me of something my mum used to say when we were kids: *As long as I have my eyes on you, you'll be fine.* I was always too scared to test the theory, so I stayed close, and true to her word she never let me come to any harm. I only hoped we could do the same for Frankie now.

He stayed put for a little while, every now and then performing a step or two for his invisible audience, the style slightly changed now that Phoebe had left the room. His movements were bolder than before, closer to the kind of thing we were used to seeing him do: the alpha male working his crowd, every move considered, the performer skilful enough that it really felt like he was doing it all off the cuff; that it was all inspired specifically by the people who just happened to be watching. 'Everything we do is for the fans,' they'd often say, and to watch Frankie in action was to believe it. He knew how to work a crowd even when there wasn't one there.

Eventually, his bursts of movement slowed, and he headed towards the door, bags left where they lay. We all froze. The timestamp in the corner told us that it was 17:32. Five minutes still remained before the police were called. That was plenty of time for Frankie to find him. Plenty of time to make it from the studio to the roof.

'Where is he going?' Gemma's accent sounded harsh against the tense silence we'd fallen into.

Screen-Frankie left the room, and the shot of the empty studio felt ominous.

'Are we going to follow him?' Jas asked, and Gemma, one step ahead as she had been the whole time, was already zooming back out to the full screen. She pulled the cursor along the bottom, speeding through the footage, but Frankie did not materialize in any of the boxes, even as the time bar drew closer and closer to 17:37. It was like he'd completely vanished, disappearing into the darkness somewhere between the studio and the street. I didn't know if that was a good sign.

'Is this a good sign?' Jas asked.

Gemma shrugged her shoulders. 'No idea. He's obviously somewhere the CCTV's turned off. Let's keep eyes on the studio. He might just walk back in like nothing happened.'

'I wish we knew where Phoebe had gone,' I said, my mind returning to her. 'The police must know something about her that we don't, right? They must have seen this footage, too, but they clearly don't suspect her for some reason.'

I pulled up Phoebe's Instagram on my phone, and looked at her latest photo. This one, unlike most of her recent offerings, didn't feature Frankie, instead showing her leaning against a fence on the edge of what looked like a huge field, a horse visible over her left shoulder. The caption, though, was very much in the style we were growing used to from her.

Hey, everyone – I just wanted to check in to say that since taking some time away I'm feeling much better, and know that people are just reacting in the way they know how. When something like this happens, we learn a lot about ourselves, and what I'm learning is that I owe it to Frankie to be here, and to make sure I'm supporting him and all of you in the best way I can. Some people close to me have warned me against coming back online so soon, and I know they're only looking out for me, but I also know that I have to do this. Staying away would only make it worse. As ever, I hope you're all looking out for each other, and being kind to yourselves, and I'm here if there's anything I can say that might help xx

'God, she's really going for the earth-sister, best-friend, innocent thing, isn't she?' Jas said, looking over my shoulder. 'And everyone's falling for it. *We* fell for it.'

'Well, it might be true,' I said, and Jas rolled her eyes.

'Harri, even if she didn't push Evan, she was at the studio that day. She's not telling any of her followers that, though, is she? She's basically lying by omission. You just don't want to believe any of them are capable of actions outside what you'd imagined for them, do you?'

I didn't think she was gunning for another fight, but I didn't want to risk it.

'You're right,' I said. 'It's a bit much.'

She was easily placated. Jas liked being right.

'Oh crap.'

I had almost forgotten we were still connected with Gemma until she spoke, and my eyes flew straight to the screen, where the rehearsal studio was still empty.

'What? Have you found him?' I asked.

'No, but I have to go. My parents just came home, and they get weird when I do things that are legally questionable. I'll pick this up later, I promise. Keep me updated if you find anything, too.'

She was already clicking out of the browser window, and it felt weirdly like a loss. We had been just a couple of minutes from the time of the police call. Knowing that Frankie could have walked back into shot at any moment had been keeping me calm. Suddenly I felt completely adrift again.

'We will,' Jas said, and Gemma gave a little four-fingered wave and disconnected the call.

I picked up my phone where I'd placed it on my dresser, as if it might help me think of our next step. Phoebe's photo was still open on the screen, and an idea began to form, slowly and then with certainty. It was stupid. It would draw far too much attention to what we were doing, surely wouldn't give us any answers, and was definitely a terrible plan.

'You're thinking too hard,' Jas said, peering at me. 'It scares me when you do that.'

'We want to know what Phoebe was doing there, and where she went when she walked out of that shot.'

Jas just looked at me expectantly.

I waggled the phone in her face. 'Then let's ask her.'

TRACK EIGHTEEN

'No.'

The immediacy of Jas's answer, and her complete conviction, surprised me. We both just wanted Frankie to be free, didn't we? Weren't we both absolutely ready to do whatever it took? It appeared not.

'Why not?' I asked.

'We can't just *ask her if she killed him*, Harri. What's she going to say? "Oh yeah, caught me!"'

'Wasn't gonna phrase it quite like that, but cool, thanks for the input.'

'All right, what were you going to say?'

'I was going to say we know she was there, we know she wants to help Frankie – was there anything she saw that might do that?'

Jas's face softened in apology. 'Do it.'

'Really?'

'Yeah. Do it. She said she's here for anything that might make us feel better. If she can somehow convince us

199

Frankie left that studio and went *anywhere* but up on to the roof, I'll feel better.'

'Her too,' I said. 'I really want to believe she didn't follow Evan up there.'

'I know. You're right. Do it.'

I began to type quickly. I didn't want to overthink the message or I knew I'd never press send. *She probably won't reply*, I thought. *She probably won't even see it. I bet she's absolutely inundated with people private-messaging her because they think it'll get them closer to the boys. This is probably just going to get lost in the pile, but at least we'll know we tried.*

'There's nothing on your profile that'll tell her where we are, is there?' Jas asked, and I raised an eyebrow quizzically. 'I'm just saying, if she *is* involved, I'd rather she didn't know where I currently am, thanks.'

'No. There's nothing on my profile that'll tell her where we are.'

'What are you saying to her?'

I finished typing, and turned the phone screen so that she could see for herself.

Hi Phoebe,

You don't know us, but we think you might be able to help us, and Frankie, with something. You see, we know you were at the rehearsal studio the day Evan died. We're not going to tell anyone, because I think you know that doesn't look good for you, but we want to know why.

What were you doing there? And why haven't you told
anyone? What happened, Phoebe? You can tell us.

Jas laughed as she read it.

'It wasn't meant to be funny.'

She reached out and lightly touched my forearm. 'God,
I know. I'm sorry. It's a great message. Let's do it. What
have we got to lose?'

Quite a lot, I thought as I pressed send. 'She won't reply –'

'Harri, she's typing,' Jas cut me off, and I half threw the
phone at her in shock.

'What's she saying?' I scrunched my eyes shut as I heard
the notification come through. *Had this been a really
stupid idea?*

'*I'm not having this conversation with you*,' Jas read
out loud, and I kept my eyes closed, waiting for another
sentence that didn't come.

'Wait, that's the whole message?'

'Yup.'

I opened my eyes so I could see for myself. Seven words
that told us nothing at all. Grabbing my phone back, I
began to type furiously.

'Harri, what are you doing?' Her eyes were wide, and I
let out a laugh.

'Do I look that unhinged?'

'Yes!'

We saw you on the CCTV. You went in, danced with
Frankie for a few minutes, then disappeared. We saw you

201

walk back out, and go round the corner where the stairs
to the roof are literally minutes after Evan did. You don't
get to tell us you're not having this conversation.

I pressed send before Jas could stop me.

She put her head in her hands and groaned. 'Well,
you've done it now. No going back.'

Only as she spoke did I realize what was happening.
Suddenly my face was hot. I had to remind myself to breathe.

'Oh my God. Jas, what have I done?'

I sank on to the edge of the bed, and she looked at me,
concern all over her face.

'Are you all right?'

'*No*. I've basically just accused her of killing him! Why
do I keep doing this?'

'Well, do you think she did?'

'I don't know! Probably! Not! I mean probably not! The
police don't seem to think so, right? Oh God, Jas!'

I felt the mattress dip as she sat down beside me, and
took my hand in hers.

'Harri, don't panic. Let's just see –'

She was cut off by my phone, one message and then
another two immediately after.

'I don't want to read it,' I said, my words wobbly in the
air between us, and Jas sighed and took the phone out of
my hands.

'Then I'll do it.'

She let out a long breath, and began to read aloud.

'I don't know if you'll believe me, and I don't want to say what you think you saw isn't what you saw, because it is.'

'Good job I had plenty of sleep last night or that would have really messed with my brain,' I said wryly, and Jas grinned.

'That's more like it.'

'So you know I was at the studio with Frankie. But the police know that, too, and they cleared me on Friday. I got into a taxi and, as we drove away, the driver recognized me, said his teenage daughter was a fan and would I take a selfie with him? I snapped it on his phone, and that's how I was able to prove to the police that I'd left the studio by the time Evan fell. They found the driver, checked the time the selfie was taken.

'As for why I was there, it was because he was helping me learn some choreography. Not that I owe you any kind of explanation, but that is the truth. He was teaching me a dance for an audition, and I didn't tell anyone because this industry is not kind to women, especially women who refuse to stay in their box. I really want this part, and I don't want to be the girl who got it just because she's got Instagram followers. I wanted to get it because I was good enough, and he was helping me get good enough. Does that answer your question?'

'No,' I said.

'Hang on, H. There's one more.'

'And following Evan? I have no idea what you're talking about. Evan wasn't even there by the time I left. I walked *out of that building, got into the taxi and went home. I can prove that. Sorry if this doesn't fit into whatever narrative you've come up with, but this is my life. You're messing with real people. Remember that. I can't just let this go.'*

'Do you believe her?' Jas asked, but my mind had latched on to something else entirely.

'What does she mean she can't let it go? Is she going to tell the police?'

I felt nauseous, and reached over to throw the window open a little wider.

Please don't tell the police. I watched as Jas typed, as if that was going to help if Phoebe had already decided we'd gone too far. Her reply was almost instantaneous.

I'm not going to waste the police's time. Don't be so stupid. Look, I agree with you that he's being set up, but, trust me, it isn't by me.

'What did she mean then?' I half wailed, and Jas turned off the phone screen, stood and pulled me up.

'Harri, I don't know. We have exactly the same information. Now come on.'

'Where are we going?'

'To eat something. I can't think when I'm hungry, and playing detective makes me *very hungry.*'

Worrying about Phoebe could wait. Jas had a point. I was ravenous.

TRACK NINETEEN

I was in the kitchen, refilling our teacups, when I heard Jas scream.

I skidded as I ran back across the hall to my room. Jas was sitting on the edge of the bed, my phone gripped in her hand.

'What?' I asked, and she held it up without speaking.

'You got an Instagram message.'

'And you screamed about it?'

'And I screamed about it.'

I reached for my phone. She pulled it back.

'Listen, H, we've not had a whole lot to be happy about lately, have we? Well, maybe you did last night, but apart from that. Anyway. Let me just have this moment, OK? Let me see your excited little face when I tell you it's from Jack.'

My face froze momentarily, like it was taking my brain a little longer than usual to process what it was hearing, and then I broke into a smile so wide it almost hurt. I crossed to the bed in a second and sat down beside her.

The notification was still on the screen when she handed over the phone. It wasn't that I hadn't believed her, or thought for even a second that she was joking, but I hadn't prepared myself for how seeing it would feel. It was as if we'd crossed over into a world we'd spent so long on the fringes of. Like we'd always suspected the boys were real, but this proved it. I snapped a screenshot and Jas laughed.

'Do you think I haven't already done that?'

Of course she had.

'Well, read it, then!' she urged, and I swiped into the message quickly.

> Hey Harri. A friend – Phoebe Shaw – pointed me in your direction, and we both think it's gone too far for us not to be in touch. Nobody is telling me anything and I want to help. Whatever else, I don't think he did it. Of course he didn't do it. Neither did Phoebe. Can we meet?

The phone slipped out of my hand without fanfare. I expected Jas to reach for it immediately, but she left it where it lay at my feet.

'Crap,' she said, and I laughed.

'What? You think he's angry?'

'Well, Phoebe doesn't exactly love us, does she? But no, I meant more like . . .'

'Yeah. Crap,' I filled in.

She picked up the phone then, and handed it back to me. *You're supposed to be ecstatic*, I told myself. *Why does this feel so weird?*

'Because we never imagined it would be like this?' Jas offered.

'Did I say that out loud?'

'No, but I know you. I get it.'

She was right. That was exactly it. We had dreamed of this for so long, and none of the dreams had ever looked like this. Still, I couldn't entirely damp down the feeling of excitement as I typed out a reply altogether more cool than I felt.

Hi Jack. Thanks for getting in touch, and we're so sorry about what happened with Phoebe. Yeah, we should meet. Tell us when you're free. Love Harri & Jas x

'What shall we do while we wait?' I asked, desperate for a distraction, and when the phone chimed in my hand I was surprised all over again to see Jack's name pop up.

'Bloody hell, that was quick,' Jas said. 'Read it out!'

'*Constantly free right now. All band stuff's on pause, as you can imagine. Probably best for me to come to you? Keep it inconspicuous? Can you text me your address?*'

'Can we really ask him to drive all the way to Brighton?' I asked, worrying my lip between my teeth.

'We're not asking him to do anything – he asked us. And anyway, like he said, he's not doing anything else. Send the address.'

I typed it in quickly.

He said he'd be with us in a few hours. There were so many things to consider before then – what would we say? What would *he* say? Would he be angry we'd planted ourselves uninvited in the middle of his huge personal crisis? Or might he be grateful? Might he understand what we were actually trying to do? I couldn't think of any of those things quite yet, though. There was a much more pressing matter at hand. *Jack*, whose face had been on my walls through so many of my most formative moments, was coming to my tiny bedroom. He was going to be *here*.

'What the hell am I going to wear?'

The sky was getting dark when my phone chimed again where it was still tangled in the duvet on my unmade bed. My face was inches from the mirror, make-up almost finished, and the noise made me jump, the mascara brush in my hand colliding with the corner of my eye and smudging at least ten minutes' worth of work. My shaking hands weren't helping to speed things along.

'Crap. He can't be here yet, surely?'

Jas was lying in the middle of the floor, having seemingly finished her own make-up in fifteen seconds flat. Her electric-blue eyeliner glinted as she opened her eyes and reached for the phone.

'You look great, by the way,' I said.

'Thanks. No, it's not him. It's a Tumblr message.'

'Anything interesting?'

I wasn't exactly hopeful. Since Jas's post, hordes of fans had been in touch, some to thank us for what we were doing, some to let us know they'd been to Jack and Frankie's house and seen nothing suspicious at all, and, yeah, a few telling us to back off, to leave the boys alone, to let the police do their job. We were choosing to ignore those ones.

'Not really. Just another girl who went to the house and says the only people in or out that whole time were the boys and Georgia.'

'Lucky Georgia. But what are we missing here?' I asked as I fixed the black smudge spreading further over the side of my face the more I tried to wipe it away. 'Unless Jack took that shirt off somewhere other than his own home, whoever is setting up Frankie must have taken it from there.'

'Whoever it was must have gone in when no fans were watching. I know they're a bit much, but I think they probably do sleep occasionally, H. Anyway, we can ask him, can't we?'

'What the hell are we going to say to him?'

'To Jack?'

'Well, obviously not Frankie,' I snapped, regretting it immediately. I was suddenly nervous again, my stomach in knots. I let out a shaky, staggered breath, which seemed to fully pique Jas's interest.

'You're not having an anxiety attack, are you?'

'No, I'm anxious about a thing I actually have every reason to be anxious about. That's normal. I should probably be celebrating.'

'Oh. Well, good. Congratulations. And what we're going to say to him is that we're sorry this is happening, and that we love him, and that we're trying in the best way we know how to help.'

'You always know exactly what to say, don't you?'

'Yes,' she said, pulling herself upright and holding out my phone. 'Now reply to this girl and say thanks.' She looked more closely at my face and grinned. 'Actually, *I* will. Fix your make-up.'

(▶)

How We Met – Jack

We met in a broken-down lift, of all the ridiculous places. I had my eyes down, focused on my phone, so I didn't even notice at first when we slowed, and jolted, and eventually came to a stop. I only realized what was happening when I heard you mutter, 'Crap.' I looked up, ready with a reassuring smile for a nervous stranger, but it wasn't a stranger who looked back, shy beneath the brim of a baseball cap. It was you.

I had always thought I'd be able to tell if we were on the same street, let alone locked together in a non-moving cage with only two other people. I thought I'd be able to feel your energy. I don't know why. I've never felt anybody's energy before.

I think you knew I'd recognized you by the way my cheeks immediately turned red. You smiled. You must have been used to it. I knew I had to say something. It wasn't like either of us could get away and, even if we could, I never would have forgiven myself for passing up an opportunity like this.

The man in the suit and the woman with the headphones hadn't even turned round, didn't even flinch as I stepped closer to you, but I whispered anyway. For some reason, I didn't want them to hear.

'Hi,' I said.

'Hello.'

'I'm Harri.'

'I'm Jack. And I'm . . . sort of freaking out right now. I'm so sorry.'

Something in me sprang into action. You were freaking out. I was always freaking out. I knew exactly how to handle this. I stepped closer still.

'I get it. I know my way through this. Freaking out how?'

You gulped and closed your eyes. 'Just like . . . hot. Head is swimming. Just . . . not good.'

'Do you need me to stop talking?'

Your eyes flew open at that. 'No, I need you to keep talking. Please. Tell me about you, Harri.'

So I did, but in doing so I really told you about you. I told you about uni, and my essay on queer female identity in fandom, because I thought you'd like that one. I told you about Jas, and Alex, and my friends all over the world; how I felt like I'd seen cities I might never set foot in, because of the places Half Light had taken me, even if just through pixels on a screen. And I told you about anxiety.

'You're actually one of the things that grounds me when I'm feeling bad.'

You looked up, reached out and stroked my wrist. 'Well, now you've done it for me. So thank you.'

It can't have been more than five minutes before the lift started moving again. The man in the suit hadn't looked over once. The woman hadn't taken out her headphones. It was just us. I knew straight away I would never tell the internet. Not everything is for an audience. You taught me that, too.

We met at a wedding, the groom a distant family member of my dad. I went reluctantly. Spending an afternoon making small talk with strangers was far from my idea of fun, and it was too hot to get all dressed up and put on a full face of make-up. I was coerced with the promise of a free bar and a night in a fancy-ish hotel, but I did not have high hopes. I'd never even met the bride. Perhaps that would explain why nobody thought to tell me that Jack from Half Light, he who had adorned my walls for years with no signs of stopping, was her cousin.

I saw you at the bar, surrounded by men I guessed you knew well, but didn't see often, if the back-slapping, and hollering, and one-armed hugs were anything to go by. I hovered for a moment, but then decided it was not the time. I'd catch you alone, after a few more glasses of champagne. That would be altogether less terrifying than the prospect of walking over at that moment.

You barely had a second to breathe all night. There were reunions with red-cheeked aunties, and selfies with friends of the bride, which you took in surprisingly good spirits. There was dancing with your mother, and a rowdy attempt to get you to join the band, which you wriggled out of with

212

the expertise of someone who has had to do it a million times before, much to the relief of the actual singer.

The night was winding down by the time I saw you sloping off towards the huge French windows alone, and I had sipped enough liquid courage to follow you. You must have heard my heels on the hard wood floor, because you turned as I approached, and your eyes widened, obviously expecting someone you knew and instead being met by a perfect stranger.

'Are you OK?' you asked, and I grinned at hearing your voice in real life for the first time.

I was more than OK.

'I'm good. I'm Harri. I didn't want to bother you before, but I just had to say when I saw you on your own that Half Light . . . well, you all mean a lot to me, and I just needed to say that.'

I knew I was talking too fast. Knew I had barely stopped for breath. Knew that what I had actually said did not even begin to encompass all of the things I felt. I like to think you got it, though.

'Do you want to take a photo?' you asked, once we'd finished talking about how beautiful the bride was, and what a lovely day it had (actually unexpectedly for both of us) been.

I thought about it for a second.

'No,' I said. 'I won't forget this.'

We met in the back of a taxi, at a time I'd call the middle of the night, but for you was probably somewhere closer

213

to the beginning. I was on edge, having confidently ignored my parents' advice never to use the Pool option on those taxi apps before considering that maybe it could actually be quite dangerous for a teenager on her own.

I didn't look up as the door opened, but when you said, 'Hi, mate,' to the driver, my eyes flew to yours in a second. There was no mistaking that voice.

I must have gasped, because you looked over and smiled, and it was only as I returned your grin that I realized you were shuffling closer; that someone else was climbing into the car behind you, his fingers tangled in yours. It wasn't Frankie. For a second, I was disappointed that it was someone else you were leading hand in hand through this night, but I knew you'd get there eventually. For now, you could step into a taxi, with a complete stranger already inside, holding hands with a man you seemed fond of, without worrying who was watching at all. It felt like a victory.

'Hello,' you said as you settled into the middle seat and plugged in your seat belt, your arm brushing against mine.

'Hi.'

'Hi,' your friend said, and I think I smiled in what was supposed to be a greeting, but I didn't look away from you for a moment.

'I'm Harri,' I said, and you laughed, although not unkindly.

'Hi, Harri. I'm Jack, and this is Paul. Sorry, I've just never had someone introduce themselves in one of these things before.'

I didn't know what to say next, the London streets blurring on the other side of the window as we sped along them, so I said nothing at all. I tried not to stare as you carried on a whispered conversation with your date, tried instead to look out of the window at all these places I would now associate with you forever.

'Don't tell anyone where he went,' Paul said as we pulled up at your destination, and I don't think he meant it to sound as menacing as it did, but I appreciated the way you reached out, touched my arm.

'He's joking.'

He didn't have to worry. I had no idea where we were. All I could see for miles was you.

We met when you arrived at my bedroom door, stubble rash and red eyes and a sad-looking smile. Your boyfriend, if that was still what we were calling him, was in prison. We were going to help you get him out.

TRACK TWENTY

It sounds ridiculous, but it felt like he arrived on the wind. The windows were clattering in their frames, and I didn't have to leave the flat to know it was freezing outside. The buzz of the entry system sounded louder than it usually did, aggressive almost, as if it was announcing the beginning of a battle. *Might be apt*, I thought. We still weren't sure if he knew the truth about what had been a dream relationship for us. Or how he was going to feel about our involvement in all this.

'Hello?' I said into the speaker, desperately trying to remind myself that *he* was coming into *my* space; that I should be comfortable here.

Well, I thought as my voice shook, *that pep talk definitely didn't work*.

'It's me,' he said. 'Um . . . Jack? Law?'

It was a struggle not to laugh out loud. As if I wouldn't get it from just *Jack*. As if I wouldn't know his voice anywhere.

'Come up.'

I felt Jas rise from the bed behind me, and turned to see her smoothing down the duvet before she joined me at the door. It seemed to take him an eternity to make it to my corridor. Enough time to wonder if we'd crossed the line to in-too-deep. If we were putting him in danger by involving him in whatever this was. If we were going to tell him the truth, supposing nobody else had.

He looked like hell as he rounded the corner, skinny jeans slightly too baggy, the oversized black hoodie he was wearing one I recognized as Frankie's. He smiled when he saw us standing in the open doorway. I felt very young suddenly. Jack was only a few years older than us, but he seemed like a proper grown-up compared to Jas and me. *Occupational hazard*, I thought. *I guess you have to grow up fast if you're whipped away from everything you know to become an international pop sensation.*

'I'm Jack,' he said as he approached, again completely pointlessly.

'We know,' Jas said as she held out her hand. 'I'm Jas, this is Harri.'

He looked down at her hand as if it was going to burn him, and pulled first Jas and then me into a hug that verged just on the wrong side of painful.

How are we going to find out if he knows? I tried to ask Jas just by widening my eyes over Jack's shoulder, and it must have worked because I watched her decide to do it, steel herself and speak.

'Jack, how much do you know? About . . . what was going on with Frankie? And specifically . . . you.'

No ceremony, no time for politeness, no question of if it was sensitive, or harmful, or our place to speak. We were here to help Frankie. Jas was just speeding that along.

Jack gulped and released me from his grip.

'Shall we go inside?' he asked. And then: 'I know it wasn't real, if that's what you're asking. But shouldn't I be asking how *you* know that?'

The silence should have been more awkward than it was as Jas arranged herself on my bed and I sank to the carpet beside Jack, pulling a pillow with me to rest my back.

'Sorry, I don't have any chairs,' I said, and apparently in Jack's eyes that made me a comedian, if the way he laughed was anything to go by. 'What's so funny?' I tried and failed to sound offended, which I wasn't in the slightest.

'Like you not having *chairs* even registers on the list of things I'm worried about right now. My boyfriend, who it turns out wasn't *actually* my boyfriend – but don't worry about telling *me* that, I'll find out in my own time, thanks, Frank – is in prison. The band, which was the only thing I cared about even close to how much I cared about him, is probably destroyed beyond recognition – sorry, that's probably hard for you to hear and I shouldn't have said it, but it's true – and I'm holed up in student halls with two strangers, who I've only been put in touch with because they accused one of Frankie's friends of murder, no less, trying to work out how we're going to untangle all this, and how on earth they seem to find out my secrets before I do.'

218

He wiped his eyes, still laughing. 'It's fine that you don't have *chairs*, Harri.'

I didn't know what to say to any of that. He had a point.

'We're really sorry,' I said. 'About . . . Phoebe.'

Jack nodded. 'Well, you're lucky she's a sensible person and came to me rather than anyone else. *God*. Why did you think it was *Phoebe*?'

'The CCTV,' I explained. 'She walked round the corner and disappeared. That's where the stairs to the roof are. We just –'

'Took a giant leap in the wrong direction,' Jack said. 'Did you really think the police hadn't watched the CCTV? Hadn't made her prove that she left when she said she did? She told you about the taxi driver, right?'

We nodded, a little sheepishly.

'How did *you* get the CCTV anyway?'

'Our friend Gemma hacked it,' I said, and Jack raised an eyebrow, then laughed.

'Of course. You know, though, there's nothing of any use on those cameras. Most of them don't even work! It's one of the reasons we used that studio . . . no secrets can get out if there's no evidence of the secrets. That's ironic.'

'How did you find out?' Jas asked, changing the subject. 'About Frankie, I mean. And . . . um . . . you.'

'Molly told me.'

'That must have been awful for her,' I said, remembering how upset she'd been at my interview. 'For both of you obviously.'

He sniffed and nodded. 'Yeah. It was.'

'Did you suspect?' I couldn't help but ask.

Jack shook his head, and slid his body down further until he was almost horizontal, his head tipped back to rest against my bed.

Still weird.

'God, no. I thought we were absolutely solid. Never crossed my mind for even a second. It felt like a proper relationship, you know? Everything was completely normal, except better than normal because it was *Frankie finally*. He's not *straight*. That part wasn't a surprise. I wasn't the first. Doubt I'll be the last now. I've known for a while he was open to the idea of men, just . . . never me. Until suddenly it was me, and I was so *happy* I didn't stop to question what had changed. Why, suddenly, I was good enough.' He glanced up at us quickly. 'Please don't tweet any of that.'

'As if we *would*.' Jas's voice was tinged with genuine offence, but to be fair to Jack he didn't actually know us. We could be those girls. God knows there were enough of them out there who *would* take that information and run with it.

'What happened?' I asked. 'When she told you, I mean. Is that OK to ask?'

Jack shrugged his shoulders.

'Yeah. What have I got left to lose at this point? It was yesterday afternoon. I'd been pretty hysterical up till then, I guess – crying a lot. I think Molly was worried the press would see me, although I'm not sure why that would have been such a terrible thing. It's normal to cry when your boyfriend is arrested for something you're sure he didn't do, isn't it? I just couldn't work out why they'd ever think it – nobody who'd ever seen those two together would believe for a second that he did it. Just because he was in the same building? A building he had every right to be in? It wasn't adding up.

'I became *obsessed* with the thought of working out what was wrong. And, when the police said Frank's shirt was evidence, I wasn't as quick as I should have been, but I realized, *No way – I wore that, you know, afterwards.* So I called Molly and said I was going to go to the police and tell them that he was being set up, but she told me not to. She said that there was more going on. That Evan knew something, that he was going to spill. And that Frankie really wanted to keep him quiet.'

'And then she told you what Evan knew,' Jas interjected.

'And then she told me what Evan knew. And suddenly going to the police was second on the agenda to crying a lot – again – and wondering how the hell I fell for it.'

I reached out and gently touched his hand. 'I'm so sorry, Jack. We wanted it to be true just as much as you did.'

He laughed. 'Almost as much, but, trust me, not quite. But that brings me back to my first question. How the hell did *you* find out? No offence, but who told *you*?'

'Frankie,' I said. 'Well. Sort of.'

TRACK TWENTY-ONE

He was silent as we played through the recording, which was only slightly less difficult to listen to the second time around. I pretended not to notice the way he winced when he heard Frankie's voice admit what Jack had only heard paraphrased by Molly.

'So a girl you'd never met happened to be in the same bar as them, recorded this and sent it over just because you asked?' he said as the audio stopped.

'Kind of,' I said. 'There was a little bit of getting her to trust me, but essentially we all want the same thing, don't we? She wanted to help.'

'But you'd never met her? You don't know her . . .'

'Still haven't met her actually. And no, we don't really know her at all. But that's how fandoms work, isn't it? When they're at their best? We don't really need to know each other, because we all know you. There's already one thing – that most important thing – we definitely have in common. How bad can a person be if they love the same things you do?'

I was impressed at how well I could articulate it with him sitting right in front of me.

'It's insane to me that we did that without knowing, or trying,' Jack said, the look on his face somewhere between proud and confused.

'Well, it might just be the thing that saves Frankie, if we can work it out, so let's stop being nostalgic and get on with it.' Jas stood up and manoeuvred my laptop out of my arms and on to her lap. I was amazed at how pragmatic she was being, but I knew that sometimes, when she was really nervous, she could get like this, all pushy and sharp. I didn't mind, though. She had a point.

'What are we missing?' Jack asked.

He was stretched out on my bed, and I marvelled at how normal this seemed until he moved, even slightly. It was as if, when he was still, I forgot that the cells and bones *sitting on my bed* belonged to Jack. Then he twitched, or stretched, or shook out some tension, and it was like his molecules were *everywhere. There you are*, I thought as he settled again. *In my bedroom, as if it's a completely normal thing; like you have no idea how many times I've imagined this.*

'Could there *really* not be a second shirt?' Jas asked for about the fourth time, and Jack and I shook our heads so perfectly in sync it was as if we'd rehearsed it.

'No, it's custom. I . . . I had it made for him actually. Long before we were anything more than friends.'

I smiled at that, and caught Jas's eye. She returned the grin. He definitely noticed.

'Yeah. He never let that slip, did he? There was a time we didn't like the rumours, hard as that is to believe now. So I'm sure there's only one shirt like that. I know there must be something we're missing here, but it's useless. I promise you, nobody came or went from that house except me and Kyle, and they've kept us so deeply in each other's pockets since it happened that I can tell you with certainty he's not the one that went back there and hid that shirt.' He smiled at us wryly. 'I don't know why I'm telling *you two* that, of all people. You probably know exactly where we've been every waking second since.'

'And people from Pure, right? Could they have seen anything you missed?' I asked.

'People from Pure what?'

'When they were coming and going from your house. Could they have noticed anything unusual?'

'No,' he said. 'No one from Pure's been there. It's just us. That's their compromise. Our homes are our own spaces. They never come inside.'

'Well, that's something, I suppose,' I said, and I hoped he didn't notice the way my voice caught mid-sentence when the thing that wasn't sitting right hit me.

I tried to calculate how long I had to leave it before I excused myself to go to the bathroom to check out the theory that was rapidly blooming in my head. My skin was prickling, my hands beginning to feel clammy where I'd curled them into loose fists. *It's probably nothing*, I told myself. *Yeah, but you should just check*, I silently replied a split second later.

I pulled myself to my feet. The movement was definitely too quick, I knew, and probably looked suspicious, but I couldn't wait.

'I'm going to the bathroom.'

The beauty and curse of university halls was that I barely had to take a step to shut myself in the half-room that was essentially a small shower, sink and a toilet. I locked the door, flipped down the toilet lid and sat. I could hear Jack and Jas talking on the other side of the door, so ran the tap as I pulled out my phone. I didn't want them to hear the silence and realize I was just sitting here.

Navigating to the Tumblr app, I flicked through the few messages from fans who backed up exactly what Jack was saying: that nobody but he and Kyle had entered or left the house Jack and Frankie shared the entire time. I was glad they still had their own places to just be human instead of Half Light; to just be with each other rather than under the scrutiny of the whole world.

But finally I landed on the message I was looking for.

Hi Jas and Harri!

I'm sure loads of people have told you this already, but I think you're gonna have to widen the search from people who came and went from Jack and Frankie's house. It was only Jack and Kyle, usually getting in cars right outside the door and not talking to anyone, and once Georgia from Pure, when none of them were there, which I'm guessing she didn't realize because she was in and out within, like, five mins. Maybe she was using the loo? I don't know. Anyway, just wanted to say I wish we could help more, and if we go back and see anything weird we'll definitely let you know. Love what you're doing! Thank you for not judging – we're all just doing what we can, right? Emily x

I turned off the tap and called through the door: 'Jas, could you grab my make-up bag off the chest of drawers and bring it here, please?'

I heard shuffling as she approached and cracked the door, grateful she was standing right in front of where Jack was lying so he couldn't see when I mouthed, *I . . . maybe . . . found something.*

She gently pushed me back, stepped into the bathroom, which was now beginning to feel genuinely claustrophobic, and closed the door.

'In your make-up bag?' she asked.

'Oh no, that was just an excuse to get you in here. I thought if he thought you were bringing me a tampon or something he wouldn't question it,' I whispered.

Jas rolled her eyes. 'You're ridiculous. OK. What?'

I turned my phone so she could read Emily's message.

'This girl saw Georgia enter the house when nobody else was in it, stay for five minutes, then leave again. I think that might be something.'

'Yeah, management checking up on them, H. Obviously they want the guys to *think* they get moments that are just for them, and the house is a safe space or whatever, but *of course* they're keeping an eye.'

'On an empty house? Wouldn't it make more sense to be watching the boys themselves?'

'Harri, what are you saying?' Her whisper sounded more like a hiss now.

'I'm saying Georgia was in the house and the boys had *no idea*. You heard what Jack said – Pure never go inside.'

'So, if Georgia was going in and out without them knowing, who else was?'

I knew that what I said next, whether I was right or not, would be a catalyst. We would not get to walk out of this bathroom and pretend that nothing had changed.

'Harri, what?'

Here we go.

'Exactly what I said. That *Georgia* was in the house, and the boys had no idea. She knew about Jack and Frankie, Jas. She knew none of it was real, and she knew that Evan knew that, too. She must have. She saw Alex talking to him at that party, and she broke it up straight away. She was desperate to make sure it didn't get out. To prove herself. She was under pressure at Pure, right? That phone call with Scarlett I overheard before the press conference?'

'So . . . she took it upon herself to make sure Evan couldn't tell anyone else?' Jas finished.

'Maybe,' I whispered.

'But she has an alibi. The photo with Molly, remember?'

'We can't be sure it's her. All we know for certain is that it's a girl with a similar taste in rings.'

'But why would she frame Frankie?'

'Jas, I can't . . .'

'Is that enough to –'

There was shuffling, and then a knock on the bathroom door.

'Um, girls? Is everything OK?'

Before we could discuss it, Jas pulled the door open, and Jack sprang back in surprise.

'Sorry, carry on. I was just –'

'Jack, Georgia was in your house,' blurted Jas.

I was going to do it sensitively. I would have steered them back towards the bed and sat us all down, and then asked if maybe there was any reason Jack could think of why Georgia would have been there when nobody else was. Perhaps it had just slipped his mind that she had a key. Perhaps she did that occasionally. Dropped something off when the place was empty, or came to pick something up when she knew it would be quiet. *Well, maybe that's what she was doing*, I thought. Now that the words were out, though, just hanging there heavily, there was no time for sensitivity. Apparently, we were going to do this standing on the threshold of my bathroom, Jas and me crammed into the tiny space, Jack standing aghast on the other side of the open door.

'What do you mean?' he asked.

'We put a post on the internet. Asked the girls who've been waiting outside your house who they'd seen. Almost

228

everyone who replied said the same thing – that it was only you guys coming and going, and they didn't see anyone else at all. This one girl, though, got in touch to say she was sorry she couldn't help more, but, as she was sure we knew by now, it was only you guys . . . oh and that one time you were out that Georgia popped by.'

'The intern Georgia?'

I nodded.

Jack looked confused. 'What was she doing there?'

'We don't know,' I said, squeezing past Jas and gesturing for them both to follow. I sat on the edge of the bed, waiting for them to join me before I turned back to Jack.

'But she could have known the truth about you and Frankie, couldn't she? Someone could have told her that it wasn't real between you two, and that Evan didn't like it one bit. She loves you guys together. She would have done anything. Maybe she took it upon herself to keep it quiet.'

'Would she?' Jas asked, looking at Jack.

'Would she what? Sorry, I'm a little . . . what are you asking?'

I glanced at Jas, who nodded. I took a breath. 'Jack, is there any way that Georgia could be involved in this?'

TRACK TWENTY-TWO

Jack didn't need to say anything. His face said it all – his pursed lips, and the pained look in his eyes. Part of him – however deep that knowledge was buried, however much we all wished it could not be true – thought that there was a chance that Georgia had played a part in what had happened. I didn't know how he was going to react to my question, but I didn't expect him to take a deep breath and calmly say, 'OK. So what do we know?'

He was methodical. Practical. It was as if it wasn't his life at all. As if he was playing a game – figure out who the killer is, and at the end there might be a prize. Except the prize was Frankie's freedom. But it wouldn't change the fact that Evan was dead. None of them would ever really recover from that.

We went back through what we knew, over and over. Frankie had been worried about sales, so faked a relationship with Jack because it was what the fans wanted (that part made Jack wince, so we didn't linger on it too long). He told Evan, who – with Frankie's best interests at heart, as always – wanted him to get out of it, and made Frankie confess to Molly. Frankie and Molly were worried that Evan would spill to someone else. Somehow Georgia found out – Georgia who was desperate, *desperate* to prove herself to the rest of Pure – and saw keeping Frankie's secret as her mission, whatever it took.

'But why would she frame *Frankie*?' Jas asked as we recapped for the third time. 'She loves Frankie. Everyone loves Frankie.'

'She loves Half Light,' Jack pointed out. 'Probably Frankie the most, sure – doesn't everyone? – but it's not just him. She might sacrifice one of us to save the whole. We know how it goes with the girls who do that internship. Almost all of them are fans. They just have to play the game, and act like they're super professional about all this celebrity stuff, to get through the interview.'

'Well, yeah,' I supplied. 'I've applied every year so far.'

'Right,' Jack said, nodding, as if he'd seen that coming.

But Jas was shaking her head. 'Putting one of you in prison for murder seems counterproductive. Her thinking she had to keep Evan quiet, I can sort of believe, but there are so many things she could have done that weren't *killing him*. Why didn't she just make him sign a contract to say he wouldn't spill? Surely you guys serve people with those all the time?'

Jas knew more about things like that than I did. It sounded legitimate to me, but Jack shook his head.

'No. I mean, *yes*, obviously we do, but not for Evan. Not for our friends. Frankie would never let that happen.

He's so black and white about it – no contracts for the people in our personal lives, no exceptions.'

'So what?' I asked. 'You think she thought she had no other choice?'

Jack huffed out a little laugh.

'People who work for Pure always think they have no other choice. It must be in the job description. None of them have ever taken it *this* far, though.'

I was silent for a moment, turning it over in my head. We seemed to be homing in on Georgia, but I was well aware that a few hours ago I'd all but accused Phoebe, and before that Alex . . .

Alex.

'We need to call Alex,' I said, and Jack screwed up his face.

'Who?'

'Our friend,' Jas told him. 'Also Harri's first-choice suspect, but I think we've moved on from that theory.'

'She knows Georgia,' I continued. 'Well, we all know Georgia, but she and Alex were actually pretty close at one point.'

'So what? We try and get her to admit it to Al?' Jas stood as she spoke, and reached for the bottle of gin from the shelf above my bed. I watched her glance around for glasses but realize that getting them would mean leaving the room – mugs would do just fine. 'Remember, you did *accuse* Al last time you spoke to her, H. What makes you think she still wants to be involved?'

232

'Can someone explain to me what the hell is going on?' Jack interrupted, and I turned to him.

'Right. Sorry. I accidentally accused our friend Alex of . . . killing Evan maybe . . . well, that's exactly what I did, but I didn't mean to. She met him at an awards party – she's a journalism student – and he made some comment about his best friend being in a fake relationship. Al thinks he reckoned she didn't know who he was, but obviously she did, and she worked out he was talking about you and Frankie. She kept it secret, which upset us, and I took it too far.'

Saying it out loud made me realize just how deep we'd got ourselves into this.

'Right,' Jack said slowly. 'And Georgia?'

'Was also there,' I cut in. 'At the party. She told Alex that whatever Evan had said was best forgotten. Make sense?'

'Does any of this make sense?' Jack asked; at the same time I heard Jas say, 'Alex, hi.'

She'd taken the plunge and called while Jack and I were speaking. Now she held a finger to her lips to silence us as she explained what we'd discovered. Once she'd finished, she put Alex on speaker.

'So what you're asking is, did Georgia hear what Evan said to me?' Alex asked.

'Or did he tell her, too?' Jack said, and I wished I could see Alex's face as his voice proved this was actually happening. Jack was really here, in my bedroom, trying to help us get to the bottom of all this.

'She definitely didn't hear him. She couldn't have. I was facing her the whole time – she didn't come over until she pulled him away.'

'But why did she pull him away if she didn't know?' Jas wondered aloud. 'And why did she tell you that whatever he said was best forgotten?'

'Wait, wait, wait. Remember what we heard Frankie say on that recording?' I said. 'That he and Molly could ask Georgia to keep an eye on Evan, stop him talking to anyone outside the inner circle – but that they wouldn't say what it was about. Maybe Georgia knew there was a secret to protect, but not what the secret was?'

'Frankie would never have told her what it was,' Jack cut in, nodding. 'Especially not when he and Molly were trying to keep it from spreading any further. If she knew, she found out by accident. Or . . . or Evan had already told her, I suppose – before he told you at the party, Alex? He crosses paths with everyone at Pure fairly often.'

We all sat silently for a moment, trying to fit the pieces together. Finally Alex sighed. 'Are we . . . are we saying we think *Georgia* could have done this?' she asked.

Jas, Jack and I glanced at one another. 'That is kind of where the three of us had got to when we called you,' Jas admitted, and I was so glad she was the one to say it. I had, after all, accused the wrong person twice already. I was hesitant to do it again.

'What do you need me to do?' Alex asked.

TRACK TWENTY-THREE

Jack was almost completely silent as Alex, Jas and I hashed out a plan.

'What are you typing, Al?' I asked, hating the fact that she wasn't in the room with us.

'*Hi, George, hope you're OK. Listen, can we talk about that party where you saw me with Evan? I don't know if you heard what he told me, but I'm feeling pretty weird about it and want to chat with someone who was there. Drink?*'

'Sounds natural enough,' Jas said. 'Let's hope she bites.'

I looked over to where Jack was sitting and noticed his face had paled. I crouched beside him, trying to silence the part of my mind screaming, *This is so weird.*

'What's wrong?'

He looked up at me; the panic on his face was something I recognized all too well from my own mirror.

'She was on our team. We let her into our world. I can't believe we didn't see this.'

I wriggled into place beside him, my back against the

wall, and fought the urge to take his hand. I guessed he wasn't feeling particularly trusting towards fans right now.

'You can't blame yourself for that, Jack. You didn't hire her, nor –'

Alex's voice interrupted me before I could continue: 'Jas, she's calling me! What do I do?'

Jas leaped into action almost literally, springing to her feet from where she was perched on my bed, and began to pace the definitely-too-small-for-pacing room.

'OK, Al, let it go to voicemail. Hang up with us, then Skype us from your laptop, call Georgia back and put her on speaker so we can all hear her, too.'

Her cool answer could not have been more in contrast to her chaotic energy. I looked at her, jaw slack in awe, and I felt so lucky to have a Jas in my life.

Alex's Skype call came through almost immediately, the shrill ringtone from my laptop making me jump even though I was expecting it.

'All right, so now I call her back?' she asked, her face filling the screen, and Jas nodded as the three of us moved closer, making sure we were in the frame. I kept my eyes firmly on Alex as she noticed Jack in person for the first time. Her smile was almost worth all this. He'd noticed, too, I knew. He raised his hand in a tiny wave, and her smile grew even wider.

'Yeah,' Jas said, still calm and focused, 'call her back. We'll be listening. I'll type if you need help knowing what to say.'

Alex nodded, and the sound of a dialling tone filled the room as she pressed the call button.

'Hello?' It was a stretch to say I'd recognize Georgia's

voice anywhere, but the high trill from Alex's phone was unmistakably her. Alex looked in our direction, and I gave a thumbs up.

'Hi, George, sorry I missed your call. You all right?'

'I got your text,' Georgia said, and I felt Jas grip my knee. 'What's the problem?'

Do you know what Evan told me? Jas typed at lightning speed, and I held my breath as Alex repeated it to Georgia without missing a beat.

'How could I know what he told you?' Georgia replied, and Jas leaned forward to type again, but I pulled her back. It was too risky to get involved and say something that would give the game away. Alex had to handle this part on her own.

'You just seemed *very* sure that I'd do well to forget it,' Alex said, and glanced at us, raising her eyebrows as if to say, *How am I doing?* Jas and I both grinned and nodded in encouragement.

'Alex, what are you asking me?' Georgia sounded impatient.

'Well, you've got to admit, George, it doesn't look good for Frankie that his best friend knew his biggest secret and then suddenly his best friend is dead. I feel this weird guilt. Like knowing what we know implicates me somehow.'

Georgia was quiet for a moment.

'So. That *is* what he told you,' she said when she finally spoke. 'Frankie and Jack.'

'See!' Jas hissed. 'She knew!'

'So you knew,' Alex said, taking Jas's cue.

There was another silence before Georgia said, 'Yes,

fine, I knew. If Evan was spilling to me, the intern, I thought everyone knew. At that party alone he was wasted enough that he told me twice!'

'Everyone absolutely didn't know,' Jack said, then immediately clapped a hand over his mouth when he realized what he'd done. I heard Georgia draw in a sharp breath.

'What the hell was that?'

Jas closed her eyes. I covered my mouth. Alex's expression was wild with panic.

'Alex? Who's with you?'

'Nobody,' Alex squeaked. 'I'm alone.' Even though that was technically true, it could not have sounded more like a lie.

'Alex, what is this? Tell me who you're with or I'm hanging up.'

Alex was crumbling before our eyes, and I could not see a way out of this one. It was excruciating to watch. It seemed Jack felt the same way. He gritted his teeth.

Sorry, he mouthed to Jas and me, and, before we could stop him, he was speaking again.

'Georgia. It's Jack.'

Oh fine.

'And Harri,' I said.

'And Jas.'

Georgia laughed unkindly. 'I should have known. The Fangirl Detective Society. How did you rope *Jack* into this? What did you tell him?'

'We told him the truth, Georgia.' Jas sounded braver now than I knew she felt. I could tell by her slightly shaking hand, close enough to my arm for me to feel it, that she was wading into completely uncharted territory.

'And what's the truth? That I did my job? That I pulled Evan away from a fan because he was in a vulnerable situation and I recognized that could be bad? I can't apologize for that.' The way she spat out the word *fan* riled me. She'd been one of us. She still was. I'd forgive the icy facade she'd thrown up hastily when Pure first hired her. I'd forgive her distancing herself, and playing it cool, and pretending that loving something loudly wasn't how she'd found her dream job in the first place. I would not, though, forgive her for saying *fan* like that.

'We know you were at Jack and Frankie's house, Georgia,' I said, and the look on Alex's face suggested that maybe I should have warned them that I was about to go there. 'We know you're involved in this.'

The room was so quiet that I feared for a moment Georgia might have hung up. Alex was completely still. Beside me, I could feel Jack breathing. Jas wrapped an arm round my shoulder and pulled me close. *Still here*, her body said.

'Fine.' Georgia sounded defeated. 'You're right. You're absolutely right, of course you are. I was at the house.'

'What happened, George?' Alex asked gently.

'Georgia, if you took anything, we need to know,' Jack said softly as if he was trying to coax her on to our side.

'I'm not doing this on the phone,' Georgia replied, the power returning to her voice. 'Meet me. I'll text you the address.'

TRACK TWENTY-FOUR

The drive to London was quiet. If this worked, we knew, it could *actually* save Frankie. It felt like I was nervous in reverse: as if meeting Jack had happened so quickly and unexpectedly that we hadn't had time to be anything but matter-of-fact about it, and now all the feelings we had skipped – all the fear and the guilty joy – were arriving at once. I tried to think of things to say that wouldn't feel completely contrived, but I couldn't.

How is it possible, I wondered, *that I've spent so many years wishing I could tell this man how I feel about him, and now he's here I can't think of a single thing to say?* So I kept quiet.

Did I hear you leave? Stef had texted as we hit the motorway, and I had no idea how to tell him what we were up to this time without totally terrifying him, so I sent back a string of kisses, and hoped they'd hold him at bay until I was ready to say more.

All three of us would go, we'd decided. Strength in numbers, speeding towards the address Georgia had texted to Jas.

'Should we really be meeting her at her house?' I'd asked. 'Is her own territory the safest place to do this?'

'We're all here.' Jack looked at me in the rear-view mirror as he spoke. 'She's not going to hurt us, Harri. I'd never let that happen.'

'Can we put the radio on?' Jas asked when the silence became too loud, and Jack flicked through a few stations, settling on one that played the kinds of songs we'd all sung along to at parties at the end of the night. The music somehow made it even more obvious that we had nothing to say; that we didn't know how to navigate this. It was getting weirder rather than more normal.

'We're nearly there,' Jack said as we drove down the kind of residential London street where the homes looked like they'd been in families forever. They were imposing and *old*, nothing like where I'd imagined Georgia would live.

'Shall we go over the plan again?' My voice was too high-pitched, too fast.

'Are you all right?' Jack asked, looking quite alarmed, and Jas reached for my hand and squeezed it.

'I'm fine. Just . . .'

'I know,' he said. 'Yeah, let's recap.'

'So we go in together. We tell her we know she's involved, hope she straight-up confesses and we can go to the police peacefully. If she doesn't, we call them anyway?'

'What could possibly go wrong?' Jas deadpanned from beside me.

'I asked Kyle to come, too,' Jack said, matter-of-fact. 'I

thought an extra body, especially if it was his body, wouldn't hurt.'

Jas and I glanced at one another, and I put my hand to my mouth to cover my smile. It felt inappropriate somehow, to still be letting these little flashes of happiness through. Despite what we were about to do being all kinds of terrifying, there was suddenly a buzz in the car.

Jack slowed to a halt outside a large house. None of the lights were on, although the curtains were open, the street lamps shining into what looked like the living room. From out here, it didn't look lived in at all.

'We're early,' Jas said, the light from her phone screen lighting up the car as she took it out to check the time. 'She'll be here in a bit.'

I took out my own phone and tapped out a message to Gemma. We'd promised, after all, to keep her updated, and a lot had changed since we'd last hung up. *Was that only a few hours ago?*

Wait GEORGIA? Her reply came so quickly she must have already had her phone in her hand. So not Phoebe?! Damn, we got that one wrong, didn't we?

I'll tell you everything later, I promised in response. The idea of a mythical later, when all this was just a story to be told, made me feel calmer than I had in a while. *We can do this,* I thought.

Well. We don't really have a choice.

TRACK TWENTY-FIVE

'I can't decide if this should have stopped being weird by now or it isn't weird *enough*,' Jas said as we sat huddled in Jack's car opposite the house, our heads snapping up every time the road crunched under car tyres, our bodies relaxing every time it wasn't Kyle.

I knew what she meant. A few hours ago, Jack had been sitting in my bedroom and it had become normal remarkably quickly. Now we were waiting for his bandmate and it was right back to *completely bizarre*. I couldn't keep up with how we were supposed to be feeling.

'Imagine how it's going to feel when it's Frankie,' she continued, rolling her eyes when she saw the look on my face. 'Harri, it's *going* to happen. He's getting out. Haven't you spent the last week promising me that? And, when he does, we're going to do whatever it takes to get in a room with him, and tell him how *completely* he ruined everything. And how irritatingly badly we still love him. He owes us that much.'

'I hope so.'

'Oh, he definitely owes you,' Jack interjected. 'We all do.'

Another car rounded the corner, and this time the passing lights did not sweep across our faces and carry on down the street, but zeroed in on us as it stopped on the opposite side of the road to Jack's, and Kyle waved tentatively from the driver's seat.

'Let's get in his car,' Jack said, gesturing for us to follow. 'More space to talk.'

Kyle's car was warm, and the air freshener hanging from his mirror made it smell of bourbon and honey. He was quieter than Jack. My paranoia told me he seemed more wary, but I had to remind myself he was known as the quiet one. This was probably just how he was when the cameras were off and he wasn't putting on a show. Still, the silence made it feel awkward.

'Are you sure this is a good idea?' I asked, desperate to fill the quiet with my doubts, and for the others to promise me that we were doing the right thing.

'It's not a good idea in the grand scheme of ideas, but given what we have to work with it's a good idea,' Kyle said.

'Do you think –' Jas cut herself off.

'She did it?' Kyle filled in, and Jas nodded.

'I know Frankie didn't.'

It was as good an answer as we could have hoped for.

'Guys.' Jack had been silent since we got in the car, exhausted, I thought, by the events of the past few hours. Now, though, his voice was alert, his eyes wide when I turned to look at him, then past him to whatever had made him speak. Georgia seemed small as she walked alone along the wide street, pulling her oversized coat more tightly round her, steady as ever on her thin-heeled silver boots.

Right. Showtime.

'Are you ready?' Kyle asked.

I nodded.

'Yeah,' said Jas.

Kyle turned on the light above his seat, and tapped on the window to draw Georgia's attention.

'Wait.' They all turned to look at me.

'We need to get out. I can't do this if we're contained – I need –'

'She's right.' Mercifully, Jack interrupted before I had to try to articulate further that if I sat still any longer, with this amount of energy coursing through my body, I might actually combust. I opened the door, and raised my hand in a wave, the people-pleaser in me unable to resist a weak smile despite the conversation we were about to have.

Georgia stopped outside the address she'd given, and sank down on to the low wall as we crossed the road to join her.

'Hi, boys,' she said, not even looking at me and Jas.

'Hi.' Jas positioned herself in front of Jack. *Good*, I thought. *She's taking control.*

Except then she fell silent. We all stood there for a second, nobody saying anything, Georgia's expression unreadable. *Come on, Jas. Say something.*

'What were you doing in my house, Georgia?' In the end, it was Jack who was the first to speak, and Georgia closed her eyes before she answered, as if looking at him would make this conversation too hard.

'What are you really asking me, Jack?'

'Exactly that. I never gave you permission to be there. What were you doing in my house?'

'Are you asking me that because you think it's related to all this somehow? Because you think I've done something wrong?' Her voice was quiet now, and she opened her eyes to look at Jack, as if she was pleading with him to let her off gently. *No such luck*, I thought. I wanted him to make this hard on her.

'Georgia, I have no idea, but if you being there has anything to do with what happened to Evan you need to tell us.'

A look passed across Georgia's face at this, and I couldn't place it, but I knew I didn't like it. Something was wrong. She hadn't crumbled. She looked . . . powerful almost. Like she knew something we didn't.

'Oh my God,' Georgia said quietly. 'You seriously think I've done something wrong. You actually have no idea what I was doing there.'

'Can you please just tell us what the hell happened?' Jas snapped.

'All right. Fine. I'll tell you what happened.' Georgia stood up. 'I went to the house on Sunday to pick something up, yes. Some clothes. I was just doing my job. Then I brought the bag of clothes back here.'

246

'What do you mean, doing your job?' I asked, at the same time as Kyle said, 'Actually, why are we standing in the cold when we're right outside your front door? I'm freezing.'

Georgia held up her hands to silence us.

'One at a time, except the two are actually related. I was doing my job in that my boss asked me to pick up the clothes. I'm an intern. I'm asked to do menial tasks all the time. It didn't seem odd. And why are we standing in the cold? I don't have the key because this isn't my house. It's Molly's.'

TRACK TWENTY-SIX

It was so quiet I felt like I could hear the air. Nobody said a word, all staring at Georgia as if she might crack and say she'd been joking. But there was no way, I knew, that any of this was a joke.

'Don't you want to know what happened?' she asked eventually, and it was Jack who broke first.

'I can't see any way that knowing what happened will make me feel better.'

I wanted to reach out to him. Wanted to put my hand on his arm, hope he could feel it through the thick fabric of his coat, and tell him with my touch that everything was going to be OK. I didn't quite believe it myself, but I really wanted to be able to do that for him. *It's still Jack*, I reminded myself. *Things haven't changed* that *much in the last few hours that you can just casually touch his arm. He's not your friend.*

Georgia nodded, and sank back down on to the wall with more impact than I thought she'd intended. It looked sort of painful.

'Jack, we have to let her explain,' Kyle said. 'We're so close now. We have to know the truth, if it can get him out.'

'The truth will set you free,' Jas interjected, and I wasn't entirely sure what she was quoting, but knew from her deadpan tone that it was something.

Jack nodded. 'OK, Georgia, what happened?'

He took a seat beside her on the wall, gesturing for the rest of us to follow suit. The brick was cold on the backs of my legs, even through my jeans. I shivered.

'I honestly don't know why this is such a big deal,' she began, and that was all it took to push Jack from sad to seething.

'Georgia, we don't have time for this. My boyfriend has been arrested for something I'm now certain he didn't do, and you have information that could help him. Tell us what happened!'

Georgia gulped, and just for a second I almost felt sorry for her. She'd built a life round these boys. I'm sure she'd never imagined it would end up quite like this. I also couldn't help noticing that Jack had called Frankie his boyfriend, even after everything. *They're all going to need some pretty intense therapy when this is over*, I thought.

'All right. I'll tell it as it happened. Molly asked me to go to your house, Jack, on Sunday afternoon and pick up a few clothes. She said there was a chance the paps would get nasty, and that if they did we'd have to be ready to check you in to a hotel. She said you would be out –'

'Kyle and I went for massages,' Jack cut in. 'Molly

booked them and came with us … Said we needed to relax.'

Georgia nodded. 'So Molly gave me a key. She said she'd had it cut for emergencies only, and that whole weekend definitely counted as an emergency. Anyway, I let myself in, grabbed a few things from the bedroom, stuffed it all in a bag.'

'And you brought it here?' I asked. When Georgia nodded, I continued: 'Didn't you think that was weird? Why would clothes for Jack be delivered to Molly's house?'

'Oh, it's not that weird,' Kyle cut in. 'You've just got to get things to the person expected to see us next. That's more likely to be Molly than anyone else. Bringing them here wouldn't have been a red flag. Sorry, Georgia, carry on.'

'Well, she told me where she keeps her spare house key. I opened the door, put the bag inside and left. That's why I was in your house, Jack. Completely innocent.'

'Except it isn't.' My voice was small, and everyone turned to stare at me at once, a parliament of owls zeroing in.

'Why not?' Georgia asked. 'I've just proved to you that I wasn't in the house under false pretences. I'm innocent, Harri.'

'I know *you* are,' I said, and turned to look at Jack. I wanted to see his face, hoped I wouldn't have to spell out what I'd just realized. 'My interview at Pure was on Monday morning. Molly was supposed to be there, but she was late. Accident at the end of her road, she said.'

Jack's face had gone ashen. 'Georgia, did you look at what clothes you'd picked up?' he whispered.

Georgia shook her head, confused. 'I was rushing. I didn't really –'

'You picked up the shirt. The one they're using as evidence,' Jack said, his voice still barely audible. 'Frankie's shirt. I'd been wearing it on Saturday. I threw it back in the drawer on Saturday night. It would have been right at the top. And . . .'

'And Molly asked for the clothes to be brought here,' Georgia finished. 'I felt like something was off, but I didn't know it was . . . that.'

'She got lucky,' Kyle said quietly. 'Could there have been a more *Frankie* shirt in there?'

We were silent. We all knew what had happened next. The shirt had been found at the scene of the crime. Molly had planted it there.

'But Molly couldn't have killed him,' I said, the pieces not quite fitting together as I remembered. 'She wasn't there the day Evan died. She was with you.'

Georgia looked confused. 'Was she?'

'Yeah,' I said. 'In a bar? She posted a picture.'

The perfect team-mate as ever, Jas had already pulled it up on Instagram, and thrust her phone in Georgia's face.

'That is my hand, yes, but that wasn't the day Evan . . . That wasn't *that* day,' Georgia said, her voice confident.

'Are you sure?' Kyle asked, and Georgia nodded.

'Definitely. That's at Ember. It doesn't even open till ten

thirty. It's a club. I was there with Molly, yeah, but maybe three weeks ago. Not that day.'

'So what does this mean?' Jack asked.

Jas took her phone back and turned to face him. 'It means Molly posted a selfie that we thought was an alibi but wasn't at all. It wasn't even taken on the same day. It doesn't prove she wasn't at the studio that day. If it proves anything, it's that she was lying about where she really was.'

'Where *were* you that Friday?' I asked Georgia.

'In a meeting at Pure, with Rich and Scar! We were starting on the international tour dates. You can –'

'We don't need to check,' I said. 'We know about that meeting. Sorry. I don't know what I was thinking.'

'So what now?' she asked, and I stayed silent since I didn't have an answer.

'Wait a sec.' Jas's voice was loud in contrast to the silent street. 'You said you brought the clothes *here*?'

Georgia nodded.

'And Molly told you where she kept the spare key?'

'Jas, no.' I'd spoken before I even realized I was going to, and Jas turned away from Georgia to look at me.

'Harri, one of us has to go in there. There might be more evidence. We said we'd do anything, remember? It's time.'

'I hate to say it, but she's right,' Kyle said, and Jas flashed him a grateful smile.

'Harri, we've got to,' Jack added. I looked over at Georgia, who had her head in her hands as if she couldn't quite believe how this was playing out. I knew the feeling.

'Fine. Georgia, where's the key?'

'Under the second-biggest flower pot.' She didn't lift her head as she spoke. I guessed she was thinking about everything she stood to lose if this went wrong.

'Right, so what? We flip a coin to decide who goes?' I asked.

There was silence. I could tell from the way they all looked at me that we were not going to flip a coin.

TRACK TWENTY-SEVEN

The key was exactly where Georgia had said it would be. *Is it still breaking and entering if no actual breaking happens?* I wondered, pushing the door, which opened with a loud creak that made me jump even though I knew exactly where the sound had come from. A quick call from Kyle to the Pure PR offices had confirmed that Molly was on a video conference with the Half Light LA team until eight, which gave us at least a few hours.

How did it end up being me doing this? I asked myself as I crossed the threshold. Why had they all looked at me at the same time? Why was it so obvious that I should be the one to go in?

I understood why it couldn't be Kyle or Jack. Molly was their friend, after all. If we were proved wrong, there was no coming back from the fact that, even if just for a moment, we'd thought she was capable of murder. Georgia, too, had a lot to lose. Besides, I didn't trust that in her current emotional state she wouldn't get us caught immediately.

Jas, though? Why had it been so clear to Jas that it should be me? Weren't friends meant to go into battle for each other? Why, when it came to it, had she been so quick to just let me go?

I couldn't dwell on it too long. I couldn't think of a single possible answer that would have helped.

The hallway was narrow but airy, the kind of place that managed to feel cosy and spacious all at once. There was one of those plug-in air fresheners running close to the skirting board, I noticed. Vanilla. It made the house smell far too sweet. The wooden floorboards creaked as I stepped further into the hall and I laughed that I found myself tiptoeing even though I knew with certainty that I was the only one here. There was a rug on the floor that looked threadbare, but intentionally, stylishly so. *Jealous much?* I asked myself as I stepped over it. Even the carefully distressed edges made everything I owned seem tired and worn in comparison. The boys said she hadn't lived here long – not even long enough for them to have been invited round yet – but somehow it already felt like quintessential Molly. Cool without trying.

Upstairs, I pushed open the first door I came to, and was met with more artistically threadbare rugs on gappy, painted floorboards, and a copper bedframe with fairy lights twisted through the headboard. I glanced out of the window and, once I saw that the room backed on to the garden, I turned on the lights. And *oh*, that was the perfect finishing touch. The lighting made it look like something straight from a boho-chic vision board.

'What am I actually looking for?' I whispered as I glanced around the almost tidy space. There were piles of books on the floor, and a few clothes strewn around where I guessed they'd fallen as she peeled them off at the end of the day, but besides that I was going to have to *actually look*. She hadn't left anything glaringly obvious to be found.

I turned to her dressing table, my eyes widening as I saw something I recognized glinting from among the lipsticks and perfume bottles. I reached out, and ran the tips of my fingers across the top of the BRIT Award. Half Light had won numerous in their time, but a closer look told me that this had been the first. *British Album of the Year*. It felt like I was touching a little bit of history.

My phone buzzed in my hand, lighting up the room with a text from Jas.

> Kyle says check the wardrobes.
> She used to have boxes where
> she put important things, and
> that's where she kept them in
> her old place.

Back to work. I crossed the room and pulled open one of the built-in wardrobes, then the other. Kyle was right. The shelves above where her clothes hung were completely stuffed with boxes of various types and sizes. Shoeboxes, the pretty kind you gave gifts in, ones that used to hold kettles, and games consoles, and one that previously housed a set of incredibly sharp knives, which sent a shiver through me.

Chill out, H, I told myself. *She's allowed to have knives. She has to cut things.*

Still.

I pulled down the biggest of the boxes, still unsure about what I was actually looking for. It was full to the brim with receipts, and what looked like random knick-knacks. I threw it on to the bed behind me, and heard a surprisingly heavy clunk as the box hit the duvet.

I turned and pulled the duvet cover aside. An iPad. It was only when I picked it up, planning just to slip it back where I found it, that I realized the true weight of what I was holding in my hand.

'An iPad will have messages on it,' I said aloud to the empty room. Heart beating in what felt like double time, I sat tentatively on the edge of the bed.

If I could just get past the lock screen, I'd probably have her entire life at my fingertips. Text messages, emails, social media – if Molly had said an incriminating word to anyone, chances are I was holding the evidence.

'Where the hell do I start?' I whispered. I closed my eyes and rested my forehead against the screen in my hands as if it might act as some sort of information transfer. Unsurprisingly, that didn't work. I wasn't good enough at maths to work out the probability of me being able to crack the combination, but I knew it was ridiculously low. Part of me wanted to get out of there as fast as I could, and go back to my safe little life where we didn't commit crimes to save international pop sensations.

Wouldn't be your safe little life without him in it, though, would it? The niggling voice at the back of my mind cut through all my logical thoughts. It was true. Going back to my life and leaving Frankie locked away for something he didn't do wouldn't be going back to *my life*. Not without him.

For God's sake, I told that mind-voice. *Why do you always have to be right?*

I lifted my head and trailed my fingers across the screen. As I grazed the home button, the whole iPad lit up, four dashes appearing like a game of hangman. *And someone actually has died*, I thought wryly. *Don't think. Just use your instinct. What's the code? Maybe she hasn't changed it from the factory-set one. Those were usually 0000, right?* I typed it in quickly and jumped when the device vibrated in my hands to let me know I was wrong.

OK, think. What's her birthday?

A quick scan of her Instagram told me, and I briefly considered how safe putting our entire lives on the internet for the whole world to see actually was. I typed in the date carefully, and was again greeted by the vibration. I had no idea where to turn next; I realized I knew almost nothing about this woman that didn't involve her connection to the boys. I tried the date their first single was released, their first album, the date of their first number one. Each time, the buzz announced my failure with something like smugness. *Wrong again.*

I gritted my teeth and slammed the iPad on to the bed in frustration. It was completely pointless, and the longer I sat here, recklessly typing in numbers, which would eventually lead to me locking the iPad entirely, the more creeped out I was becoming. As I turned, my eye caught the photos jammed in along the top of her mirror frame.

I smiled, as a sudden pang of recognition struck. The circumstances were different, of course, but they were exactly like my own. Photos in a woman's bedroom of the guys that she adored. Granted, she was actually in those images, snuggled up to Jack on a boat that I recognized from similar photos, champagne flutes in their hands, celebrating the end of the Lights Up tour. Or laughing with Jack by a Christmas tree, both looking considerably younger than they did now. Or a selfie with . . . Jack . . . both pulling stupid faces.

A picture in one of my scrapbooks – Jack on a talk-show stage, Molly looking on with the warmth of a thousand suns – suddenly appeared in my mind in a brand-new context. I glanced again at the mirror, just to check, but I knew I was right. All the photos were of Jack.

This won't work, I told myself as I began typing in the numbers. *Don't get excited.*

1

6

0

2

The screen immediately sprang to life, a triumphant chime telling me straight away that Molly had notifications to read, and that Jack's birthday was the key to getting into her most intimate correspondence.

Jack, I thought. *Of course. She's doing all this for Jack.*

Not allowing myself to waste time celebrating yet, I clicked the calendar icon, part of me hoping I'd be faced with an alibi. It felt juvenile, and silly, but as much as I'd rather it be Molly than Frankie, I *really* didn't want it to be her. Molly had represented everything I'd aspired to be ever since she first began appearing in photographs, smiling through gritted teeth at the edge of a frame as she tried to corral Frankie away from the fans and into a waiting car, or at the side of the stage, watching in wonder as the boys performed, human for a second rather than the management machine she immediately transformed into the moment they walked off and were back in her care. She was as close to Half Light as anyone, almost as much a *part* of Half Light as the boys themselves. It seemed strange to say that I'd become a fan of Molly, too, but it was the closest I could come to articulating what she meant to me. *If she can make it in their world*, I'd thought, *maybe I can.*

Scrolling back to Friday, the day of the accident, I offered up a silent prayer to the universe.

Please, just let there be something. Something we have to look into, even if all it does is delay us from finding out the truth for a minute or two. Anything. Please.

I looked down at the screen and gulped.

No such luck. Either she'd beaten me to it, deleting all evidence of her movements, or her days for the last two weeks at least had been completely empty. I found that impossible to believe.

OK. Next. I flew quickly back into action, opening every messaging app I could find on Molly's home screen. I started with her text messages and, as I began scanning the list of names that appeared, a brief shudder of excitement passed through me. I could read messages from Jack, and Kyle, and Rich, and, I was sure, if I scrolled back far enough, Frankie himself. None of those were what I needed now, though. If I was going to work this out, I had to find out what connected her to Evan. Typing his name into the search bar at the top of the screen was frustratingly unfruitful, and I let out an irritated growl when I saw that their last text messages had been in February. There was nothing. This wasn't going to work.

My own phone vibrated in my pocket, and I fished it out with one hand as I clicked into Molly's emails. Gemma's name on the screen gave me comfort, and reminded me that even though physically I was alone here, I wasn't really. I still had people in my corner. They'd help if they could. I let the phone slip out of my hand on to the bed beside me. I'd text her back when all this was over.

Then, quickly, I grabbed my phone again. *Gemma*.

> Gem. I need help. Can't fill you
> in properly right now. No time.
> I'm in Molly's iPad but it seems
> like loads of her messages
> have been deleted. Is there any

> way we can get them back? Can
> you try?

To her credit, she asked no questions.

> Yes. I can. Send me the email
> address she's logged in with,
> and get yourself on to the
> backup recovery screen. It'll
> take seconds.

I fired over the email address and waited. *How would I know when it was done?* I assumed Gem would tell me, but part of me hoped for the dramatic satisfaction of the iPad screen bursting into life, all the deleted evidence recovered by my genius friend, half a world away. I didn't have to wait long.

> Her iCloud password is
> HomeAgain2308. I'm in too.

The opening date of the Home Again tour had been 23 August, I recalled as I fumbled with the iPad and typed it in. How much random information must there be in my brain because of these boys? It made my heart hurt for Molly. I knew she loved them just as much as we did.

I almost got my dramatic moment when I pressed submit and the messages came flying on to the screen, Evan's name still in the search bar. The older messages were completely innocuous, unless I was missing some sort of secret code, which, I decided quickly, I was not. They talked about concerts, and flight times, and always Frankie in some capacity – the glue binding them together even when he wasn't the subject of the message. I flicked quickly through a few of these, wishing I had time to linger, to see what tiny new details I could pick up from their words. My eyes fell on an email dated just over a week ago from Evan. The subject line: Sorry/Frankie.

Bingo.

I read slowly, wanting to take in every word just in case there was a clue hidden there.

To: MollyJenkins@PurePR.co.uk
From: EvanDByrd@yahoo.co.uk
Subject: Sorry/Frankie

Hi Mol,

Lovely to see you the other night, and sorry about how it ended. I'd had one drink too many and didn't mean for it to come out like that. Been thinking about it today, though, and I still reckon we've got an issue. He's not OK. You can't tell me you think dragging Jack into whatever this is is the sign of a healthy state of mind? Frankie's in too deep, and it isn't his problem. All he should be worried about is singing the songs. Not telling you how to do your job here, but you need to get him out of this quickly. Whatever that means.

Evan x

'Go, Evan,' I whispered. Everyone should have someone like that in their corner. Scrolling up the screen, I came to Molly's reply. Her tone was breezy, whether through deliberate denial or because that was just how she wrote emails, I couldn't be sure.

To: EvanDByrd@yahoo.co.uk
From: MollyJenkins@PurePR.co.uk
Subject: Re: Sorry/Frankie

Hi love,

Good to see you, too, and don't worry. We all had one too many! Going to have to disagree about FW, though. He's honestly fine. You know how he gets, wants to be the one to make everyone happy. He genuinely enjoys it! Don't worry about your boy. We're looking after him, promise. See you soon?

Molly x

My phone chimed on the bed, and I picked it up to see a text from Jas.

Meeting finished early. She's on her way back.

There was a delay where my brain tried to process what that meant, and how Jas could possibly know that. Then I was on my feet, but in my panic to get out I accidentally knocked the box off the bed – leaving a mess of papers and trinkets on the floor. *Crap*. I busied myself throwing things back in the general direction of the box before I realized that this was our only chance. If I walked out now without reading the rest of these emails, we'd probably never know what they said. There was no time to think; I picked up the iPad with trembling hands and scrolled up the email trail to the top. I'd get the gist from the last thing they said to each other surely? Wouldn't that be the moment when they decided to quit the screens and meet up in person?

Evan's last email sent a chill through me. I read it twice and both times tried to swallow down the nausea in the pit of my stomach.

To: MollyJenkins@PurePR.co.uk
From: EvanDByrd@yahoo.co.uk
Subject: Re: Re: Sorry/Frankie

Molly, I'm going to spill. Not just to Jack, to everyone. I've got a journalist interested and I'm selling this story. I know you're not gonna like it, and Frankie won't, either, but it's gone too far. It isn't fair that he can go through life doing whatever the hell he likes, never stopping to think about the consequences. I'm sick of it. This is not my friend, and I won't let it keep happening. If he has no regard for anyone else, why should I? I'm meeting him tomorrow at six outside Albany Road. I'm going to try and talk him into doing the right thing. If he won't, I will. I'll take what I can get, and none of you will ever have to see me again.

Molly's reply was time-stamped less than two minutes later.

To: EvanDByrd@yahoo.co.uk
From: MollyJenkins@PurePR.co.uk
Subject: Re: Re: Re: Sorry/Frankie

Meet me first. The roof. 5.30. Let's talk about this.

As far as I could see, he'd never replied.

On the bed beside me, my phone went off again, one text and then immediately another. I picked it up with trembling hands, already knowing what the messages would say. That I was running out of time.

> Harri, NOW. She texted Jack
> saying she was walking back
> from the station five minutes
> ago. If she comes straight here,
> you have SECONDS.
>
> Where the hell are you?
>
> > Jas, she asked Evan to meet her
> > on the roof.

My fingers flew across the keys, hoping she'd read what I hadn't had time to type: **We were right.** I had just pressed send when I heard the front door swing open, a key being quietly pulled from the lock as if whoever was there knew they were not the only one in the house.

A notification from Gemma popped up on the screen.

> She didn't delete them until
> Sunday night. Trying to cover
> her tracks? Harri, are you safe?

I wished I had time to reply, but luck was no longer on my side. A final message from Jas came in – JUST HIDE – but it was too late. I looked up to see Molly at the door, taking in the scene.

'*You*? What on earth are you doing here?'

The silence was heavy as I weighed up my options. To confront her? Or to make up some kind of lie? There were so many ways this could go. I ran through them quickly in my head.

Possible outcomes of trying to get Molly to admit to Evan's murder

1. She actually had nothing to do with it and doesn't understand why I'm here at all. She'll probably think I've lost the plot, or that I'm so desperate to help Frankie that I won't rule out anything. Both of which, to be fair, are true.
2. She actually had nothing to do with it, but *does* realize what I'm trying to make her say. She'll be

massively offended and will probably call the police, which is far from ideal, but at least we'll know she's not a killer. Silver lining?

3. She *is* trying to frame Frankie for some reason, but she isn't the killer. Why? Not sure. I haven't got that far. Blackmail? Loyalty to whoever *is* the killer? Because for some misguided reason she thinks it will save Half Light, which is how we all ended up in this situation in the first place? Should I be concerned that trying to get inside the mind of a would-be murderer seems to be coming pretty easily?

4. She's trying to frame Frankie because she is the killer. She killed Evan. Whether that was to shut him up, or to take Frankie down, or for any other reason that a person capable of murder goes ahead and actually commits the crime, I don't know. I don't really want to know. (That's a lie. I've come this far. Of *course* I want to know.)

5. In all these scenarios, I'm alone with her. In all these scenarios, I'm the only one who hears her say she did it (or that she didn't). Possible outcomes of that? She's remorseful, and she's scared, and she lets us get her the help she quite clearly needs.

The other option? Well. She kills again.

'I know what you did, Molly.'

Oh, I thought as the words came out. *Guess I'm taking that tack, then.*

She folded her arms across her chest, hugging her body as if she was cold. 'What did I do?'

Another beat. Another decision to be made. If I steamed straight in and accused her of murder, the window for getting out of this intact all but disappeared. But if I started softer, and asked why she was setting Frankie up, there was a very real possibility that we wouldn't get what we came for, and that all this would have been for nothing.

'Well?' She stepped towards me, twisting her face into a look I knew should have threatened me as she closed the door behind her. A week ago it probably would have, but – after everything we'd seen, and heard, and done – my threshold for fear had shifted. We'd come this far. We'd done this much. An intimidating glare on a pretty face was child's play at this point. It angered me so much that I made my decision. *For Frankie*, I reminded myself as I dropped my phone on to the bed behind me, then I stood just a little bit taller and stepped towards her. *Two can play at that game.*

'You killed Evan.'

She almost got away with it. The facade barely dropped, but I saw it. A twitch of her lip, her cheeks sagging as she let her pout become slack, just briefly, but it was there.

We were right.

'Why on earth would I do that?'

'Well, this is how we have it plotted out so far.' My voice shook. *Come on, Harri. Don't let her see you have any doubts about this at all. She's the one that's meant to be scared, not you.*

'You killed Evan because he knew the truth about Frankie's relationship with Jack, and he was going to tell the press. Then you set Frankie up to make it look like he was guilty.'

'And I'd do that to my friend why exactly?' Another step forward. She was looming over me now. My phone chimed where it still lay on the bed but I didn't dare reach for it. 'Why would I do that to Frankie?'

Final decision time. If I said this and we were wrong, it was over.

But you know you're not wrong.

It wasn't my voice, this time, spurring me on. It was the girls – it was Jas, and Ruby, and Alex, and Gemma, and the many others who had no idea where I was, or *who* I was, or what on earth was happening right now as they scrolled through old photos, hoping that soon something would come to light to prove Frankie's innocence. It was all of them saying, 'Come on. The person that's going to prove this is you. It was always going to be you. You've just got to do it.'

But it wasn't just me. It was *us*. I was standing here because of all of us. *OK*, I thought. *Let's go.*

'You did it for Jack. You're in love with Jack.'

She didn't answer, but I knew from her face that I'd hit the nail on the head.

Is it over? I wondered, but reality's answer was like a bludgeon. *No. There's no way she lets you walk away from this.* I didn't realize that Molly could get much closer without touching me, but somehow she managed to take another

270

step forward, into my space. It was almost more threatening than if she *had* touched me. I moved back, my knees hitting the bedframe and buckling slightly. Instantly, her hand was on my arm, gripping tight, holding me like a vice.

'Don't sit down.'

'I wasn't going to.'

My phone was doing its best to demand my attention now, the text tone barely stopping before it began again. A quick glance told me they were almost all from Jas, but the most recent one was from my dad.

One text a day, I'd promised. *Of course they're checking I'm safe. I've broken my end of the bargain. If only they knew why, and could help me somehow.*

'And don't think about grabbing for that, either. I'm guessing you got in here of your own volition? Nobody forced you?'

Was there ever a choice with Frankie?

I knew that wasn't what she meant, though, so I nodded.

'Well, none of your fangirl friends can help you now.'

Please let that not be true.

'What are you going to do to me?' I asked. I couldn't disguise the tremor in my voice, and she laughed. She actually laughed.

'What do you want me to say? That I'm going to kill you, too? Admit to it by accident? Well, you're out of luck, sweetheart. I'm not falling for that. You have no evidence to prove I've done anything wrong at all. But me? Well . . . you're standing in my bedroom and I definitely didn't give you a key. That doesn't look good, does it?'

I raised my eyes to meet hers. A new theory was forming and, as we stared at each other, I realized I was right. *She doesn't know I've seen the emails.* Her eyes had been so closely trained on me from the second she'd entered the room that she hadn't even noticed the iPad, screen still alight, on the bed. And anyway, as far as she knew, all the evidence was gone.

You underestimated us, I thought. *Your mistake. I could buy myself some time here. Let her believe she's winning.* It was a struggle not to look in the direction of the evidence, just to check, but I knew her eyes would track my every movement. I had to keep her attention on me, no matter what.

'Why haven't you called the police, then?' I asked, and she pursed her lips.

'I was hoping it wouldn't come to that. I was hoping we could help each other.'

There was something in her tone that felt fragile, like she knew her own way out of this wasn't as easy as calling the police and reporting me. Hope swelled in my chest. *I could still walk away from this.*

'How do we help each other?'

Footsteps clattered up the stairs, shoes slapping hard on the wooden floorboards before coming to an abrupt halt right outside the room. And then silence. It didn't sound like all four of them, but I knew it had to be some combination of Jas, Jack, Georgia and Kyle standing on the other side of the door. I didn't want to move, didn't want to so much as breathe in case it ruined whatever they had planned.

Please have something planned.

'You can come in, Jack.'

Jack? How could she be so sure?

She sounded as though she'd been expecting this all along. There was no movement for a moment, and then the door swung slowly open, and he was standing there, Jas behind him. Relief flooded my body. Molly didn't turn; she kept her back to him as she spoke.

'I had a lot of theories about how this circus came about, but I never imagined you, of all people, would be in on it. Kyle, I'd accepted. Charlotte told me he'd called the office and I knew straight away something was going on – but *you*? That seemed like a leap too far.'

'How did you know it was me?'

She turned, her attention on Jack now, and I reached for my phone, careful not to ruffle the duvet, flicking it to silent mode as quickly and quietly as I could.

'Come on, Jack. I know what your aftershave smells like. You're wearing enough of it.'

I'd learned from an interview years back what Jack's favourite aftershave was, and all of us had gone through phases of spraying samples on our scarves. I hadn't recognized it. Weird.

'And why wouldn't I be in on it?' asked Jack.

She took a step towards him. 'Because *you* have more reason than any of us to want him locked away. He played you for a *fool*, Jack. And it *worked*.'

'And that's why you did it? For *me*?'

'I haven't *done* anything. You're not telling me you

273

believe their silly story, are you?' Her voice was softer now, meant just for him.

'Moll, come on.'

He's playing a dangerous game, I thought. *Trying to get her to just come out with it – genius if it works, but dangerous for all of us if it doesn't. Which . . . it won't.*

She moved closer still, barely even flinching when Jas crept into the room to stand beside me. We watched as Molly's hand reached for Jack's cheek and she nodded almost imperceptibly.

'I couldn't watch him hurt you like that,' she whispered. 'Couldn't see you embarrassed when it all came out, Jack.'

'So you killed Evan, and framed my best mate for it so I wasn't *embarrassed*?'

She looked resigned suddenly, her shoulders slumping in the manner of a person close to giving up. She hadn't yet, though. There was still something in her stance. She was hanging on for a way out.

It appears to be a long, long time before the dawn, I thought, recalling a Crosby, Stills and Nash song that my dad loved. *Let's hope I get out of here coherent enough to tell him that, when it came to it, it wasn't Half Light's music I was singing in my head. It was his Saturday-morning house-cleaning song.*

'Evan's death was an *accident*, you stupid man. I shoved him too hard and he *fell*. Do you actually think I'm *that* into you that I'd murder someone cos they threatened to expose your relationship?'

Sort of yes, actually.

'Molly, what are you saying?'

I ghosted my fingers over my phone screen, bringing it to life, but did not dial.

'He was going to spill. At first it was all "*Frankie should only have to worry about singing the songs*" and "*I care about Frankie's wellbeing so much*". Then it became "*It's not fair that he gets to do whatever he likes with no consequences*".'

'Mol, if he was really going to tell – tell *anyone at all* – he must have believed that Frankie needed it.'

'He was going to tell *you*,' Molly snapped, stepping further into Jack's space so their faces were almost touching.

'Well, I'm glad *someone* was. If you hadn't been scared that I was going to talk to the police, you'd have kept it quiet forever!'

'And he was going to go to the press,' Molly told him. 'Don't tell me that selling your secret would have been for your benefit, Jack – or for Frankie's. He was going to reveal all to a journalist. Take the cash, disappear. Frankie's loyal best friend. You know what would have happened then? Everything would have absolutely imploded. What? Would you rather I just stood by and let that happen? I'm meant to look after you, Jack. It's my job.'

'I'd rather you hadn't killed him, yeah.'

His voice was slow, quiet, full of remorse. It sounded, to my trained ears, tuned in after years of listening to him speak, that he was blaming himself. I wished I could reach out my hand and brush the hem of his jumper, to remind him we were here, and we were on his side.

275

'Don't you dare put all this on me!' She was shouting now, her voice reverberating off the high ceilings. 'It is *just* as much Frankie's fault as mine.'

Jack sighed, a breath that shook his whole body, and closed his eyes.

'Molly. Our friend is *dead*. Frankie made a stupid mistake, and maybe Evan made a mistake, too – but what you did and what they did aren't even in the same *universe*, let alone on the same level. *Evan died*. None of us are *ever* going to recover from your actions, Molly.'

'I have *never* done anything that wasn't in the best interests of this band, Jack.'

I screwed up my face and looked at Jas. *Was she serious?*

Molly went on. 'Never in half a decade of dealing with your missteps and fixing your idiotic choices have I let you down. And then this *huge* test comes along and you're saying you wish I'd *left it*?'

'You've never done anything that wasn't in the best interests of this band?' Jack's voice was incredulous.

'You know I haven't.' Molly was all but growling now as she reached behind her and, without looking, grabbed the award statue from her dressing table. My first instinct was to laugh. *What's she going to do, hit one of us with it?* I sobered quickly as I realized that yeah ... that was exactly her plan. Jas squeezed my hand. It was strange. I'd forgotten until I saw Molly holding something that could hurt us that we were in any danger – that she had *killed someone* – and now here we all were, standing in front of her.

I really hope Georgia and Kyle are getting help right now, I tried to mentally convey to Jas.

When Jack spoke again, I could tell there'd been a shift. He wasn't scared any more, but I couldn't pinpoint why. 'Molly, there is no band. There's nothing left to protect. You killed Evan and you broke us forever.'

'No, I didn't . . .' There was genuine confusion in her voice, and Jack choked out a strangled laugh.

'Of course you did! One of us is in prison, the others are under constant scrutiny and *our manager killed someone.* On what planet do you think we can carry on?'

'I was *helping.* You're all better off without him! It was never my plan to frame Frankie, but when the press did it for me – first good thing they've ever done for this band, by the way – it was just a bonus! You're the star, Jack! Half Light is nothing without your songs! You've been in his shadow for so long that I think even you've forgotten how good you are. This way you get to go out on your own. The jilted hero showing them all what he's actually worth. It's perfect!'

What? I had struggled to find any reason for her to frame Frankie, but that hadn't even been on my list of far-fetched possibilities.

'Was that really your plan all along, then? Kill him and hope nobody noticed? Let Frankie go down and all the while you're planning my comeback?'

Both their voices were raised now, his gruff one meeting her shrill one in mid-air and creating a cacophony of sound that made me want to cover my ears.

'Jack, I told you, it was an *accident*. There wasn't a *plan*. We argued, yes, and he went to grab me, so I pushed him. I didn't mean for him to fall!'

'If it was an accident, why did you ask him to meet you on the roof?' My voice was shaking; so were my hands, and my legs, and it felt like every single nerve in my body, too, but the question had come out before I'd had time to think it through. I had never believed the cliché that the air could turn cold. Turns out it was true, though. I shivered, waiting to see her response. She spun to face me and roughly grabbed my arm in her hand.

'How do you know I *asked* him to meet me *anywhere*?' she snarled.

I twisted my face into a pained expression, knowing I'd said too much, but not really sure that I had anything left to lose. Whatever she was going to do, she was going to do. Nothing I could say could get us out of this now.

'I saw the emails,' I said, meeting her stare.

'What are you talking about? There are no emails.'

'There *were* no emails,' I corrected her. 'You deleted them, but we got them back. You were right: if anyone could clear Frankie, it's us. The ones who love him. Who really care.' I noticed that my voice was no longer shaking.

She turned back to Jack, venom written all over her face. *Isn't it funny*, I thought, *that someone so beautiful can be so ugly?* As she spun round, something caught my eye. I didn't know how I hadn't seen it earlier, but before she could say a word it all just *clicked*.

'It was hers,' I said. 'The blood on the shirt. The reason

they couldn't match it definitively to Evan is because it wasn't his. It was hers.' I pointed to the bandage on her arm, the spot where a pool of red had clearly seeped through. 'I'm guessing you and Evan fought on the roof, Molly, and he hurt you? It must have still been bleeding on Monday, when you went back to the studio and planted the shirt, to make sure Frankie went down for the murder – but you didn't realize until after the police found it. That's why she didn't want you to go to the police, Jack. She heard there was blood on the shirt, and she knew it must be hers, and she *had* to stop them looking into the idea that he was being set up.' I thought of something else. 'She had a bandage on at my interview, but it didn't even click! How did I not think of that before? I'm right, aren't I?'

Molly looked at me blankly. 'What shirt?'

'Oh, give it up, Molly,' Jas said. 'We know you planted the shirt.'

'How would I have –'

Jas interrupted her before she could finish the sentence. 'Monday morning, when you were meant to be doing the interviews. We know you lied about the accident. I rang British Transport Police while we were waiting outside – sounded like a complete idiot when they didn't know what I was talking about. Nothing involving a motorcyclist in this area at all. But, hey, you weren't in this area, were you? You were at Albany Road, planting Frankie's shirt after Georgia left it here. You tripped the alarms, tipped off the police. That's why they searched the place again.'

'Jack, do you believe that?' she asked, turning to him. 'Have you seen the emails, too?'

279

'No,' he said. 'But I know they're telling the truth, Mol.'

Jas nudged my shoulder hard, raised her eyebrows, mouthed, *Do. It.*

I pressed the keys as quickly as I could, but I wasn't fast enough. Molly threw herself at Jack, award raised high above her head and a snarl contorting her face, and as they collided he was launched towards me, knocking the phone hard out of my hand before I could dial the final nine.

My fumbling fingers were pressing all over the screen as it fell, and the last thing I saw before my legs gave way under Jack's weight, and my head hit the bedframe, was the message I'd ignored from my dad.

Hope you're having a nice night?

TRACK TWENTY-EIGHT

I didn't know I'd blacked out until I woke up to find Jas standing over me, switching between hysterical screaming and terrified silence in the space of a second.

'Oh thank GOD! Jack, she's awake.'

I tried to turn my head in the direction she was looking, but it hurt too much, so I resigned myself to lying completely still. I heard the click of what sounded like handcuffs, and then Jack was standing over me, too, his face deathly white, his lips bitten and red with the rush of blood.

'Are you all right?'

'I think so . . .' My voice was hoarse and unsure, but it didn't hurt to speak. 'How long have I been down here?'

'Seconds, Harri. Don't be dramatic.' Jas was grinning now, relief flooding her features as she crouched down beside me.

'Do you think you can sit up?'

I tried to nod but winced at the effort. 'I think so . . . my head hurts, but . . .'

'Do it *slowly*, Jas,' Jack pleaded and, of all the things I should have been thinking in that moment, my first thought was how strange it was to hear him saying Jas's name.

She must have loved that, I thought, but from looking at her face it wasn't clear if she'd heard it at all. With Jas's help, I inched upward until I was sitting with my back against the wall. That was when I saw her. Handcuffed to a rickety chair in the corner of the room, Molly looked defeated.

'Where did you get handcuffs?' I asked, and Jack sank to the ground, joining me and Jas.

'*That's* your question?'

I shrugged, ignoring the pain.

'Someone threw them onstage once, I guess. Thank God for teenage girls. Molly brought a box of stuff back here after a gig, and *you* emptied that box of stuff so it ended up in the middle of the floor. A true example of teamwork.'

'And that girl will never know what her handcuffs did for you,' Jas said.

Although my head was pounding and I had no idea what was going to happen next, I felt calm. Happy even. I began to laugh. It started as a bubble in my chest, just a giggle at first, which quickly rose to a booming kind of laugh that made my whole body shake.

These fans are magic, I thought. *These brilliant girls, who thought it would be a laugh to bring handcuffs to a concert, maybe just saved us all. Even when we're not trying, we're making the world a better place because of how we love them. I wish I could tell them all about this.*

But that, I knew, could never happen.

'Why was it me?' I asked Jas, and she raised an eyebrow.

'Is that the whole question?'

I pulled a face that let her know exactly what I thought of her sarcasm in that moment.

'Why was it so obvious that it had to be me that came in? I get why it couldn't be Kyle, or Jack, or George – so many reasons why any of them would be a bad idea – but why was it so obvious to you that I should go?'

I didn't really know why I was asking, especially when I still couldn't think of an answer that would make me feel better. I just wanted to know the truth.

'Oh my God. Are you joking?'

I shook my head, and grimaced at the pain.

'Don't move, idiot,' she warned, but her voice was full of affection. 'It had to be you because from out there I could protect you.'

My jaw dropped, just a little, but enough to make her smile. 'What?'

'Did you seriously think I'd send you into danger, Harri? Just a "see you later, go and find the evidence, we'll wait here"?'

I shrugged, again forgetting that would hurt. 'Well, you did! Sort of?'

Jas rolled her eyes. 'If I was out there, I could warn you when she was coming. From out there, I could pull you out if I needed to. I have to be in *control*, Harri. I couldn't do that from in here. Anything could have happened to you, and I wouldn't know.'

I pulled her into my side, not even caring about the pain this time.

'That's the sweetest thing anyone has ever done for me, Jas.'

She lightly tapped my leg. 'Good. Let's never do it again.'

'All right, cute love-in, but can someone undo these damn things? I'm not going to hurt you.' Molly's voice had lost all sense of edge, but she was trying, I knew, to sound like she was in control.

'You've already hurt us,' Jack said, not looking in her direction. 'I'm not giving you the slightest chance to do it again.'

'So what? You just run off back to Frankie and let him get away with it? He hurt you, too!'

He turned to face her now, his eyes full of fire in a way completely different from all the other times I'd seen him passionate about something.

'He did. But he hurt *only* me. Nobody else in my name. That's the difference. And, if I did run back to him, it would be none of your business. You're nothing to me, Molly. It's over.'

I didn't know how she wasn't crying, but she remained stoic and silent.

'How did you get Evan's DNA on the shirt?' I asked. For some reason, I thought it would be my dad's first question.

'Seriously? It was an *accident*. I didn't rip the hair from his head if that's what you're implying. It must have been on my coat from when we fought.'

So it was hair, then. At this point, knowing that didn't make me feel better. It changed nothing, after all.

'What, and you plucked it off and put it on the shirt when you hid it?'

'I won't let you paint me as a murderer!'

You are, though, I thought. *And that doesn't answer my question.* Her lack of a proper response told me I was probably right.

'What happens now?' I asked, turning back to Jas and Jack.

'The police are on their way,' Jas said. 'Gem had already called them as soon as she read what was in those emails. When you stopped replying, she guessed something was wrong.'

Of course she had. I closed my eyes and let out a breath. The way these girls had never once let me down would always feel like a miracle.

'Will we get in trouble?' I asked.

'I won't let that happen,' Jack said; at the same time Jas was saying, 'I don't know.'

To their credit, the police were quite gentle as they guided us into the back of the cars – Jas and me in one, Jack in another – to go to the station where Kyle and Georgia were waiting. They'd been driven ahead, while the officers checked our injuries before finally deciding we didn't need a pit stop at the hospital. *Good.* That would just have been delaying the inevitable. I noticed that Jack's car was the only one with tinted windows. I guessed the police didn't want him to be seen going into a police station. That would start a whole new world of rumours.

I hadn't seen where they'd taken Molly. I hoped, though, that they wouldn't go easy on her. I wanted her to suffer, for Evan, and for Frankie, and for everything she'd ruined. *Whatever they do to her won't be enough*, I thought. But it was almost over.

We had to state our names for the tape. That was the part that made it feel real. Not Detective French, who'd led us into the interview room, nor the part where he asked if we thought we needed a lawyer. I hadn't known what to say to that, but Jas had asked what he thought, and he'd said from what he knew so far we were probably fine because we weren't minors. I knew it was supposed to have the opposite effect, but that made me feel worse. I wanted my dad to come and get me out of this.

'Will you stop us if you change your mind about that?' I asked, and his smile was kind rather than condescending.

'Of course I will. If it's verging on dangerous, it's not in my interest to question you without one, either. I want to reassure you, though: we're not treating you as suspects. We just want to hear your side of what happened.'

I decided that was probably OK.

'Where do you want us to start?' I asked, and he opened his hands wide in a gesture that said, *You decide*.

So I began at the beginning. Every now and then, he would stop me, and ask for clarity, or interrupt with a question. I told him about gate-crashing press conferences, and screwing up interviews, and recordings taken in secret in expensive bars.

'And then you entered her house?' he asked when we got

there, but it didn't sound like he was trying to accuse me of anything. It sounded like he was just looking for the truth, and his voice was gentle and matter-of-fact all at once, in a way that made me feel like telling it would be fine. I started to explain why we had to, but a commotion in the corridor pulled our attention. Doors ricocheted off walls as they were thrown open far too quickly, and the too-loud voices of the police officers echoed along the corridor.

'That's him, isn't it?' Jas asked. 'That's Frankie. They're bringing him in.'

Detective French's nod was almost imperceptible.

'Why are they shouting?' she continued, and he shook his head, presumably to stop her going any further down the line of questioning I knew was already forming in her head.

'Because if we got this wrong . . . if it was really nothing to do with him, that is *not good*. Let's carry on, please.' His voice drew our focus back.

'Why is he here?' It was me that spoke this time. Why, I wondered, did they have to get his hopes up like this? Why couldn't they wait until they were absolutely sure, then pull him from wherever they were holding him once we knew he'd never be going back? I couldn't let myself imagine how it would feel if this didn't work.

'More questions,' Detective French said. 'We have to make sure that his story about what happened with Jack matches yours.'

'But he doesn't know our story,' Jas said, confused.

'Exactly.'

There was a quick rap on the door, and the officer who'd driven us here put her head round the frame.

'Labs came back,' she said, and I sat up straighter. 'The blood belongs to Molly Jenkins.'

Detective French nodded. 'All right. I think that's everything we need.'

He stood, his chair screeching as its legs scraped along the floor, and made for the door. We didn't move for a moment after he left, not sure what we were supposed to do next. Was that it? Could we leave? I hated myself for thinking it, but it felt like a bit of an anticlimax. After all this, I wanted to know how it ended. I wanted to know if we'd cleared Frankie's name. That he'd be free.

The door opened again, and the officer from the car came back into the room, her calm face putting me at ease once more. 'OK?'

'We're fine,' Jas answered for both of us, and the officer gestured for us to stand.

'How are you feeling?' This time she addressed me directly, and I moved my neck from side to side. The pain was lessening, even if it was definitely still there.

'I'm all right.'

'You can wait outside,' the police officer said, guiding us back through the heavy door to the cold, empty waiting room. I wondered where they'd taken the others. I chanced a look over my shoulder, despite the pain, but nothing seemed untoward. The corridor was empty, all the doors closed. *Isn't it strange*, I thought, *how everything can look completely normal, but behind one of those doors they're questioning actual Frankie Williams?* I closed my eyes, just for a second. I couldn't decide if I wanted to forget this ever happened or remember it forever.

'Will we get in trouble? Detective French didn't really . . . say,' Jas asked, and I'd never heard her voice so thin. I had not once, I realized, seen Jas scared before today. She'd always been the strong one. Jas was always fine.

Check in on the strong ones, I thought. *Because nobody ever does, and sometimes they need a hand, too.*

I took her fingers in mine and squeezed. I hoped she felt everything I couldn't say in front of the police officer.

'Not if you're right.' Her voice was ominous, and then she was gone.

We sank into the cold plastic chairs without discussing it. We were silent for a long time. I wondered what Jas was thinking, but didn't ask. It felt like the silence was too heavy for a voice to break through.

Me? I was thinking that I'd long believed loving a boyband brought with it a wealth of transferable skills.

That I'd never imagined solving a murder would be one of them.

TRACK TWENTY-NINE

After

I remember reading somewhere that fifty per cent of the cells in your body are not your own. I can't remember the context, but that was the gist of it – that half of all the cells inside you are not made of *you* at all. *You can't choose what you're made up of*, I think, *but if that's true then my fifty per cent must belong to him*. I try to remember if I ever knew the science, or if I'd heard it told just like that and stored it away in the ever-growing mind palace of thoughts I could project on to Frankie Williams. In this moment, it seems more logical than anything I ever came across in a textbook, despite making absolutely no sense.

We wait.

It feels like one of those stop-motion montages you see in arty films. Every time I look up, it seems as if Jas is standing somewhere else. The sky gets darker. The hands on the clock move, but I don't notice it happening. Each time the door swings open, the air that hits gets colder. Jas sits back down.

'We could just get up and go, right?' I say, knowing I'm

not going to. 'They say that all the time on police dramas. If you're not actually under arrest – if you're just helping with enquiries – you're free to leave at any time.'

Jas laughs. I'd missed that deep cackle.

'Harri, stop being dramatic. We're sitting in the waiting room. Nobody actually cares that we're here. Yes, we could walk out any time we want. Shall we?'

'Did you know that fifty per cent of the cells in your body are not your own?' I ask instead of answering, as I link my arm through hers and snuggle closer.

'Yes . . .'

'I think mine must belong to –'

'Not what it means at all,' she interrupts.

'You don't know what I was going to say,' I argue, but she does. She always does.

'This is not another opportunity for you to bang on about how inevitable it is that we're here for him. Not this time. He doesn't defy *science*, Harriet. Weren't you almost a scientist? You should know that. He's not that powerful.'

'I was a terrible almost-scientist, but it *is* inevitable,' I say, only half joking, and she hesitates before replying.

'Yeah . . . it kind of is.' Then another half-beat of silence before she whispers, 'But not because of *cells*, you weirdo.'

We wait. The sky gets darker still. Jas stands and sits. The clock hands move. I can't take the silence.

'What a story,' I say, just to break it.

'Long story,' Jas replies. 'I'd like to know how it ends now.'

If this was one of those arty movies, what happens next

could not be more perfectly timed. Maybe, I think, those arty movies would make sure it happened *any other way* than the way it actually does, because it feels a little too clichéd. The door separating the waiting area from the rest of the police station swings towards us with a creak. The harsh light softens. Perhaps someone steps in front of the bulb, I don't know, but in a moment the whole room is washed with a warm yellow glow. Detective French walks out, smiling.

'Are we done?' Jas asks, and I think she's trying to sound empowered, but she actually just sounds tired.

'You can go whenever you like, girls,' he says. 'I just thought that, since you got him off, you'd like to meet him.'

And then he steps out of the light, and Frankie Williams steps into it.

⊙

How We Met – Frankie

We met in a bookshop. I had always dreamed of meeting a cute boy in a bookshop (actually, I had always dreamed it would be you) and now here we were, your back to me in the fiction section, hand reaching out for a fat paperback whose cover I couldn't quite see. Not that it mattered. There wasn't a single book on those shelves as interesting to me as you were.

It sounds weird, and please don't judge me when I say this, but I recognized your earlobe, or at least the way your hair fell round the closely hugging silver hoop. We'd been obsessed with that hoop when it first began to appear in photographs, a hole in your skin where there wasn't one before, just another reminder that there would always be more things to notice about Frankie Williams.

'Good book, isn't it?' I gestured to the one now in your hands. I'd never read it, didn't know what I was planning to say if you asked about its nuances, or characters, or twists. You turned, and when your eyes met mine they were exactly like I'd expected. You smiled. I locked my knees in place just in time so they wouldn't buckle under your gaze. I don't think you noticed.

'Haven't read it yet,' you said, and I laughed like you'd made the funniest joke I'd ever heard, which, I'm sorry, you really hadn't.

'It's good,' I said again, invested now in this book I still didn't know the title of, hoping that if you bought it you would agree with my completely uninformed opinion; would remember the girl in the bookshop who introduced you to the greatest thing you'd ever read. It was still in your hand as you walked towards the next shelf, smiling over your shoulder at me.

'Thanks.'

'You're welcome,' I said, proud at the way my voice didn't shake.

We met at a party, inching towards the end of the night, and as soon as I saw you standing at the bar, your face twisted away from me, but your body recognizable even so, I was amazed that we'd been sharing this space for hours and I hadn't felt it. I'd always imagined I'd be able to feel it. I stood beside you and picked up a menu, which, being the kind of party where the drinks are designed to fit a theme, had about three things on it. I knew I'd been staring at it aimlessly, trying to figure out my next move, for far too long, when I felt your eyes on me, and looked up to be greeted with a smug but kind smile.

'Interesting menu?'

'It kind of is actually.'

You took the menu out of my hands, placed it down on the bar and held out one of yours to be shaken.

'I'm Frankie.'

'I know.'

You laughed. 'You're meant to tell me your name.'

'Harri,' I said, aware that I was blushing, aware that you were kind enough not to mention it.

'So what brings you here, Harri?' you asked, taking slightly longer than would have been considered usual to let go of my hand.

'I'm an intern here.'

'We never get to meet the interns.' Your face lit up, and I'd never been prouder to be at the bottom of the food chain, the people you never get to meet because we're far too unimportant to ever be in the same room as you.

Until now, I reminded myself. Don't pretend you didn't take this job just a tiny bit because you were hoping it would lead to this moment.

'Well, *we're* not important. Not like you. You're the reason we're all here.'

Your friend appeared at your shoulder, then, because for this moment to have lasted any longer would have ruined it. It had to be brief. Had to leave me wanting more, but then any moment with you would have left me wanting more.

'What's taking so long?' he asked, a glance between us where our hands rested on the bar, close, not quite touching.

'I should go,' you said, your eyes still on me. 'It was nice to meet you . . . Harri.'

'You too,' I said. As you walked away, I thought about how nice would never even come close.

We met on the Tube, somewhere towards the tail end of rush hour, still busy enough that the passengers blurred into one, but not so busy that I wouldn't notice the wing of a butterfly tattoo creeping out from the sleeve of your sweater, hand holding the pole at almost perfect eye level to my seat, smaller than imagined.

(Because I had imagined.)

I had to stop myself from reaching out; from grazing the hem of the sleeve, the raised edge of the tattoo. That would be weird, right?

I pulled my hand back. Perhaps you felt the movement because you turned, and looked down, and when your eyes met mine they were nothing like I'd expected at all. I smiled, and thought that in another universe it could be just that –

just a girl smiling at a boy she thought was cute. Of course it wasn't, and you could tell from my expression that I knew. It was you who said hello first. I didn't trust myself to start the conversation, so I waited and you obliged.

'Hi.'

'Hi,' I replied. Hardly an inspiring beginning, but I like to hope you knew the weight that one word carried.

'I'm a huge fan,' I said next.

When you came back with, 'Well, I'm a huge fan of our fans,' it somehow didn't sound cheesy at all. We pulled into the station and it was your stop. Of course it was your stop. I asked for a photo because I couldn't think of a quick enough way to stop myself, and you said, 'With pleasure,' just as the doors slid open. I treasure it above most things. It came out blurry.

We met backstage at gigs, and walking down streets you'd never have reason to be on, and sometimes in my own kitchen at the end of a particularly exhausting night, exactly where I needed you to be right in that moment.

We met in a police-station waiting room. You'd just been cleared of murder.

Because of us.

I'd imagined it so many ways.

But never like this.

TRACK THIRTY

He looks so tired and so beautiful. That's the order that the thought comes in: tired first and then beautiful, and I'm surprised. I never imagined anything would prevail over his beauty.

I see the moment he turns it on – that fool's-gold charm that's the reason we're here in the first place. A light behind the eyes, a slight shift of the hips to a position that's only subtly different, but allows him to bring a completely changed energy. He breathes in, and that's the transformation complete: the fragile boy in the cold waiting room with the dark circles under his eyes becomes Frankie Williams from Half Light. Supernova. I watch it happen and still it disarms me. I know it isn't real, and I'm still blindsided by all the things I feel for this character he plays. I wish I could tell him he doesn't have to do that. I wish I could tell him he'd better hold on hard to the real parts of himself while he can. That he's fooling no one.

I don't, though. Because he's still Frankie Williams and because of history, and nostalgia, and love of the kind you build hopes and friendships and identities around; because of all those things, and because he's so beautiful, and so tired, when he reaches out his hand and takes a step towards us, I begin to cry.

I'm crying because I'm exhausted, and because we did it. Because *we specifically* did it. Me and Jas, Alex and Gemma, and even Georgia, using all the things we know how to do best to try to get him out. Becca, in a bar she'd never been to before. The girls in the crowds. The girls on the internet.

'We'd do anything,' we said, and fate said, '*Prove it.*'

I'm crying because we proved it.

He thinks I'm crying because I'm overwhelmed to finally meet him, and I let him.

'Can I?' He twists to speak to the police officer, who nods, and then Frankie is embracing both of us at once, pulling us into his arms. He says nothing until he lets us go, never removing his hands from our arms.

'Thank you.'

'Nothing to thank us for,' Jas says. 'We just did what was right.'

'Most people wouldn't,' he counters, and we have to agree. No, they wouldn't. I'm not sure if that makes us special or stupid, and perhaps by now it doesn't really matter. We're done.

'Can you forgive me?' he asks, and it's me who speaks this time, finding I almost mean it when I say,

'Nothing to forgive.'

'There is,' he presses, and I wonder if thinking you're

doing the right thing can count for something, even when it all falls down.

'We forgive you.'

I speak for both of us. I remind myself that forgiving and forgetting are not the same thing at all. I remind myself that forgiving doesn't mean we have to keep pretending. I remind myself that sometimes making a person feel better is more important than telling the whole truth. I don't know, when I say that we forgive him, if it's the whole truth.

'Are you going to tell everyone?' he asks, and I hate that we have to be the ones to stand here and witness the heartbreak on his face, not through fear of everyone hating him, but through fear that he's let us down. We don't need to make it worse for him, or for the girls who have only ever had faith that he was good, and kind, and right.

'No. We're not going to tell anyone,' I promise, and this time I'm sure of my words.

He rubs his eyes, smiles weakly. 'I just wanted everyone to believe this was real.'

'I think believing it and feeling it are different things,' Jas interjects, and the love I have for this brilliant woman floods my body, replaces the tension with calm. She always knows exactly what to say. How did I ever imagine she wouldn't?

'I think we felt it,' she continues, 'and maybe that's enough.'

The police officer hovering behind Frankie's left shoulder takes this as his cue to leave.

'Look after yourselves,' he says, and it sounds comforting

and disapproving all at once. The door squeaks, and he's gone.

'No more police,' I say.

Frankie sinks into one of the hard plastic seats. He's free. At any point, he can walk out into the evening, no longer shackled by the law, but forced, I suppose, to face his new reality. That Evan is dead. That Evan had planned to betray him. That Molly – someone he trusted, someone he loved – has killed his best friend. When I think about it like that, I guess the chairs might not seem like the least comfortable option. I sit down on one side of him, and Jas takes my cue and sinks into the seat on his right.

'Does Jack hate me?' he asks.

'I don't know if he hates you,' I answer, sure that the answer is not a simple yes or no. It's somewhere in between. I have no doubt that Jack loves Frankie; that maybe he always will. But love and hate are not mutually exclusive. The last twenty-four hours alone have taught me that.

'I doubt it,' Jas supplies, and I'm glad because I'd been trying to find a way to stop myself adding, '*Probably.*'

'I need to see him.'

'You do,' I say. 'He was here. I don't know where they took him, but . . . he was here. He fought for you. I don't know if that helps.'

'I was going to tell him.'

'We know,' I say, not quite believing it.

'No, I mean . . . that day. I was going to tell him. I sat on the stairs inside Albany Road, and I pulled his number up

300

on my phone, and I tried to do it. But I couldn't make myself dial. I just . . . wasn't ready.'

'That's where you went?' I ask, remembering the way Frankie had disappeared from Gemma's screen. 'When you walked out of the studio? To call Jack?'

'Is there anything you *don't* know?'

So much, I think.

'What'll happen now?' Jas asks, and Frankie finally looks up from his lap; looks right at her. I know her well enough to recognize the flutter as their eyes meet. She hides it so deftly, but I know it. I feel it for her.

'They called Rich to come and get me. I guess we have to talk about it. About what I did. And how Evan is dead. Because of me.'

A strangled sound escapes his throat, and he drops his head into his hands. He looks absolutely shattered. We let him sit for a while, breath laboured and body shaking. I want to tell him it isn't because of him. I want to tell him that Evan is dead because Molly killed him – nothing else. I want to. I really want to.

I can't.

'I meant what'll happen now with the band,' Jas whispers after a few moments, and he sits up, slides one hand into mine, and takes hers with the other.

'I have no idea.'

The door does not so much open as succumb to Rich throwing his whole weight at it as he hurtles into the waiting area, Scarlett barely a step behind. Frankie doesn't stand, even as Rich skids to a stop in front of us. I loosen my grip and his immediately tightens. I think I should, but I do not let go of his hand.

'Frankie,' Scarlett says, and the wobble of her voice makes me look up from her killer patent boots just in time to see her burst into tears. I let go of his hand as he flies towards her.

'I didn't know,' she says, and he rubs her back as he assures her.

'I know you didn't.'

They repeat the whole exchange twice, three times, and she's crying and Rich stands there as if he has no idea how to navigate this situation, or how to act like a human being, both of which are probably true. I look at Jas with a *maybe we should leave them to it* raise of the eyebrows, and she gives a slight shake of her head, which I think means *imagine how awkward it'll be if we get up and walk out now.* She has a point. They pull apart and Frankie finally turns to Rich. In this moment, he is terrified, I know. He took the thing they all built together and he tore it down so spectacularly, just by trying to keep it alive.

'Did I ruin it?' Frankie asks.

'Yeah. You did.'

'Can we fix it?'

'Do you want to?' Rich asks.

'Of course I do.'

'Well, then we can,' Rich says, 'but I don't know if we should.'

I wonder if they've forgotten we're there, and just as I think it Frankie is twisting his body back towards us and gesturing for us to stand. My throat feels tight and my legs trembly.

'This is . . .' Frankie begins, pulling us both forward by the wrists, then stops. 'I didn't even ask your names. Why didn't I even think to ask your names?'

'Because it didn't matter,' Jas says, and reaches out to shake Rich's hand. 'Jas Sidana, and this is Harri Lodge.'

Didn't matter? I think. *Yes, it did. Of course it did. We risked* everything *for him, and he didn't even ask our names.*

I can hardly believe I hadn't noticed until now.

Jas gestures in my direction and I step forward, taking Rich's outstretched hand.

'Thank you,' Scarlett says, and Rich seems to remember that he's supposed to be polite, and grateful.

'Thank you,' he echoes, dazed, shaking my hand. 'At some point, I'd be very interested to know how you did it, but . . . thank you.'

'You're welcome,' I say.

He drops my hand more gently than he took it.

'The others are waiting,' he says, turning back to Frankie whose face flickers between relieved and terrified before he speaks.

'They want to see me?'

'They don't have a choice – they're under contract with you. But yes. Luckily they want to, too.'

'Even Jack?' Frankie asks, and his voice breaks. Scarlett drops her gaze to the ground. Jas clears her throat. We wait.

'Even Jack,' Rich replies.

'He doesn't hate me?' Frankie pushes, and now, finally, he is weeping. Finally he's feeling something.

I feel unexpectedly relieved. Because, if it was the thought of Jack hating him that broke Frankie, then at least a little of it must have been real, right? We hadn't put everything at stake for a complete fantasy.

'Of course he hates you,' Rich says, and Frankie's chest begins to convulse. 'Because he loves you so much, you idiot. You had it all and you almost lost it . . . for *what*? Isn't he the most important thing? Because he should be. You're so *stupid*.'

'He still loves me?' Frankie asks.

Scarlett huffs and says, 'So much, you fool. Jack hating you is the least of your worries. What about them?'

She waves a hand in the general direction of where Jas and I are standing, and Frankie looks over, confused. 'They don't hate me . . .'

I shake my head because no, I don't hate him.

'Not them,' Scarlett clarifies. 'People like them. The girls. What are they going to think when this all comes out?'

'We're not going to tell,' I promise her as Frankie drops his head into his hands.

'We can get them to sign NDAs,' Rich says, and if it's supposed to be of any comfort it does not land, because Frankie's head snaps up immediately.

'We're not going to do that. They *saved* me, Rich. This is not a business transaction.'

304

'Frankie, you know they have to,' says Scarlett firmly.

He doesn't respond. Instead, just closes his eyes. 'I can't believe how badly I messed this up.'

No, I think. *Neither can I.*

'Then let's do what we can to fix it.' Scarlett sounds defiant.

'What about Evan's family?' Frankie asks.

'What about them?' says Scarlett, her tone more gentle now.

'Are they ever going to speak to me again?'

He steadies himself as his knees start to buckle, and Scarlett reaches out and grips his arm.

'Frankie, this is *not* your fault. Your friendship with Evan was a *gorgeous* thing. I don't know how much they've told you, but he was so worried about *you*, and all the things this crazy bloody life was doing to you, and that's why he was meeting up with Molly that day. Because he loved you. And they love you. No matter what else Evan thought he wanted to do, or what else he thought was right, that doesn't change.'

'But if I'd done things differently . . . he'd be alive.'

His voice comes out in a whimper, thick with tears, and I want to turn away. *I shouldn't be witnessing this*, I think. *It's all too much from this close.*

'Maybe,' Scarlett says, soothing and firm at once. 'But you didn't, so you can't know that. If you'd done things differently, perhaps none of the brilliant things that made you and Evan what you were would have happened, either. That's not the thought you drive yourself crazy with, Frank. All you need to decide now is what you do next.'

'The car's here,' Rich says. 'All we have to do is walk out.'

Frankie lifts his head, nods and opens his arms, gesturing for Jas and me to come into them. To say goodbye. I sniff the collar of his shirt. Don't judge me. I just know it may be my final chance, and I've always wanted to know if he smelled like cinnamon and cloves, like fabric conditioner and flowers. He actually smells like days-old aftershave clinging to unwashed fabric. I realize I'm not surprised. He is only human. He squeezes our shoulders as he speaks, too quietly for his handlers to hear.

'Thank you,' he says.

Jas says, 'It was nothing.'

'It was *everything*.'

He unwraps his arm from round my back and I feel something end. They make for the door. Only Scarlett looks back. Smiles. I am so sad for her in that small movement of her mouth. Everything she loved has gone. *I know the feeling*, I try to tell her when I smile back.

But then they leave the room, and Jas is still standing next to me. They leave the room, and all the magic stays inside. They leave the room, and my best friend is still here.

So no, I don't know the feeling. Not everything I loved is gone.

Not even close.

TRACK THIRTY-ONE

We take a train back to Brighton in near silence. My hands are cold, and my eyes are heavy, and my mascara is halfway down my cheeks, but I can't bring myself to care. I have an essay due that I haven't even started. I wonder how I'm supposed to ever write about 'artist and brand management' in any kind of academic context now.

Why is brand identity important?

Well, I think, it's supposed to keep everyone safe and in their box, right? And yet an innocent man ended up dead. That went well. I make a mental note to check how many essays I can miss without failing the year. I think maybe I'll write a counterargument for that one. *Why is brand identity important? It isn't. It's completely toxic.*

It's only as we walk from the station that I realize I've barely spared a thought for Stefan. How am I supposed to explain everything that has happened since I left his room as the sun came up, promising to return as soon as all this was done? I know he tries to understand, and he comes so close, but I find myself not wanting to explain to anyone who doesn't *absolutely* get it. Not when there are so many people in my corner who do.

'What are you thinking about?' Jas asks.

'Stef.'

She waggles her eyebrows and I laugh.

'Not like that, Jas!'

'Like what, then?'

'I don't know,' I admit. 'Like I know he isn't my big love story so . . . am I wasting my time? I don't want to tell him about this, you know? Aren't I meant to, if it's really something?'

'Harri, we're eighteen.'

'What does that mean?'

She stops walking.

'When you're our age, every love story can't be a huge romance, and maybe that's OK. Maybe he's meant to teach you something, or help you heal or whatever, or maybe he's just fit and he fancies you and that's as good a reason as any. Don't write him off just because he isn't your big love story.'

'How are you so wise about all these things?'

She grins. 'Romance novels.'

Obviously. It's just so classic Jas.

When the statement lands, we're both sitting on my single bed, surrounded by the kinds of self-care they don't tell you about in magazines – empty cans of sugary drinks, chocolate wrappers, old Half Light interviews. We'd realized pretty quickly that the latter were a form of self-sabotage, but every now and then one of us picks up the scrapbooks I've spent half a decade curating, waiting in a package from my parents when we returned, a note saying, 'We thought you might want to take these.'

We scratch briefly at the scab, just in time to stop it from completely healing. We're largely ignoring the new stuff: the photos of Molly being led from a police station in tears; of Jack and Frankie walking side by side, but pointedly not touching as they leave their house, heads down, faces serious. The press aren't telling the whole story, and I'm not sure if that's because they don't know it, or because Rich and Scar have made it go away somehow. Either way, I'm grateful. As far as the world is concerned, Molly killed Evan in some kind of freak accident. Her real crime, it's being reported, is that she tried to hide it. There's no mention of Jack, no mention of the way she tried to set Frankie up for the fall. An accident from all angles. It's completely implausible, but people seem to be buying it. I can't decide if I'm glad we know the truth, or I wish we could forget it.

Jas's phone vibrates where it's tangled somewhere in the duvet, and she kicks half-heartedly until it bounces out, its screen lit up. I see Frankie's Twitter handle at the top of the screen.

'What's he saying? Is he allowed to tweet? I'm surpri– Oh God, it's a statement.'

Jas doesn't move. I pick up the phone and it's warm in my palm, as if it's about to explode.

'Read it to me?' she asks, and I shake my head.

'I don't think I can. I'm going to put it down and we can both read it, OK?'

I turn up the brightness and place the phone between us, the screenshots from his notes app filling the screen as Jas scoots closer.

'You ready?' she asks.

Obviously not.

I don't know how to begin this statement or how to say sorry that my actions put our fans in a position where they ever had to consider my innocence. I know I cannot blame myself for the things our former colleague Molly has done, but I've always felt a responsibility to protect the people who have given us so much, and recently I've exposed you to an ugly world that I never wanted you to have to see. For that I am sorry. I hope you can remember Half Light as we were before this, because trying to be those people you fell in love with, and to keep going for each and every one of you, is all that has ever mattered to me.

I also ended up irreversibly hurting my soulmate Jack. I don't want to go into details, because that's between us, but the last few weeks have been more of a challenge for our relationship than I ever could have imagined, and at this time we have decided to go our separate ways romantically, and to remain the best of friends, as we always were. Your support of our friendship has been the most extraordinary thing, and we'll always love you for it, but we need to do this part alone. I don't expect you to understand this, but I hope that you'll try, for him more than for me.

Most importantly, and most tragically, my best friend Evan has died. I can't help thinking that was because he was close to me, and for that I can never apologize enough. Nothing I can say can ever bring him back, but I will have only the best of things to say about Evan for the rest of my life.

I know you're all wondering what will become of the band and, while it breaks our collective heart as well as mine personally to say this, we've come to the mutual decision that it's time for Half Light to take an extended break. To continue performing as a band right now would not be positive for any of us, or for our fans. We'll be playing a 'goodbye for now' gig, with details to be released later this week. We really hope to see you there, and we can never thank you enough for all the support you've given us.
All my love, always,
Frankie x

'He didn't write that,' Jas says after a moment.
I agree entirely.

TRACK THIRTY-TWO

The articles get even more ridiculous after that, which I guess is not a shock, but still feels like it's *our* lives they're infringing on, *our* story they're twisting. The speculation is ludicrous, newspapers claiming everything from Frankie getting Molly pregnant, to Jack being the one to cheat, and with Evan of all people, which had forced Molly's hand. It's the most invasive, disrespectful, completely unbelievable pile of rubbish I have ever read. *If it feels like this for me, I can only imagine what it's like for Jack and Frankie.*

I hadn't really expected it, but it stings just slightly that they haven't been in touch.

'Someone should have checked we're OK,' I say, and Jas looks up from whatever she's reading on her phone and smiles.

'We don't need them. We've got each other.'

'What are you reading?' I ask.

'More tabloid crap speculation.'

'Interesting?'

'I'll read it to you,' she says.

'*After a week behind bars for a crime he didn't commit, Half Light heart-throb Frankie Williams has been released without charge as manager Molly Jenkins admits to killing Evan Byrd in an argument that went too far. According to reports, Molly arranged to meet Byrd to discuss a misunderstanding relating to the band. Unable to resolve it, they fought, leading to Evan's accidental death. Miss Jenkins is now in police custody, awaiting sentencing, and tragic hero Frankie Williams has been released back into the arms of now ex-boyfriend Jack and his adoring public. What did Evan know that had Molly so rattled? What could Frankie possibly have done that would threaten Half Light to the extent that Jenkins was prepared to kill to keep the secret?*'

'Actually kind of close,' I say as she finishes.

'Yeah. Definitely the closest yet.'

'They really don't know it wasn't real. Jack and Frankie.'

'So it seems.'

'I don't know how I feel about that,' I admit.

'Nice to have one up on the press,' Jas says, 'but I know what you mean. It feels dishonest of us. Like we should be telling people.'

'We shouldn't,' I say, the conviction coming as the words do. 'We promised. Life is hard enough, Jas. This has all been hard enough. Let's give the fandom this one thing. Let's allow them to believe it was real, if only for a little while.'

I turn back to the article before she can answer, but the way she slides her hand over mine tells me she agrees.

'The things we could tell them,' I say as Jas puts down the

phone. 'Like . . . the stories we could take back. It's like we're travellers, and we've been on this adventure, and our families and friends are going to be waiting for us when we get home, expecting all the details . . . and I don't want to share.'

'Why not?'

'I'm not sure,' I admit. 'Kind of because I want to keep it just for us. But also . . . I don't want to ruin it for everyone else. It's not our place. I get what Alex meant now. Why she didn't tell us about Frankie and Jack. I don't want it to have to be us.'

'Not all of it would be ruining it, though,' Jas says. 'There were some really wonderful bits, right? We could tell them those.'

'Like Jack in my bedroom . . .'

'Hugging Frankie in the police station.'

'*Sniffing* Frankie in the police station,' I correct her.

'Weirdo.'

'I just thought it might be my only chance, and that's always the first question people ask, isn't it? *What did he smell like?*'

'Like stale aftershave and *prison* . . . might not be the answer they want.'

'Doesn't matter. It is the answer.'

'I don't want to forget any of it,' she admits quietly.

'Then let's make sure we don't.'

All the things we could take back to the fandom, but won't

1. That Kyle has a whisky-and-honey air freshener. It would be fun to watch them zoom in on photos of his

car, and work out which brand it was, and sell that baby out. But I don't want to tell them what his car smells like because then I'd have to talk about sitting in it outside Molly's house, no idea that what we thought we were getting into, and what was actually about to happen, were not the same thing at all.

2. The look on Jack's face when he talks about Frankie, close up and unfiltered. We've all seen it a million times, of course, but, when the cameras are turned off and the studio lights give way to daylight, it changes. I didn't know that until I saw it happen. I didn't know how it looked, at such close proximity, when a person's in love and is trying not to be; holding on when there's nothing real to hold on to. Scared and hopeful all at once. I don't think I could properly describe it if I wanted to.

3. The way that Frankie-in-person is nothing like the man we thought we knew. That anyone who ever tries to emphasize the point that you can never really know a celebrity should use this man as a case study. When he realizes he doesn't need to turn it on any more, that there's really no point, and he fades back into Frankie-the-human, he becomes less than what we thought, and so much more. More fragile. More raw. More and less beautiful all at once. Younger and older, more and less Frankie Williams, at exactly the same time. An enigma, and a daydream, and a man who hasn't showered for days, in a police-station waiting room, smelling nothing like we'd spent all that time imagining he would.

315

4. So, when they ask what happened with Kyle, we'll say the conversation was brief but lovely. His car was warm when the night was cold. Air freshener? Sorry, we can't remember.

5. When they ask about the way Jack feels for Frankie, we'll tell them they see it exactly as it is, in magazines, and on the internet. The way he lights up when Frankie is near, and someone snaps a picture? That's real. He loves him. It's as simple as that. Hasn't that always been obvious?

6. When they ask about Frankie, and about the way we met, we'll tell them it was a dream come true. That he was just as charming as we'd always thought, and as gorgeous, and mysterious, and kind. He was as much as we'd imagined, and more. An enigma. A daydream. What did he smell like? I didn't think to check. I'm sure, though, that the answer is *delicious*.

Jas finally leaves after three days of being right by my side at all hours. She says she's going because she can't ignore her responsibilities any more, but I know that, if she's feeling anything like the way I am, this is becoming too intense. I desperately need a break from thinking about Frankie, and the boys, and what happens next and, as long as Jas is here, that can't happen. But then she goes and I miss her immediately, and I have no reasons left to avoid reality – the other reality, I mean, where life is not police stations and boys in bands with tired smiles, which is how I find myself knocking on Stefan's door at 9 p.m. on a

Tuesday, hoping he can tell I'm sorry, and scared of what this could be because I think it could be good.

He opens the door with a confused expression on his face, like anyone who bothered to knock rather than just barging right in must be bringing bad news, but he softens when he sees me, and I know immediately we'll be OK.

'Harriet Lodge . . .' His voice is slow, reprimanding in a way that drips with affection. 'Fancy seeing you here.'

'I'm sorry,' I say, and he raises an eyebrow and steps aside to let me in.

'You don't have to be sorry. But I'm glad you are.'

I perch on the edge of his bed, and he joins me, his expression tentative, like he isn't sure what this is, or at least what I want it to be. We're quiet.

'Are you OK?' he asks eventually, and I turn to look at him, smile, and find that I really am. I'm fine. The whole world fell apart, and we kept on living. *Doesn't that mean they weren't the whole world after all?*

'I'm good, really.'

'Harri, what are you doing here?'

'We proved Frankie's innocence,' I tell him, and he gestures to his laptop, open on the bed, where an article telling him a not-quite-true version of what happened is on the screen.

'I know. Just because you weren't talking to me didn't mean I stopped paying attention.'

'Stef, that's really sweet.'

He places a hand on my knee, holds it there for a second

317

and then retracts it, as if he isn't sure what he's allowed to do any more.

'I'll say it one more time. I like you a lot, Harri. I thought we were getting somewhere, then you pulled a vanishing act that made me feel like I'd got it completely wrong. I can't compete with him, and I'm not going to try. I was happy to wait until all this was over, but now it is and you still didn't come so . . .'

'I'm here now,' I say. 'I'm here now, and he wasn't who we thought he was, and it's over. It's really over. I promise.'

He nods and tilts his head towards mine, stopping just shy of touching. I understand that the next move has to be mine.

'Are you going to tell me what happened?' he asks.

'Later,' I say, and close the gap between us.

OUTRO

Some people have been queuing since the early hours of the morning. Some were scoping out the gig venue last night. We, though, had not felt the need. We arrive just as the doors are thrown open and the crowds surge. We're in no rush.

Isn't it cool to be late to your own party? Because this *is* *our* party.

My rallying call in the group chat had worked perfectly, and almost the whole gang is here, flown in from all over the planet to say goodbye, and thank you, and no hard feelings. We talked a big game about just walking away, but that was false bravado. We would not have missed this for the world. They're live-streaming the show globally for the fans who couldn't make it. In bedrooms in Japan and Australia, fans will be woken by alarms in the middle of the night for one last performance. Over drinks in Italy, people we'll never meet will join us for this last farewell. Gemma is watching from her desk in LA. I hate that she's alone for this, but know that she isn't *really* alone. Nobody who presses play on the stream will be. We're in this together, one last time.

I feel a hand on my shoulder the moment we enter the arena. It's as if she's been waiting, which, I assume, she has. Scarlett looks much more poised than the last time I saw her, no tear tracks on her cheeks, no smudges in her eyeliner. We smile in the way that people do when they've seen each other vulnerable, but neither of us mentions it. She doesn't look sad, but maybe that's because she's good at twisting the narrative to suit her. She works in PR, after all.

'Harri,' she says, pulling me into a hug that takes me by surprise. 'Rich asked me to look for you guys. He wants you to come up.'

'Up?' I ask, one eye on my friends ahead of me, making sure not to lose them in the crowd.

'To VIP.'

'I don't know . . .' I begin, half gesturing towards my friends in a way I hope conveys that I've come here to be with them. To say goodbye to a time in our lives, but not to each other. To see this out together.

'Just for a little bit, at least,' she sort of pleads, and then Alex is at my shoulder.

'Harri. Go. We'll be here.'

I nod as Jas is pushed towards me, and Scarlett takes off. We follow, past gawping fans we've never met and people we vaguely know, stopping in front of a heavy red door.

'You ready?' she asks, and I have no idea what I'm supposed to be ready for.

'Let's go,' I say, and nobody notices that I haven't answered the question. She knocks, and Rich appears from behind the door, smiling when he sees us.

'Welcome,' he says, then steps out of my eyeline to reveal the whole crowd below.

It's the most beautiful thing I've ever seen. We're on a large balcony at the left-hand side of the stage. It's the kind we've always stared at and wondered what we had to do to get invited up with the friends, and the family, and the Important People that the rest of the fans took blurry photos of, just to prove they were in the same place. Insert ourselves into the middle of a murder plot, it seems. I'm not sure that it feels worth it.

Georgia appears and holds her arms out to hug me. It's strange, I think, the way an experience like the one we had can change everything. We'd accused her of being involved with a major crime, but then we'd won Frankie his freedom, and that trumps everything. She still wants to be friends. I hug her back tightly.

Moving away from where Georgia and Jas are now talking in whispers, I look down over the railing at the crowd below. Blond heads touch black, small hands hold larger ones, and in every group my eyes fall on I see all of us. The girl dancing even in the space between songs on the playlist could be Ruby. It could be Alex standing there, sipping a drink with a nonchalance that can't be learned, which I know will fall away the moment Half Light take the stage. The one taking photos of everyone is Jas, in another version of this universe. If another girl was telling this story. I know all of them, even though I've never seen most of them before in my life.

My eyes scan the arena for the *real* version: our *actual* friends. It's a general-admission show, so they could be anywhere, but it takes me only a second to spot them, somewhere towards the back of the crowd, where we have more space to dance.

'Screw this,' I mutter. I grab Jas's hand and start to pull her towards the exit.

'Where are you going?' Rich asks as he steps into my path. 'They're about to come out!'

'Where *are* we going?' Jas asks.

'We need to be with our friends,' I explain. 'It's all of us or none of us. That's the whole point. It's the whole reason this works.'

'But the boys want to see you, after the show,' Rich says as I pull the door open. To his credit, he makes no move to stop me.

'Well, you know where to find us,' I say, and I grab Jas's hand and we run to where our friends are waiting.

The thing about an arena like this one is that, when the lights fall, a bubble of magic follows straight behind, exactly the right size to cover the whole of the crowd; to hold them tightly through what's about to follow. Some people are immune, of course. Maybe they're tired, or sad, or just think that they're too cool to be there, but that's all right. That magic holds them anyway. At any point, they're allowed to change their mind and, when they do, they'll be in it with the rest of us. We'll be ready for them.

The thing about an arena like this one is that when the music starts, right from the very first note, there's an electric charge that binds us to one another, crackling in the spaces between us and connecting us hip to hip as we surge forward, and find room where there definitely wasn't any a moment before. Two hours earlier, you never would have been able to tell what was going to happen when the cold, hard floor is filled with people, and coats are shed to combat body heat, to reveal T-shirts bearing the faces of whoever is about to take the stage – another way to scream their names.

Before, if you'd stood on opposite sides of the room and called to one another, there's no chance you could have been heard – probably no chance you'd even be able to make out the features of the person trying to reach you – but the thing about an arena like this one is that, when the doors open and the crowd streams in, the space grows bigger and smaller all at once and, when you scream, everyone can hear you. That person on the other side is so far away, and maybe you still can't see their face, but you can feel them. You know they're there.

And then the show begins properly, and it's as if a shower of forgetting falls like rain. No more sadness, or anxiety, or self-conscious embarrassment about your dancing. All your fears are gone.

The thing about arenas like this one is that for the rest of the day they're nothing special at all. It's these hours that turn them from artless to astonishing, that people travel from all across the country to be a part of, that transform them from empty hangars in the middle of nowhere to the centre of the goddamn universe.

⊙

We see them before we hear any music. It's never been that way before – those boys have always been a fan of a dramatic entrance, a riff of a song they know we love, and screams that could power a city in response. But this time they walk out before the lights are even fully dimmed.

They take their spots, Kyle first, then Jack and, when Frankie shuffles into position behind the microphone, I find myself *praying* that this still works. Praying they have a little bit of magic left to give us, and that my tired heart has enough room to receive it, just for a few hours longer. Frankie raises his head, shifts backwards on his heels, smiles.

The place erupts.

Should we have forgiven him so easily? I want to scream. *Are we really going to let him off for lying to us all this time? For what he did to Jack? I don't know how to deal with this. Someone give me a freaking sign.*

Jas puts her hands on my shoulders and twists me towards her.

'Harri. Stop thinking so hard.'

'But . . .'

'Don't you want this? Cos in two hours it'll be over and we can't get it back.'

'I don't know what I want.'

The music kicks in. They're opening with 'Home Again' and, despite everything, that is still how it feels.

'Yeah, you do,' says Jas. 'You want to dance with me.'

I wonder if there's a limit to the amount of times I'll forget-and-then-remember that Jas is always right.

And so we do. We dance. Until the straps of our tops are

sliding off our shoulders, slick with sweat. Until our mascara is almost entirely gone from our lashes, wet with tears of sorrow and laughter and mostly joy. We hold hands, and we dance and scream and sing the words. It's for them, and for Evan, and for all the girls who wish they were here but can't be. I dance hard enough for every last one. I don't know if the boys can see us, from way up there. I don't care. In some ways, it feels as though they never really could. We were just faces in the crowd to them. Funny, I think, how from down here you can see so much more.

We jump, and sway, and raise our hands, and the whole time I'm trying not to think of childish games, where the people who lose are the ones still dancing when the music stops.

True to his word, Rich is waiting as the seemingly endless screams for the boys to come back finally fade, and the arena is transformed back to a cold hangar in a part of north London that you'd never go to if you didn't *really* have to.

'You coming?' he asks, and I gesture to the group standing around me, waiting to see what's going to happen.

'All of us?'

He does not hesitate. 'Of course all of you.'

I turn to face my friends, and am a little bit surprised at the jolt of adrenaline as I say, 'Hey, girls . . . wanna go to a party?'

He has his back to me when I first pick him out of the crowd. Not like it was difficult, because it never is.

Is it a real feeling, I wonder, *the way my body tells me when he's close, or do I feel like this because I already know he is? What comes first, the beating heart and shaking limbs, or the knowledge?*

It doesn't matter. The result will always be the same. No matter how much I want to be the girl who can walk away from all of this, he's still Frankie, and I'm still me. I'm just not there yet.

He's talking to Phoebe, heads bent close together, her smiling, his hand on the top of her arm.

'Is that happening again?' I ask Jas.

'God, I hope not. He needs to be on his own.'

'He doesn't know *how* to be on his own,' I say. 'He's been surrounded by people for so long. Being on his own is going to absolutely shatter him.'

'It's so sad, isn't it?' she says.

'What is?'

'All of it. His life. What it's become.'

She's right. I don't want to think about that tonight, though. This is a party, after all.

'I'm going over,' I say to Jas.

I walk up behind him, and take a moment for the way my hand reaches out towards him, like he's just another person I know; like I'm just casually saying hi, as if any interaction with Frankie could ever be casual. There's a shift, just as my fingers come to graze the scratchy fabric of his T-shirt, and I can't name it, but I feel it. I hold my hand where it hovers, somewhere between my body and his; just hold it there, trying to stop it shaking as the next thought comes.

This is where you leave him.

I don't know how I'm so sure, but I am. I spin on my heel before I can change my mind, turning back to Jas, who is looking at me like I've completely lost it. I grin at her, and suddenly I feel like crying because, of all the people in the room, it's her I want to be talking to. Her, and the other girls, and not Frankie Williams at all. I look back over my shoulder. He's watching me with a curious expression on his face. I raise my hand. Wave. He smiles and returns the gesture. There's nothing left to say, I know. I'm fully aware that I may not get a second alone with him again in this lifetime. I'm surprised to find I'm fine with that.

I walk back to my best friend. 'Jas, we should go,' I whisper.

'Really?'

'It's time. You know what they say – do it quickly, like ripping off a plaster. How many times are we going to say goodbye to them before we mean it?'

She smiles at me. 'Come on, then. We're as ready as we ever will be.'

When we reach the door, I hesitate. 'Are we mad?' I say.

She shakes her head. 'It's just like you said, H. We've said goodbye. They've always been the ones with the power. It has to be us now, babe. We've got to walk away.'

'But I don't want to lose this.'

I gesture at the room, and Jas catches my hands in mid-air, holds them still.

'Listen to me. We're keeping more than we're letting go, I promise.'

'Tell me,' I say.

She does.

The things we're not saying goodbye to when we say goodbye to Half Light

1. To each other. Because fandom friends are real friends, and anyone who says any different just hasn't *felt* it.
2. To knowing what it looks like, and what it feels like, to really have a dream. To knowing that there isn't shame in chasing it. And to knowing that these things change, and that's all right, too. It's what you do with it while it's there that counts.
3. To seeing the world without leaving Brighton. To the girl who knows now what New York subway stations and Saturday night in LA and Berlin sunrises look like. Because those boys – and my girls – *took me places*, and for most of it I didn't even have to leave my room.
4. To feeling that *absolutely anything* is possible, because they were just three *normal* boys, and *everything happened* for them. To feeling like, just sometimes, in the midst of a nightmare, there can still be miracles. That you get to be *so happy*.

Like a fairy tale.

Or a movie.

Or a dream.

328

Except the reality is better than any of those things. And we got that. They gave us that. And that never lasts forever, but you never forget it, either.

The things we're saying goodbye to when we say goodbye to Half Light

1. Just them. Just Half Light. Which is no small thing. But it's nowhere near as big as all the parts we get to keep.

As Jas pushes open the door, I feel a hand brush against mine, and I turn to see Frankie there. It's the kind of light touch that in normal circumstances you probably wouldn't even notice, but that I know on some level I'll be able to feel there forever. My fifteen-year-old self would have sworn she was never washing again; probably would have meant it until she forgot and ran dirty hands under a warm tap. *There are some parts you get to keep forever*, I remind myself. *Hand cells renew. Memory ones are all yours.*

He doesn't say anything, doesn't even smile, just looks at me, but it was there. That's enough.

We walk out with Alex and Ruby, who are waiting for us with cheeks flushed and make-up smudged. Alex has been crying, I can tell. I put my arms round her.

'Are you OK?' I ask.

'Course I am. It's not a sad thing, not really. I wasn't

crying because I was sad. Just . . . letting it go. We're going to be *fine*,' she adds, for whose benefit I can't quite work out. 'And we've gotta go. It's almost morning.'

Part of me can hardly believe we've stayed out so late. The party hadn't felt that long at all. But then again a night like this would never feel long enough. We'd always want to hang on for just one more hour, one more minute, just a little bit longer to avoid having to say goodbye.

'OK. Let's do it,' I say with far more conviction than I feel.

We head en masse back down the stairs to the empty arena. What goes up must come down. I don't look over my shoulder. There's a chill in the air again, the heat from our bodies long departed. The girls make for the closed door, but I hang back. Only a little, not so much that they'd notice, but they are in step and I'm not, and it feels like an omen, although maybe not a bad one. I'm used to that: to being the one veering in a slightly different direction from everyone else. The difference is that these days I don't entirely hate it.

'*And I think to myself, what a wonderful world,*' Louis Armstrong croons over the speakers, even though there's nobody there to listen. I turn back to the stage just once more. Men I've never seen before, dressed entirely in black, dismantle lights and speakers like it's no big deal. Just another day.

We bundle into warm coats, swap heeled boots for trainers, ready to walk to the Tube station, to the bus stop, back to life as we don't know it, because life as we know it has been this for so long. The last of the stage lights sputter and go out behind us.

Ruby hangs back at the exit, turns and pulls me back into the arena that isn't so magic any more.

'I'm just not ready for it to be over,' she says. 'Are you?'

I have to admit that I'm not.

'Why is that, do you think?' I ask. 'We know that none of it was real. We know that, and still we're not ready to walk away. Why?'

I'm not really expecting an answer, or at least one delivered with the confidence in Ruby's voice when she says, 'Because we made this.'

'What do you mean?'

She spins on the spot, her arms thrown wide, round and round and round in an empty arena, nobody to watch her but me.

'All this was ours. A PR team in a glass building didn't make them, Harri. We did. It wasn't clever marketing, or connections they already had, or, God forbid, their raw talent. It was us, on our laptops in our parents' houses, saying, "*Look what we found.*" And we had no idea what we were doing, no idea what we even *wanted* the outcome to be, but we did it anyway because we *felt it*. Do you know how rare that actually is? To do something with absolutely no expectation? Just because you want to? Or, like, because you can't not? It's rare, Harri.'

Ruby looks over her shoulder without turning to the stage behind her, still being dismantled in the dark. The skin of the kick drum is being removed as we watch. It used to say Half Light, and now all that's left is a gaping hole that would let the noise straight through without ever twisting it into music.

'We did this, you know? We built it. And it's hard to let go of what you built.'

'Do you think we'll see each other again?' I don't know where the question comes from, but now it hangs in the air between us, no way to unsay it, and I'm scared of how she might answer. Jas, of course, I'll see. Jas is in the bones of me. Alex lives close enough that we'll give it a go, and I know there will be tweets and blog posts and Instagram comments and *so much to say* in the days that follow that it'll feel like nothing has changed at all. But the reality is that tomorrow morning Ruby boards a plane, back to a life that doesn't have Half Light in it. I don't know if I'll get to see the Berlin sunset again; don't know if this friendship or the others just like it will exist without something specific to revolve around.

They're not the sun, I attempt to remind myself. It only partially works.

'Yeah, I do,' she says, no sentimentality tingeing her voice. 'I won't pretend I think nothing is going to change, because that's naive and untrue and, like . . . I think we all need this reset.'

I nod.

'It's like . . . we built a whole world around them. They're how we know all our best friends, and how you picked the course you're doing, and how I picked the job I want to do. All our favourite songs are theirs. But we won't stop *being* just because they're gone. Those parts of us

332

won't stop existing. We're just going to have to look in different places for the new bits. That's all. The unmaking of Half Light isn't the unmaking of everything that exists because of them. That would be impossible. What?'

I gulp. 'Nothing.'

Ruby laughs. 'It's all right to be choked up, Harri. That was a good speech!'

I nod as I try to hold my face in a way that will stop it from crumpling into tears. I hope for everything that she said for us. For all of us. I *really* hope they'll be proud, but also . . . It doesn't matter what they think at all.

'You ready?' Jas shouts from the entrance, and I grin as I walk towards her.

Yeah. I am.

'Thank you,' I whisper, hoping the ghosts in the walls of this place that has meant so much to us will hear me. I breathe in deep, hoping I can take a little bit of them with me, for when I need to remember what it was like to feel something so strongly, despite all the evidence warning against it. I breathe out long and slow, hoping I can leave a little part of me behind. *Works both ways*, I think. *They needed us just as much as we needed them.*

'It's time to go home, H,' Jas says, opening the heavy black door and letting the almost-morning stream in.

I nod. I don't look back. I step out of the half-light and into the sun.

DISCOVER MORE ABOUT
Half Light

NAME: Frankie Williams

STAR SIGN: Leo

FAVOURITE PLACE YOU'VE VISITED: Japan

FAVOURITE HALF LIGHT SONG: 'Closer Than You Think'

PET HATE: Slow walkers!

FAVOURITE FOOD: Blueberry pancakes

MOTTO IN LIFE: 'Keep your eyes on the stars and your feet on the ground.'

WHAT WOULD YOU BE DOING IF YOU WEREN'T IN HALF LIGHT: I always wanted to be a marine biologist. I'm entirely unqualified, but maybe that?

NAME: Kyle Barber

STAR SIGN: Taurus

FAVOURITE PLACE YOU'VE VISITED: New York City

FAVOURITE HALF LIGHT SONG: 'Home Again'

PET HATE: People who misuse the word 'literally'.

FAVOURITE FOOD: Pizza

MOTTO IN LIFE: 'You get what you work for, not what you wish for.'

WHAT WOULD YOU BE DOING IF YOU WEREN'T IN HALF LIGHT: Definitely still something musical. Maybe production, or writing for other bands.

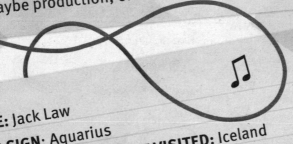

NAME: Jack Law

STAR SIGN: Aquarius

FAVOURITE PLACE YOU'VE VISITED: Iceland

FAVOURITE HALF LIGHT SONG: 'Famous Last Words'

PET HATE: People who can't admit when they're wrong.

FAVOURITE FOOD: Really good sushi

MOTTO IN LIFE: 'Everything you want is on the other side of fear.'

WHAT WOULD YOU BE DOING IF YOU WEREN'T IN HALF LIGHT: I've often thought that I'd quite like to teach.

SETLIST
Half Light
THE FINAL SHOW

1. Home Again
2. Ghosts
3. Trust Fate
4. Circus
5. Starlight
6. Closer Than You Think
7. Watch You Leave
8. Equinox
9. Things to Remember
10. Felicity
11. You Were Never Mine
12. By Any Other Name
13. Everything I Never Said
14. Distance

ENCORE
15. Trick of the Light
16. Famous Last Words

ACKNOWLEDGEMENTS

As Westlife sang in my first favourite boyband song, 'Flying Without Wings': 'Impossible as they may seem, you've got to fight for every dream.' What they didn't mention is that when it comes to the really big ones, like publishing the book of your heart, you can't do it alone. It might be my name on the cover, but *The Boyband Murder Mystery* belongs to so many people, and there's a little bit of all of them in every page. I've spent years thanking them in private. Now I'm going to do it here, in this book we all made.

To Lucy Irvine, my brilliant agent, who changed so much about this book for the better with the very first comment she made about it. I knew within a sentence that we were meant to work together. We can go from publishing contracts to boyband conspiracies in the same conversation, and that's only one of the reasons why there was no better champion for these girls and Half Light. Doing this with you as my team-mate has been one of my favourite parts. Here's to many more.

To Jonathan Sissons and Rosie Gurtovoy, for all your work to take Half Light from page to screen. Thank you for some of my most joyous professional moments of 2020.

To Natalie Doherty, my dream editor, for somehow streamlining all my thoughts about fandom into this book that I'm so proud of, and that says exactly what I want it to in about 20,000 words less than I'd managed without you! (I wish you had edited that sentence, actually . . .) Thank you for the amazing book recommendations, always checking to make sure the deadlines weren't destroying me, and the perfect title. I can't believe we ever thought it could be called anything else.

To Jane Griffiths, for bringing back my excitement when I was exhausted and had read this book about five times in a week! I'm in the best of hands with you, and I'm so pleased we've got to work together.

To Wendy Shakespeare, you are so brilliant at what you do! Thank you for somehow taking what this book was in my head and making it that on paper. Thanks also to Jane Tait, Marcus Fletcher and Jennie Roman, for their major part in making that happen.

To everyone else at Peters, Fraser and Dunlop and Penguin Random House Children's. I feel you all in my corner constantly. How did I get so lucky? It's like I struck gold twice.

I started writing *The Boyband Murder Mystery* on Faber Academy's Writing A Novel course, and truly believe that without it I may never have even got a complete draft. Thanks to all the 2018/19 Faber Owls, who gave me encouragement, ideas, and a confidence to carry on that I never would have had were I doing it alone. To Joanna Briscoe, whose weekly word-count checks guided me gently but firmly to the finish line, and especially to Tamsin Smith, who was the first person I spoke to in the first class, the first person I told when Penguin asked for a meeting, and the first person to find out I had a book deal. Thanks for being right there for all of it. You're next!

To Harry Styles and his girls on the internet for reminding me how fandom feels at the exact moment I needed to remember. To Aaron, Antony, Kevin, Leon and Mark, for teaching me in the first place.

To Sharif Afifi, Bella Eldred-Smith and Hailey Golding, who read early drafts and said lovely things that made me think maybe I was on to something good. To Rachel Berner, who did the same, but also didn't throw me out of the flat when this book was on submission and I was on edge, for which she deserves a lot of wine and her own special mention.

All my friends and family have been my personal fandom for everything I've ever written, but Chrissie Homer and Paul Spicer especially have never wavered in their belief that this was going to happen. Knowing you both is so good for my soul.

To the Montiel McCanns. You'll probably find out from your mum, who found out from my mum, exactly what this sentence says before you get a chance to read it, but, at this point, would we have it any other way? Thank you for a whole lifetime's worth of support. I'm so glad we're all friends.

To David Coverdale, who has put me in the acknowledgements of everything he's ever written. Now it's my turn – I love that we get to be writers together.

To Georgie Armour. The most magical thing is a friend who says, 'I really believe in this, and you,' and then steps up and proves it. I think you changed my life this year, and I'll never ever forget it.

To Frankie Wakefield, for everything, not least the perfect name.

To Rosalyn Curtis, Katrina Farnan, Sarah Farnan, Helen Keane, Siobhan O'Reilly, Laura Post, Emma Sales and Philippa Stennett. My 'boyband friends'. After seventeen years, we could probably drop the 'boyband', but I don't want to. I never want to forget where we came from. I hope you like our book. (And to Edith. I hope you always know how brilliant your mummy is. I can't wait until you're old enough to read this.)

To Max Tierney, who showed me a stargazing app under a Greek sky, and explained it in a way that made me want to write it down. So much of the essence of this book grew from that scene, and therefore that night. Thanks, pal. I'm so happy you're in our family.

To Nanny and Grandad, who have kept everything I've ever written. This might not be quite as imaginative as the story about the green children, but I hope you love it anyway.

To Mum and Dad, who spent a lot of my twenties trying to gently guide me away from questionable career choices, and, when it came to this, never tried to persuade me I should be doing anything else. Thank you for a house that my friends used to call 'the library', and for letting us treat it as an un-official fangirl HQ for most of our teens. Both are among the reasons I could write this book.

To Rosa Eldred. I'm pretty sure everything I know about writing mysteries came from that summer we spent making a murder radio show on our karaoke machine. I'm so glad you thought it was as fun as I did, and so glad we no longer have the tapes! (You know the unspoken part that I could never print in a book.)

To Martha Eldred. Did you think for one second, sitting on the wall outside that pub, that a tiny comment about fangirls and the boys they love would lead to this? Because I didn't. Never in my wildest dreams. Thank you.

Q&A WITH AVA ELDRED

Where did you get the idea for The Boyband Murder Mystery?

I've always known I wanted to write about fandom. I'm fascinated by the idea that everyone is a fan of something, however casually, and that the ways in which we express that can either fit neatly into our lives or completely change them. It took me a while to figure out what the story was, because for something so universal it can be experienced in many different ways. I did a lot of research around boyband fandom specifically, and was struck by the passion – some fans really would go to great lengths for the artists they loved. That got me thinking about how far that could extend, which led to the question: 'If the lead singer of a boyband was arrested on suspicion of murder, what would his fans do?' The answer was very clear to me – they'd use everything they knew about him to prove he didn't do it.

Have you always wanted to be a writer? When did you start?

I have always been a writer, even if I haven't always wanted to! I rejected the idea of writing for a long time because my teachers seemed convinced it was inevitable and I hated feeling like I had to do what they said. Turns out they were entirely right! But even then, when I didn't think it would be my career, I was just writing for myself. When I came to writing seriously, it was theatre I began with, but that never really felt like the right fit. I did that for most of my twenties before admitting to myself that I really wanted to write novels, and the only way to do that was to start! That was three years ago and I've never looked back.

The book is a real page-turning mystery. Were you inspired by other mystery writers or novels? Are murder mysteries your favourite type of books?

Karen M. McManus and *One Of Us Is Lying* were a huge influence on the book even having a mystery element! I'd picked her book up while I was trying to figure out what my story should be, and, while I loved the idea of writing mystery, it was very separate from 'the boyband book' in my head. It was only as I read *One Of Us Is Lying* that I realized there was nothing stopping the boyband book from also being the mystery book! I also read everything Tiffany D. Jackson has ever published while I was editing, which made me want to step up my game because she's so brilliant, and I wish Holly Jackson's *The Good Girl's Guide to Murder* was mine because it's *so* well done. I don't think you can go wrong with a well-crafted mystery book. If you guess the twist, you get to feel clever – and, if you don't, you get a surprise! Win–win!

If you had to pick a favourite character from the novel, who would it be and why?

The easy answer to this is definitely Jas. She has a comeback to everything, is fiercely protective of the people she loves, and behind all the quick remarks she has the biggest heart. I wish she was real so we could be friends! But would I really be a proper fangirl if I didn't say I also have such a soft spot for Frankie? He's a bit more of a complicated favourite, because he definitely does some questionable things, but I can't help loving him anyway. His intentions are good; he just needs to work on his execution!

Were you ever as much of a fan of a band as Harri, Jas and the other Half-Lighters? Did you have a boyband crush when you were younger?

Oh yes, definitely! For me it started with Gareth Gates, so not a band at all but definitely a similar level of obsession, although I can't say I was ever *quite* as dedicated as Half Light's fans! I also had a huge crush on Taylor Hanson and loved Westlife, but my major fandom was a band called V. I don't want to say no one has ever heard of them, but very few people have! One of the most surprising parts of writing *The Boyband Murder Mystery* was that I fell right back into fandom after many years away – I definitely have a few new boyband crushes now!

Music plays a key part of the novel. Do you listen to music as you write? If so, what was your playlist for this book?

I can't listen to music as I write because the lyrics always end up in whatever I'm writing! I'm terrible for it! But a lot of my ideas come while I'm walking, and there was definitely a playlist for that part of the process. 'Superstar' by Taylor Swift was a big one, as well as any live album where you can hear the crowd singing back, and, of course, practically any boyband you can name!

Harri and Jas have an incredible friendship, despite having never even met in real life before the start of the novel. Are there any real or fictional female BFFs who inspired you to write a novel with a strong group of friends at its heart?

I know a lot of my oldest friends through a boyband, so really it was inspired by them! I think there's a special kind of bond that comes out of loving the same thing, and those friendships can long outlast the bands. They were some of the most interesting relationships of my teenage years, too, so I knew I wanted to write about that – my friends and the band we loved were my biggest love story back then, and, while we've all moved on to very different lives, it's so nice to remember where it all started.

What do you hope that readers take away from **The Boyband Murder Mystery?**

Firstly, that your female friendships are some of the most important relationships you'll ever have, and that becoming who you are because of the things you love is such a gift. Secondly, that you can never really know a celebrity, but in a lot of ways that doesn't matter, because you know how they made you feel. And also that boybands are so much more than cheesy dance routines and matching outfits – if you're really lucky, they can open up your whole world.